Praise for *Six Months Later*

"An intriguing story line...readers will be drawn in to the mystery of what happened to Chloe and will never guess the ending."
—*VOYA*

"The story is well paced and beautifully written, with fully developed characters teens can easily relate to. This romantic thriller will leave readers on the edge of their seats until the very last page."
—*School Library Journal*

"An intense psychological mystery... Richards constructs Chloe's fear, paranoia, and scheming with great care. Her novel has the feel of a high-stakes poker game in which every player has something to hide, and the cards are held until the very end."
—*Publishers Weekly*

"With several twists and surprises, this is a well-plotted mystery, sure to keep readers guessing."
—*Booklist*

Also by Natalie D. Richards

Six Months Later
Gone Too Far
My Secret to Tell

ONE
WAS
LOST

NATALIE D. RICHARDS

sourcebooks
fire

Copyright © 2016 by Natalie D. Richards
Cover and internal design © 2016 by Sourcebooks, Inc.
Cover design by Kerri Resnick
Cover images © Roy Bishop/Arcangel; Valentin Agapov/Shutterstock

Sourcebooks and the colophon are registered trademarks of Sourcebooks, Inc.

Published by Sourcebooks Fire, an imprint of Sourcebooks, Inc.
P.O. Box 4410, Naperville, Illinois 60567-4410
(630) 961-3900
Fax: (630) 961-2168
www.sourcebooks.com

Library of Congress Cataloging-in-Publication Data
Names: Richards, Natalie D., author.
Title: One was lost / Natalie D. Richards.
Description: Naperville, Illinois : Sourcebooks Fire, [2016] | Summary: On a senior class camping trip, four girls find themselves lost in the woods, their supplies destroyed, and hunted by a killer.
Identifiers: LCCN 2016004463 | (13 : alk. paper)
Subjects: | CYAC: Camping--Fiction. | Survival--Fiction. | Horror stories. | Mystery and detective stories.
Classification: LCC PZ7.R3927 On 2016 | DDC [Fic]--dc23 LC record available at https://lccn.loc.gov/2016004463

Printed and bound in the United States of America.
VP 10 9 8 7 6 5 4 3 2 1

To Jody and Edie
for helping me find the artist within

CHAPTER 1

No one said anything about rain in the brochures.

Not that there were brochures. There was a handwritten sign-up sheet in the cafeteria, followed by permission slips recycled from ghosts of field trips past. I'm not really sure why I was expecting a world-class production. Must be the director in me.

I stumble under the weight of my pack, sloshing through a puddle. Cold water oozes through my boots and socks. So much for Mr. Walker's plastic ponchos keeping us dry. I guess after six straight hours of rain, dry is relative anyway.

"I hope you packed your dirty clothes in the plastic bags I handed out last night," Mr. Walker booms from the front of the line. "They might stink, but they'll be dry."

The other girls cringe a little at the idea—all except Ms. Brighton, our younger, cooler teacher guide. She's very Zen about these things, nodding along in her crystal earrings and mud-dyed *Gaia Mother* T-shirt.

I'm in the last half of the group, behind Jude with his ever-present earbuds and imperious gaze. Since I'm five-two, the back of his poncho is about all I can see, but it's better than looking at Lucas.

Anything's better than looking at Lucas.

Even behind me, I can feel him. Looming. Everyone's tall measured against me, but Lucas is ridiculous. He *towers*. If there were actually a sun to be found in this Appalachian monsoon, his shoulders would cast a shadow you could hide two of me in. I have no idea what you have to eat to grow like that. Corn? Eggs? Small children?

I trudge onward, slowing to shift my backpack. The right strap is digging a painful trench into my shoulder, and I can't find a way to move it. My poncho slips with the effort, and a river of icy water slithers down my back.

"*Holy crap!*" I say, arching in a futile effort to escape.

"Keep moving, Spielberg," Lucas says behind me.

I grit my teeth and walk on. If I respond, I might have to look at him, and I've worked very hard not to do that. I've *not* looked for sixty-two days. It's a pretty good track record. I'm not going to wreck it just because he ended up on my Senior Life Experience Mission. At the last possible minute, no less.

"Is this really top speed for you?" he asks, sounding like he's on the verge of a laugh.

I stare at the line of backpacks and ponchos ahead of me, resisting the urge to snap back at him. I need to be the bigger person here. It's not like I don't know why he's picking at me.

"Still sticking with the silent treatment?" he asks. "Gotta give it to you, you're committed. Slow-moving as shit but committed."

OK, I'm bigger person-ed out.

I whirl around. I shouldn't—I know I shouldn't—but the words blurt out. "Newsflash, Lucas! I'm moving as fast as I can. Not all of us are loping around with giraffe legs like you, so if you're in such a rush, feel free to move ahead."

He steps closer, and it happens. I see him. *Really* see him.

Fricking crap.

He tilts his head until his face is visible inside his plastic hood. How does he do it? He's just as wet and miserable as the rest of us, but somehow, he's owning the hell out of a poncho that makes me look like I need a zip tie and a trip to the curb.

I should walk away, at least *look* away. Lucas is all sharp lines and hooded eyes, and I should have learned my lesson. Because standing here brings me right back to that night on the porch. My ears go buzzy with the memory of crickets singing and the backdrop of the cast party inside. My face tingles because I remember other things too—his scratchy jaw and soft mouth and my heart beating faster than it ever should.

My gaze drifts to his smirk and lead pools in my stomach. That's what I'm really mad about. It's not his teasing or the rain or anything else. It's the fact that he turns me into the same fluttery mess I was all summer. He *still* turns me into my mother, and I hate it.

I try to move away, but he catches the edge of my poncho—keeps me facing him. "Huh."

I cross my arms. "Huh, *what*?"

"Look who suddenly remembers me," he says softly.

"Don't."

"I won't," he says, though his grin needs a parental advisory label. "I didn't then, did—"

Lightning flashes, bright enough that we both jerk.

One Mississippi.

Two Mississ—

The sound that follows is like the sky being torn in two. It ends with a bone-deep rumble that rattles the ground and bunches my spine. I close my eyes and take a breath, yoga-slow. It doesn't *cleanse* anything, so I try another.

Across from me, Lucas is searching the sky. I take the opportunity to turn and bolt ahead on the trail. Not that there's anywhere to go. Away from him is good enough.

I plow into Jude's back in my eagerness to escape. He spares me one millisecond of irritation, and then he's back to pretending we're all part of the scenery.

The trail widens here, or maybe the forest is less dense. Who knows? It gives me enough room to move past Jude until I'm next to Emily, my tent mate for the last two nights.

Emily looks back at me—a sparkle of dark eyes under her poncho—and her mouth twitches. Is she smiling at me? That's new.

"Some trip, right?" I ask.

She ducks her head. And that's as close to a conversation as we've gotten. I sigh. We have three more days of awkwardness in the woods. Three. More. Days.

"Hold up." Mr. Walker is ultra-alert. "Everybody stay right here. Don't move."

Our single file line separates, students clustering into a group. The rain is a touch lighter now, and everything's hazy and foggy.

Mr. Walker clomps ahead while we wait. I roll my achy shoulders and try to ignore how damp and sticky I am under my trash bag poncho.

I can't see much, but it wouldn't matter if I could. We all look alike. I mean, Lucas is an easy spot, towering six inches over everyone here. Mr. Walker would stand out too if he hadn't walked off—he's the only one with an actual rain jacket, plus he's got that bright-yellow plastic-sleeve-protected GPS strapped to his arm. I can't see where he went though. Being short offers few advantages.

"What's going on?" Madison asks, turning to touch Lucas's arm for the fiftieth time this hour. "Can you see anything, Lucas?"

"Is something wrong with the bridge?" Hayley this time, I think. It doesn't matter. Hayley and Madison are sort of interchangeable in my head. Like bookends. In a tent.

Ms. Brighton holds up a hand high enough that even I can see it. I focus on her short, decidedly not-earthy purple nails. "Just hold tight. Mr. Walker's checking it out."

She says that like it will solve everything. It might. Back in Marietta, Mr. Walker was a math teacher with bad breath and a collection of football bobbleheads. Out here, he's Dr. Doomsday Prepper. He's got enough gear in his pack to start a new society should we get lost. I glance around the sea of drippy trees surrounding us. Scary thought.

"He's checking the bridge," Lucas says. "Something with the ballast maybe."

Plastic rustles as Madison clings harder to his arm. "Are we going to die? Oh my God, I can't die out here."

Ms. Brighton laughs. "No one's dying. Native Americans lived in these forests for generations."

Lucas snorts. "Uh, last night, you said those same Native Americans still have guru ghosts running around. Driving hunters off cliffs."

She smirks. "Guru is a Sanskrit word. That was from my first story."

"Whatever. There *were* ghosts flinging people off cliffs in the other one."

"No, the hunters found the cliff on their own," Ms. Brighton says, correcting him. "The Cherokee spirits just led them away from the sacred animals they were hunting."

"The only thing I'm hunting out here is a hot shower and cable TV," Lucas says.

Ms. Brighton's smile goes wide. "Then I'm sure you're safe. So let's all stay positive."

I'm positive I'm soaked. I'm positive I hate hiking. I'm positive this trip will go down as the worst choice of my young life, but I'm pretty sure she doesn't want to hear any of those things, so I keep my mouth shut. I squeeze my way between Jude and my tent mate, Emily, so I can see better.

"Oh, the things the forest will teach us!" Ms. Brighton seems delighted at the prospect.

I bite back a grin. Kooky or not, I like her. Granted, the Church of Brighton would be a cobbled-up mash-up of her choice—part Buddhism, part Cherokee spirituality, and a whole lot of all-organic-all-the-time. But she's nice.

She points ahead. "Oh, Mr. Walker's headed back. See? It's probably fine."

Mr. Walker stomps up the streambed, looking grim. "We've got a problem."

Or it's not fine at all.

"What problem?" I ask.

"Bridge is out." He wipes his rain-soaked face like there's nothing more to say.

I look up at the narrow metal structure. It's a little rusty and worse for the wear, but overall, it seems intact.

"It's suspended over the water," Jude says, his soft voice surprising me. "Isn't that how bridges are *supposed* to function?"

Mr. Walker turns away from Jude like he didn't say anything at all.

"Something's wrong with the supports, smart-ass," Lucas says.

Mr. Walker nods at Lucas and points out a sagging seam and some cracks in the dirt that are apparently scary dangerous signs or something. I don't care enough to make suggestions. This is somebody else's show falling apart, and I'm just going to stand here like a stagehand waiting for someone to tell me what to do.

"OK, so now what?" Ms. Brighton asks, her oh-so-positive voice dipping a little.

"We can't trust the bridge. We'll go down and cross the river on foot." Mr. Walker taps the GPS on his arm. "We got a flash flood warning a while back, so I want to get on the other side while we still can."

"But we'll get wet if we don't use the bridge!" Hayley (Madison?) gripes.

A laugh coughs out of me.

"I'm already freezing," Madison adds. Or is it Hayley? No, it's definitely Madison. I can tell because she's the one whose arm is always snaking toward Lucas.

"I want to go home," Hayley says.

We will probably lather, rinse, and repeat this twelve more times in the next hour. These two have been a torrent of complaints. I can't blame them. This place is like woodsy purgatory.

Still, Mr. Walker has a point. It's an easy descent to the stream, and it still looks shallow, but with all this rain, that might change. And then we're stuck here. We're at the halfway point of the trip now, so any kind of delay could mean another day out here. I'd cross a leech-infested river of blood if it means getting out of this forest sooner rather than later.

"Should we just camp here tonight?" Ms. Brighton asks.

"Camping by the stream is risky. We could run into a bear. Plus, we might not be able to cross tomorrow."

Ms. Brighton takes a breath like she wants to argue but goes quiet again.

"It's a bad idea," Madison says. "I don't want to cross."

"Let's stay upbeat," Ms. Brighton says. "We could talk about what purpose this might serve."

Please let's not.

Gauging from the grumbles of my fellow campers, I'm not the only one thinking it as we scrabble down the hill, mud caking thicker on my boots with every step.

"Maybe we're going to be fish in our next life."

Ms. Brighton laughs, looking pink cheeked and pretty despite the rain. "Never say never."

Madison sighs. "This whole thing is proof that I shouldn't have signed up so late."

"The homeless shelter mission had openings too," Ms. Brighton says.

"Well, this mission had certain *motivating* factors." Madison's eyes trail to Lucas. Again.

Hayley sighs. "Also, our parents didn't want us in the bad part of town."

Lucas snorts. "You do realize poor isn't contagious."

"Isn't it?" Jude asks him. They've been at it since the parking lot. It's annoying as crap.

"Everyone, quiet. We need to move." Mr. Walker's voice is tight. Something's wrong. But he's halfway across, and the water is still below his knees. It's moving quickly, but it seems OK. So why is Mr. Walker scanning the horizon like a soldier?

When he's on the other side, he relaxes. "All right, let's move. You'll get to test those waterproof boots here. Emily, you first. Then Jude and right down the line."

I stumble to the edge of the stream, rocks slipping and scattering under my boots. Jude's next to me, earbuds in and his chin tipped up like we need a reminder that he's better than us.

Emily begins to cross with Jude behind her. Then me and Lucas and the rest of the group after. I can't help but think about what we must look like, this conga line of plastic-wrapped hikers splashing its way through the river.

Jude gasps ahead of me. Before I can ask, cold water gushes over the tops of my boots, then past my ankles. I stop when it reaches my knees. It's higher. We're not even halfway across.

Lucas splashes up from behind, rising over me. "Need me to carry you?"

I don't dignify the question with a response. Behind me, Hayley and Madison shriek. I turn to see a glimpse of all three of them, Hayley on her butt in the water and Madison and Ms. Brighton rushing back for her. The girls are laughing hysterically.

"We're almost halfway," Lucas says, ignoring them. "Keep going."

"Should we help?"

"They're fine. Move."

"Stop playing around back there! Get them up, Ms. Brighton," Mr. Walker barks, then more softly to the ones climbing out, "Good job, Emily. Jude! Earbuds out!"

Mr. Walker looks downstream, and his expression hardens. "Sera, speed up now."

I look up and wish I hadn't. I don't like the urgency in his tone any more than I like the rushing sound of water I hear off to the east.

"Is that rain?" I ask because I want it to be rain. Or hail. I want it to be anything other than what I already know it is.

Mr. Walker's eyes flick upstream, his face going pale. "It's flooding," he admits.

My hope snaps like a rubber band. Fear billows out in its place, making me woozy.

"Sera, move!" Lucas says, prodding my backpack.

"I got it!" I snap, plowing ahead.

Hayley screams again behind us. They're all three shouting. Something about a shoe. Someone's stuck. Mr. Walker is yelling at Emily and Jude to *back up, back up*! And then the rain changes, the shower shifting into a driving roar with drops so hard they feel like sand spraying down. Everything is garbled. Muffled. Fear pushes the hair up on the nape of my neck.

We're not going to get across.

"Go, Sera!"

Lucas. His voice right behind me, his wide hand just under my backpack, urging me forward. I stumble, spreading my arms wide for balance.

"Lucas, help!" Madison's cry filters through the rain, but Mr. Walker shakes his head.

"No!" he bellows. "Move, Lucas! Ms. Brighton, pull Hayley and Madison back to shore!"

The water is moving quicker and higher, and my boots are sucking down into the mud at the bottom. The current pushes back at me. Steps turn into half steps. Quarter steps.

"Forget her shoes!" Mr. Walker screams. Someone's coughing back there, but I don't look, though I can hear their garbled cries. They're struggling.

"I can't get her!" Ms. Brighton's voice is suddenly young and small, nothing like the serene woman from before. This is scared little kid voice. "Help! Hel—"

Someone else screams. Hayley maybe. I turn over my shoulder to see Ms. Brighton haul Hayley up and stumble back. Water's pushing at their thighs, but they're all three up. They're OK.

Mr. Walker is screaming at them. "Get back! Faster, faster, *move!*"

I shriek as the frigid water laps up my thighs. Then—*Snap! Pop!*—off to my right. Dread spikes through me. Something's coming downstream. I have to go. Right now.

"Come on, Sera," Mr. Walker says, sounding breathless.

I rush, feet lurching. Almost there. So close now. I stumble. Lucas grabs my pack and hauls me up, and then I'm snarling at him—"Don't touch me!"—while Mr. Walker snags one of my straps and half drags me out. Water pours down my pant legs. I'm soaked and freezing.

I take a soggy step, and my boot slips on the muddy bank. Lucas is out too, swearing and scrambling up while Mr. Walker stares across at the girls, hands in his hair, eyes wide with terror.

My knees are buckling, but I grab branches and exposed roots and, finally, Jude's smooth, dark hand. Once I'm up, I follow him past brambles that snag my poncho. My hair.

"Over here." Jude points to a vantage point near the path. No earbuds now. He's wide-eyed and utterly focused on the stream fifteen feet below us. Emily and Lucas are beside him, both shaking.

There's a tree wedged across the stream. That must have been what I heard. The water is rushing under and over it, pushing it harder and harder. And then it's loose. I hold my breath as it rolls with the mud-brown river, snapping anything in its path.

"The others," Emily says softly.

They're lined up on the other side, mud-spattered and white with fear as the log hurtles past, ripping its way through the streambed and releasing a wall of sludgy brown water in its wake. The current surges up the banks behind it, littered with smaller branches and clumps of vegetation. Madison's eyes track us across the water, finding Lucas and then me.

"They're stuck over there." I know it's obvious, but I say it anyway.

Mr. Walker barks instructions at the edge of the stream. Ms. Brighton nods along, one arm wrapped around each girl, her dark braid coiled around her pale neck like a snake.

"What's he going to do?" Jude asks.

"Nothing, rich boy," Lucas says. "There's not a damn thing he can do tonight. Can't even call for help because there's no signal anywhere with this rain."

"What will happen to them?" I ask.

"If they listen to Mr. Walker, they'll go set up camp on that ridge. We'll stay here for the night, probably farther up the path. Us here, them there. Regroup in the morning if we can."

I whirl on Lucas. "What do you mean *if*?"

"You expect us to believe he's just going to leave them?" Jude asks.

"That flood isn't going anywhere soon. And I don't give a shit what you believe," Lucas says to him. "Since someone has to set up our tent again, I need to find a clearing."

Lucas storms away, and my eyes drag back to the stream. Three girls with arms wrapped around each other's shoulders. The river gushes along, a monstrous evolution of what I just crossed, swallowing the bridge inch by inch.

It wasn't supposed to be like this. Not like this at all.

CHAPTER 2

The temperature is dropping fast, and between that and the rain, my fingers are shaking. Not helping the tent setup situation. I blame my tent stakes. Flimsy pieces of crap, they're bent to hell from the first two nights out here. I hate them. I also hate the rain and the backpack that's so heavy I might as well have a dead moose strapped to my shoulders.

And Lucas. I *definitely* hate Lucas right now.

"Give back the hammer," I say, one dripping hand outstretched toward him.

"Why? I can hammer it in for you, Sera."

I grit my teeth hard and resist responding to the innuendo he loads into every word. I don't know how anyone can turn a conversation about tent stakes into something depraved, but he's managing.

This is what I get for looking at him, for reacting. I have no one but myself to blame.

"Can you please give me back the hammer?" I ask again, voice sweet but glare dialed up to murderous.

"Your loss."

He shrugs and drops the rubber mallet on my pile of soggy tent fabric. I valiantly resist the urge to pick it up and fling it at his head.

Beside me, Emily shudders.

I unclench my fists and turn to her. "You OK?"

"Just cold. Do you think…" Her eyes drift to the path behind us. The one that leads down to the river where we left the others. "Do you think they're all right?"

"Oh, sure. Ms. Brighton is totally together. And Mr. Walker will get us out of here tomorrow. It's no big deal."

"You really think so?"

No, I think it's an *enormous* deal, but freaking her out won't help. It takes me a beat to find Emily's dark eyes inside her plastic hood, but when I do, I smile.

"She'll make it great," I say. "She'll probably have them building a new bridge out of repurposed water bottles or something."

"Maybe she'll sing the ancestor spirits song again." Emily wrinkles her nose.

I laugh, remembering Ms. Brighton's little fireside performance after all the ghost stories. "Yeah, Madison's story was better. Dead people in the trees really sets the mood."

Emily nods.

I look around, frowning. "OK, tell me the truth. Did someone really die out here?"

She shrugs. "Yeah, a girl. I mean, probably not like Madison told it at the fire. I doubt she was killed. That's an urban myth."

"God, it's a creepy one though. Left to die by your friends. A bear dragging pieces of you out?" I shudder. "Let's hope they don't go there. They can make their own cool story."

"Yeah, the night they froze to death, lost in the woods," Emily says, shivering.

I position a stake now that I have my mallet back. "For me, it might be the night I go to jail for shoving a fistful of mud down Lucas Crane's throat."

I pull back to strike the metal stake. It folds like a taco, just like the first ones. That's why I'd let Lucas take a turn with the mallet. Clearly, the break did not improve my ability. Whatever. I keep right on hammering, banging away until the bent metal is buried in mud. Success. Sort of.

This trip was supposed to be great. Mr. Walker practically promised mythical nirvana out here. We'd see mountains and ancient trees and unicorns that come to drink at sunset or some crap. Extremely remote, he said. Personally enlightening, Ms. Brighton added.

They pegged the remote part. We're in Nowhere, West Virginia, where the only thing less common than people is cell phone reception. Of course, we're not remote enough to get me away from the one boy I'm trying desperately to avoid.

"Sera?"

"Yeah?"

Emily's eyes dart to the subject of my glare. "I know you and Lucas have a history."

"We don't…" There's no way to finish because I don't want to lie. Or explain. I trail off instead, drifting into the space my lies want to fill over.

None of it would have happened if I didn't want that stupid stage scenery so badly. I could have made do, but I wanted real metal, and I have a way of getting what I want. Just like my mother.

I press the heels of my palms into my eyes, hating the way her smile forms in my memory. Oh, she would have *loved* Lucas. No. No, that's not quite right. She would have loved everything about the way *I* am when I'm with him.

I push my mother's face out of my mind, but another memory rushes in.

The scent of metal, as sharp as the hiss of the torch. Long sturdy tables and sparks that cascade to the ground, skittering like glowing insects. Our school is brightly colored murals and paint-spattered floors, but this room is different.

Lucas looks up when he sees me, the dark glass rectangle in his welding mask fixing on my face. Under the mask, he's formed with the same angles and hollows as the shop around him.

I should tell him why I'm here, but I don't. My gaze trails over his heavy-lidded eyes too long. I linger. And I know I shouldn't.

"Be careful," Emily says, pulling me back. "Do you know what he did to Tyler Kenton?"

If you're within a hundred miles of Marietta, Ohio, you know what Lucas did to Tyler at the homecoming soccer game last year. If you're smart, you remember it *before* you kiss him.

My lips quirk. "I think it's required knowledge for graduation."

I nudge each of the stakes with the toe of my boot. They're a mess, but the tent feels sturdy enough. Maybe we won't get blown away after all. I slam in the last two stakes and stand up as the rain tapers off. Mist clings to the trees and turns the air even colder.

Lucas stands up on the other side of our tiny camp, and I narrow my eyes, imagining his wide shoulders sending Tyler flying. I know nothing about soccer, but you don't have to be an expert to know Tyler went into that game a star forward senior with dreams of a full ride. Then newcomer junior Lucas showed up. One collision later, Tyler's leg snapped. Senior season over and sainthood secured.

Lucas meets my eyes across camp like he can sense me thinking about him. I turn back to my tent. My boots squish with every step, and the collar of my T-shirt is wet enough to chafe.

I tug the tent cover out of Emily's pack, and she starts pushing in the poles to lift this mess of canvas off the ground.

"I officially hate camping," I grumble. Every breath fills my head with the smell of wet tent and hard rain. Another damp night awaits, with rocks digging into my shoulders and mosquito bites keeping me squirmy and miserable. At least it will be dry inside the tent. My eyes linger on a rivulet running down the canvas. Dry-*ish* at any rate.

Emily gasps, and I look around the side to see her holding the broken string of one of the tie-downs. I sigh and start toward her, and she stumbles back desperately, her face chalky.

"I-I'm sorry," she says.

I laugh. "It's fine. Did you see what I did to the tent stakes?"

Across the camp, Lucas snarls something at Jude, and Emily flinches again. The girl's a nervous wreck.

"Poor Jude, huh?" I say.

Emily's mouth draws tight, her shoulders shifting under her poncho. "There's nothing poor about Jude."

I lift my brows, surprised at her candor. True enough though. Jude's super rich. He's also super talented on the cello. I used to roll my eyes when he'd talk about Julliard, but then I heard him play. He's the real deal. It might be cool if he weren't an elitist, antisocial tool.

I shift our tent poles to straighten them as best I can, and Emily swishes the tent cover around. It's a little lopsided, but we get it upright. I hold one hand out wide, giving Emily some jazz hands. "Ta-da!"

"You're pretty good at this."

I shrug. "We had tents in the background of one of our summer plays. I spent three nights a week setting them up on stage."

Emily helps me straighten the tent, locking the poles for security. "I thought you were a director or something now."

"I am. Usually. Which means you do all the jobs that don't get finished. Tent assembly included."

A snap-cracking in the woods to the south tells me Mr. Walker is returning from the creek, where he'd stayed to direct Ms. Brighton. There he comes from stage left, hands tucked under his backpack straps and a deep furrow over his brows. I try to imagine what lines will be his.

Except this isn't a stage, and there won't be an intermission or flowers after the curtain call.

"Are they OK over there?" I ask.

"Ms. Brighton's plenty capable of getting them through the night." He says it convincingly, but his eyes are too squinty. I don't believe him.

"Should we call for help?" Emily asks, pipsqueak soft.

"No signal," he says, and his grin has a hard edge. "I told you girls not to bother bringing your phones. It won't kill us to handle this crisis. Might even build some character."

I'm not sure how wringing out my bra or dying of hypothermia will build character, but I nod automatically.

"They don't have water, but they have a filter bottle in one of the packs." He frowns, and I can tell he's sorting supplies in his head. "I've got the bottles we filtered at our lunch stop."

Ah, those were good times. During the first hour of the downpour, all eight of us clustered around the river, trying to cover the filter with ponchos to protect it from rain contamination. Because the only thing that would make this trip more special would be a case of the trots.

Mr. Walker's smile goes even tighter. "Bad news is Ms. Brighton's got most of the food."

I shrug. The smell of wet leaves and mildewed canvas isn't doing much to whet my appetite anyway.

"I see you got your tent up without me tonight," he says, putting on an expression that makes me think of dry-erase markers and trigonometry homework. He's all teacherly pride and confidence, and as much as I want to gripe about how cold and hateful I feel, his words from sign-up week are still rattling around in my head. *You're such a leader, Sera. I'd love to have you on this project.*

So here I am. My friends are repainting the town rec center, and I'm *here* in hell, collecting enough mosquito bites to contract malaria.

Still, I keep my shoulders back and my smile pasted on. "We're regular survivalists. It's all good. Emily helped me wrench this baby into shape."

"I broke a string," Emily admits, sounding like she might cry over it.

"Great teamwork," Mr. Walker says. He moves around to fiddle with our work, shifting a couple of poles and tugging on the fabric here and there. Before I can fully figure out what he's trying to do, our whole tent is perfectly centered on the poles and tidily covered. He digs around in his pack and hands me a box of Whoppers and a bottle of water for each of us.

"That's about it," he says. "But it's safe. Sorry it's not more."

Suddenly, all the rotten earth smells whisk to the back of my mind. The promise of chocolate is heady, and my stomach growls. My fingers are actually pale and shaky when I hand Emily a water. I'm hungrier than I thought.

"You may be the greatest teacher in the history of teachers." I laugh, waggling the Whoppers.

"Well, don't tell the guys. They're stuck sharing the half-melted Hershey bar."

"Jude has his own food," Emily says, that same darkness leaking into her words. I sort of get the Jude hate. He has all the things we don't. He looks at the rest of us like we're *less*.

"You mean the macrobiotic twelve-dollars-a-pop granola bars?" He winks. "Well, unless he's evolved into a higher life form, he'll still need water."

I look around pointedly. "Huh. Where on earth could we get some of that?"

"*Clean* water," Mr. Walker says. Then he points at a spot between our tents. "I'll be setting my tent up right there if you girls need anything. Things will look better tomorrow."

I nod before unzipping our tent flap with a sigh. It might not be raining anymore, but I'm in a quarter inch of water, and I'm pretty sure I'll need six showers to scrub off the standard-issue musty *camping* smell.

The last thing we want is to get the inside of the tent wet, but getting out of our boots and ponchos is a clown show. Emily holds up her poncho as I squish my feet out of my boots and stand barefoot on top of them, wrestling my poncho off. Then it's Emily's turn. By the time we're in, I don't know if any of it was worth it. Our soggy boots and backpacks are leaving puddles inside the door. Even when I peel off my jeans and sweatshirt, my tank top and undies are wet. Unpleasant doesn't even touch this, but I put on my sleeping clothes anyway.

Emily doesn't complain and, like every other night this week, only tugs off her pants when she's got a sweatshirt wrapped around her waist. The first night, I felt almost pervy just ripping mine off, especially since I've got at least fifteen pounds on her. By day two, I was too tired and achy to care. Now as we carefully wrestle our (also damp) sleeping bags out of our packs, I roll my shoulders, feeling knots bunching at the base of my neck.

The ground slopes downhill, and there's a rock under my left shoulder, but when we turn on the lantern and split our coveted candy, it feels a little better. Not great, but all right. We try our phones next, pulling them out of the plastic bags Mr. Walker passed out with the ponchos.

"They make fine nightlights," I say, lamenting the *No Signal* indicator in the corner of my screen.

"I can use my calculator…or my camera," Emily says.

I smirk. "Memories we'll always treasure."

Emily gives the smallest smile and then rolls away, curling into a tiny ball in her sleeping bag. For a second, I see a flash of her slim shoulder and four shadowy bruises on the back of her arm. My stomach tightens as I think about her fear over the broken string earlier. Because those bruises are too old to have happened out here.

As if she feels me watching, Emily slips her arm inside her bag. I see nothing but black hair and the obvious hint that she's done talking. Just like the last two nights, the silence swells in the tent until I'm sure the canvas walls will burst. There's cricket song and night noises, but I've never been a good sleeper. Not since Mom left. At home, Dad would be in the living room, reading and eating hummus, and eventually the munching and page-flipping would lull me off to dreamland. But not here.

Here, I leave the lantern on and stare at the stained tent ceiling, sticky and cold and sick to death of this SLEM trip.

Senior Life Experience Mission, my foot. I start coming up with new words to fit the acronym in my mind. See Life Endless Monsoon. Sinister Lucas Enjoys Mischief. So Long, Enjoyable Moments.

I sigh and turn off the lantern. I don't think tomorrow can be worse.

But I'm wrong.

CHAPTER 3

I wake up warm. No, not warm—hot. I stretch like a cat, rolling over in my sleeping bag. My eyes flutter just enough to peek at a sunbeam gleaming in from the open tent flap. Wait, why isn't that closed?

I open my eyes for real, and my head swims. Pounds.

I rub a hand over my face and try to sit up. I fail, going down in a heap, that same dull ache throbbing behind my temples. I lick my lips. My mouth is a wad of sand-coated cotton.

Am I dehydrated? Is that possible? I wonder what time it is because I'm *roasting* in here.

I look over, expecting Emily to be gone since the flap is open, but she's still in her bag, sawing logs. Figures. She probably ran out to pee and forgot to zip us back in, which means a parade of spiders could've crawled into our mouths while we slept. Tasty.

Or maybe Mr. Walker just opened it, trying to wake us up. We obviously overslept. It's usually freezing in the morning, but the back of my neck is sticky with sweat. I crawl toward the entrance, looking for the telltale stripes on my backpack—where is it? Tell me I didn't leave it out there in the rain! I fumble on my boots without socks and stand, but the world tilts dangerously. I clutch the side of the open door, my stomach rolling in warning.

Whoa. What the crap is going on with me?

My brain feels fuzzy in the sunlight outside. Even foggy-headed and eyes watering in the sudden brightness, I can tell it's not morning. I think it's late afternoon, and it looks like a gorgeous day. Blue sky, birds singing, the soft whisper of leaves shifting high in the trees above.

I squint up at the sun overhead. How did we sleep this late? My vision finally slides into focus, and I look around, seeing a trail of stuff between two of the tents. Is that clothes? *Was there a bear?*

My heart leaps into my throat, sits on the back of my dry, swollen tongue. Something's not right. I spot Jude on the other side of his tent. His curly head is ducked. He's hunched over, heaving. Oh. *Oh.*

I look away from where he's being sick in the bushes and grab my own churning gut. OK, time to find Mr. Walker. A pile of stuff stops me short.

That wasn't there last night.

We wouldn't have missed this heap of... My eyes try to pick apart pieces that don't make any sense. Straps and ripped cloth and papers and bits of plastic and glass. I spot a Broadway keychain dangling off a torn bit of striped canvas.

That's *my* keychain. I take a breath, but it gets stuck halfway in. Wait—*wait*—

I stagger over on wooden legs and look down at the keychain. That's my bag. Or what's left of it. It's empty, cut into ribbons of canvas and broken straps. And those plastic and metal bits aren't *bits*. They're phones. *Our* phones. This is our stuff.

Someone swears, and I turn around, seeing Lucas sitting outside his tent. He's pulling a shirt on and looking as sweaty and miserable as I feel. When his head emerges from the neck hole, he meets my eyes. I don't know the expression he's wearing, but it scares me. Everything I see scares me right now.

I scan the whole camp, torn up and empty and just…destroyed. This wasn't a bear. Someone was here. We were sleeping, and they were in our camp. My backpack was in my tent.

Oh God.

Someone was in my tent.

My heart trips itself and then races. I can feel every beat in my head, my pulse counted out in beats of pain behind my eyes.

Mr. Walker. We need—

"Mr. Walker?" My voice cracks and crumbles like dead leaves. I swallow hard and try again. "Mr. Walker!"

This time, I'm louder because his tent flap is closed. I don't know if he'll hear. Jude stumbles back toward his tent, then sinks to his knees. He's shaking all over, one earbud dangling halfway down his T-shirt, the other still in his ear. I can see the cord isn't plugged into anything. His phone is gone.

Lucas is on his feet now, moving closer. Coming for me? Paranoid thought, but still, the fear needles into my spine. He turns toward Mr. Walker's tent, and I can't move as he unzips the door, throwing it open. Still can't move when I hear him inside, calling Mr. Walker's name. Softly first and then louder. Swearing, followed by an awful rustle and grunt.

He's hurting him!

Fear turns to adrenaline, and I sprint for my teacher's tent, my steps landing fast and sloppy. I don't know what I'm thinking when I throw open that flap, but I freeze at the entrance, some ancient nameless instinct holding me back.

"There's something wrong with him," someone says. I can't tell if it's Mr. Walker or Lucas. It's too dark in here. My eyes strain for focus, my brain still sloshing around, trying to find sense in something.

"Come help me!" It's Lucas.

My eyes adjust, shadows forming into shapes. Lucas is bent over Mr. Walker. I crouch just inside the door. Our teacher looks awful. Pale and slack, half on his sleeping bag and half propped on Lucas's knees. Is he breathing?

"Sera!" He looks urgent. "Help me!"

I jerk at the sound of my name, and our eyes lock. It's as close as we've been since the party, but this is different. Seeing him like this—face blanched and breath shaky—sends goose bumps up on my arms.

"Wake him up," I say, the words as hollow as my middle.

"I can't." Lucas shakes his head. "I can't."

Outside, someone screams.

My feet and legs wobble when I stand, and the world is topsy-turvy back in the sunlight beyond the tent door. I blink sweat out of my stinging eyes and take a step, searching for the source of the wailing. Trees. Trees. Emily.

She's in shorts and a T-shirt, her hands bunched in both sides of her hair, her mouth stretched wide, even though her scream has dribbled into silence.

30

I grit my teeth against my swimming head and start walking. Emily sucks in another breath. I think she wants to scream again, but she's empty. She backs up, up, up until she's against a tree near the pile of our stuff, the color drained from her face.

Is she going to pass out? I think she might, so I move faster, feeling the ground go wobbly. My steps thud off rhythm. Emily spots me and yelps.

I reach for her, not sure if I'm trying to comfort her or hoping she'll catch me. She scuttles beyond my reach, her eyes like bits of coal.

"Emily, it's OK!" I say, lifting my hands.

She flinches again, and I hear footsteps coming my way.

"You're freaking her out."

Jude, of all people. Puke down the front of what I'm betting is a sixty-dollar T-shirt.

He crouches, and I follow his lead. We're treating her like a cornered dog, and I don't like it. What are we going to do, offer her a Beggin' Strip?

"All right?" Jude asks her.

Emily's face hardens at him, but she nods.

I swipe a shaky hand through my hair, and my knees are too weak to hold the crouch. My butt hits the ground, so I just sit, trying to breathe. Trying to think.

"Mr. Walker's alive, but he's not conscious," Lucas says, his heavy footsteps behind me.

"Did he get sick?" Jude asks.

Lucas sneers. "Apparently, that's just you, little girl."

"Don't be a jerk," I snap, then to Jude, "I feel raunchy too."

"Like, hungover raunchy, right?" he asks.

I wouldn't know, so I shrug, but Lucas mutters something that sounds agreeable. Jude's shoulders hitch down a notch, and he finally takes that last earbud out.

"What the hell happened to us?" he asks as he's coiling the white cord, examining the bare plug with a frown.

"They did it to you too," Emily says. We all turn to her. She crosses one arm over her middle and juts her chin at Jude's arm. "Your word is different."

"What w—" He never finishes. Because when he turns his left wrist up, we all see it. The letters are ornate like a tattoo. Or maybe henna. His reads *Deceptive*.

Emily lifts her wrist, and I have to squint to make out the letters. *Damaged*.

Lucas checks his and snorts. "Of course." Then he flips his wrist up so we can all see.

Dangerous.

My turn. I swallow against the lump in my throat, and it goes down hard, bruises my insides. Just do it. *Do it*.

I turn my wrist up, praying so hard for a familiar olive stretch of clean skin. I see the black marker ink immediately. My mouth goes watery and sour before I even read it. I hold it up but close my eyes because I know they won't like it.

My word is *Darling*.

CHAPTER 4

No one says a thing. Maybe what's written on our wrists is all the words we need. Or maybe we're all trying not to throw up. It's probably both. We need to think. We need to do something.

I lumber to my feet, still spinny and sick. Lucas steadies me with a hand to my hip, and I recoil. "Don't!"

He backs away, palms raised. "Calm down, *Darling*."

"Yeah, I'd love to know why you get the nice word," Jude says, voice rough.

The letters on my wrist burn. "It's not like I wrote this."

"Then who did?" Emily asks. She's not accusing me—she's scared. "Who did this?"

Lucas palms the back of his neck. "My money's on the asshole who ripped all our stuff to shreds."

My eyes drift over the other campers. The thing is, at least some of these words fit. Lucas *is* dangerous, and one look at Emily makes it clear she's got issues. Whoever did this could have known that. They wouldn't have bothered if they didn't know, right?

Not that someone knowing us would make this logical. *Nothing* about this makes sense, not the destroyed supplies or the fact that we slept away the day or the fact that we've got personalized tattoos branded on our wrists. The only thing I'm sure of is that it all adds up to something bad.

"What's his word?" Jude asks, nodding at Mr. Walker's tent.

Lucas shakes his head. "He doesn't have one."

"How can you be sure?" I ask, feeling my eyes narrow.

His expression sharpens. "Because I think I would have noticed when I was hauling his ass around. He's wearing a T-shirt. I saw his lily-white arms pretty well."

"But why wouldn't he have a word?" I ask. It bothers me, and I know that's stupid. I'm acting like someone's made a list of rules, and in those rules, *everyone* gets a word.

"We need help," Emily says.

Lucas exhales. "Yeah, and we need to figure out where—"

I inhale sharply, interrupting him. "Ms. Brighton." Her name tastes like salvation. Jude looks up, and I take a breath and look at everyone. "We need to find her and Madison and Hayley. They have their phones! They can help us."

Lucas tilts his head with a wary expression. "Unless they're in the same shape we are."

"The bridge was practically washed out," I say. "Someone couldn't have gotten to both sides of the river."

"*We* couldn't cross," Jude says. "That doesn't mean no one could."

"Fair point," Lucas says. "If there's another bridge or even a zip line, it wouldn't be an issue. Maybe this is the mountain equivalent of cow tipping or whatever."

My face scrunches. "What?"

Lucas shrugs. "This feels like a prank, doesn't it? Destroying our crap, writing creepy words on our arms. *Let's see if we can scare the city folk.*"

I cock my head. "We're from Marietta, Ohio. Wouldn't exactly call us *city folk.*"

Emily frowns. "This is pretty elaborate for a prank anyway."

"Good pranks *are* elaborate," Lucas says. "Do you know how much planning it took to get the statue of Arthur St. Clair suspended from the rafters in the school auditorium?"

Jude turns to Lucas, brows arched. "That was *you*?"

He shrugs, and my head throbs. Of *course* it was him. I don't know how blind I was this summer, but I should have put it together. It's not like I haven't seen his type before.

My mother left my dad and me over a guy like Lucas. Hotheaded and prone to snarkiness—and mischief—but still somehow charming. Funny. They've even got the same tall, dark vibe going, though Charlie looked like he belonged in a sweater on a Macy's catalog, and Lucas…well, I can't even imagine him *inside* a Macy's.

Jude and Emily are grinning at Lucas as he explains the intricacies of the plan, but I'm thinking of when I met Charlie. It was after one of Mom's shows. He played opposite her in *42nd Street*—her biggest role—and my mom swore I'd love him to death. She was right—I really liked him.

Until I *really* didn't.

"I'm almost impressed," Jude says, sounding like he wishes it weren't true.

Lucas glowers at him, and I grit my teeth. We don't have time for this. "Can we all stroke Lucas's ego about his *many* impressive crimes *after* we find Ms. Brighton?"

"You can stroke my ego anytime, Sera."

Emily gasps before I can retort, her eyes on Mr. Walker's tent. "What happened there?"

"He's not dead, remember? Just knocked out cold," Lucas says.

Emily clenches her fists, looking suddenly pale. "Not that. Look."

Lucas and Jude must see the fear in her eyes because they follow her gaze. She's looking at something beside the tent, something we missed.

I step sideways and see it: a square formed by sticks laid end on end. The ground in the middle has been cleared of leaves, and a careful number three is gouged into the soft soil. I squeeze my eyes shut for a beat, wanting it to disappear and knowing it won't.

Lucas takes a breath. "What the hell is that?"

Jude gestures to the number and adopts a preschool teacher voice. "That's a number three, Lucas. Preceded by number two and followed by—"

A muscle in Lucas's jaw jumps. "What's it *doing* there?"

"That's how many days we were supposed to have left on our trip," I say.

"I don't think that's about our camping trip," Emily says, reading my mind. Then she looks around, shoulders hunched. "It's too quiet. Isn't it?"

A chill is rolling up my back because I think I know what she means. "You mean we should hear the others, right?"

"They'd be calling for us," Emily says. She's not wrong.

"There are three of them," Lucas says, still staring at the number in the ground.

"We should hear them," Jude says, tipping his chin to Lucas. "Madison would be bleating your name like a goat."

It's true, and the absence of said bleating is suddenly pressing fear into me. There *are* three of them. But the number on the dirt makes me wonder. Are there still three?

"OK, let's not jump to conclusions," Lucas says. "They probably took off when we didn't answer. Maybe they think we left without them. Or that we need help."

"He's right. They could have even given up earlier when we were still unconscious. We'll figure it out when we get there," I say.

"I don't want to go back to the water," Emily says.

I don't need to ask why. The terror is obvious in her tone. She's afraid of what we'll find there. A cold prickle in my center tells me I'm afraid of that too.

My eyes drift to Mr. Walker's tent. We left the flap open so he'd stay cool, and I can see the faint rise and fall of his olive-green undershirt. But he's still too pale. Worry pricks at my throat. He should be awake by now.

So why isn't he?

I lick my lips. God, I'm thirsty. "Let's try to wake him up, like Emily suggested. Just one more time. Can't hurt anything, right?"

I must look desperate. Either that or Emily and I aren't the only ones hesitant to return to the water alone.

We close in near his tent door, calling his name softly and then louder. Lucas even shifts him a little closer to the edge of his tent.

Hope springs through my chest when he groans. He's waking up! Everything will be all right! It will make sense! But his eyes don't open, and no more sound comes from his lips. I snag the front of his shirt, desperate.

We shout his name, grab at his arms and hands, but it's worthless. He's back out quickly, head tipped to the right and a pool of saliva glistening at the corner of his slack lips.

How the hell is he drooling? I don't think I could spit if someone offered to pay me. My eyes fall to the empty water bottles beside him. *Two* empty bottles. The rest of us only had one.

The rest of it rolls through me—my groggy wake-up, Jude's puking. Did someone put something in our water?

"Did you drink the water last night?" I ask suddenly.

Lucas and Emily nod, and Jude's brow puckers. "Yeah, why?"

I hold up Mr. Walker's empty bottles. "I think we felt drugged because we *were* drugged."

CHAPTER 5

No one argues about going to the river now. Mr. Walker isn't waking up, so we're out of options. We lumber to our feet carefully and search for the path we used to get up here. Everything is trees and heat and misery now, yesterday's rain leaving the air thick and sticky. Maybe we went the wrong way. Maybe the forest swallowed up the trail overnight. Or maybe—

We find it, a narrow strip of mud that will lead back to the river or—if we head the other way—to the dirt lot with Ms. Brighton's car. That's the end of the trail, but it's also a three-day hike from here.

Jude steps on the path, but Lucas lifts a hand and frowns.

"Hold up. Are all these footprints ours?"

"There are footprints everywhere," I say, gesturing at the muddy tracks all over the path.

"Yeah, but if they're not ours, maybe they belong to whoever did this."

A chill runs through me as I look around. It makes sense. Someone who wasn't us was in here, unzipping our tents, destroying our supplies, *writing* on us. I catch a glimpse of the word on Lucas's wrist and swallow hard.

"Should we check the camp too?" I ask.

"What does it matter?" Jude asks. "Knowing who it is doesn't make it unhappen."

He's right, and frankly, I have no idea how forensic crime people do this. I can barely tell what smears and indents are footprints, let alone actually pick them apart and assign them to different members of our camp. But I look around anyway, hoping I'll miraculously spot a boot print with *Bad Guy* imprinted somewhere in the tread.

"I have no idea what I'm looking at," Emily confesses.

Lucas snorts. "Me either. OK, bad idea. Let's go."

I fall into step behind him, but my eyes drag back to Mr. Walker's tent. He hasn't roused again, and I'm afraid to leave him. If anything, he seemed more deeply asleep. That can't be good.

"I wish I knew what they used to knock us out," I say, but I mean him. Mr. Walker is the one who isn't waking up, so he's the one I'm worried about.

Lucas swats at a cloud of gnats around his head. "That's the thing. Mr. Walker had the water in his pack the whole time. Who could have gotten to it before we drank it?"

Behind me, Emily scuffs her foot at the ground. "We left all the packs by that overhang when we checked out that gorge yesterday. It was raining, remember?"

"Right," Lucas says. "Because he didn't want the packs to throw off our balance with it being so slippery."

"So this is all thanks to his poor decision-making skills," Jude says with a sneer.

Lucas glares at him. "My guess is this is all thanks to a psychopath who gets his jollies from messing with the heads of privileged asshole out-of-towners like yourself."

"Careful, Lucas." Jude's voice is pure derision. "Your *Dangerous* is showing."

"Can both of you knock it off?" I ask. When it goes quiet, I can hear the stream, and a few paces after that, I can see glimpses of it between the trees. I feel like someone's watching us.

"Do you see something?" Emily asks, voice small.

"No," I say, "but we should hear them. I have a bad feeling."

"You're full of ideas and feelings about this, Sera," Jude says. "Maybe we should wonder if you aren't leading us into a trap."

His eyes are narrow, and the tip of his chin points at me like a finger.

Emily's shoulders hunch, and she tucks her gaze away.

My laugh hacks like a cough. "You seriously think I had something to do with this?"

"You did say you didn't want to come," Emily says softly. "Back at the school."

"Right, so instead of backing out and going with a different project, I just suffered through this crap for two days and then… *drugged* you? Are you even listening to yourselves? Do I look like a girl who drugs people?"

"She didn't drug anybody," Lucas says.

I throw up my hands. "Thank you!"

His expression is sharp enough to slice. "Don't thank me, and don't blame them for thinking it. Everybody heard you arguing

41

with Mr. Walker in the cafeteria. We know you tried to bail after you found out I was on the roster."

Jude scoffs. "Is this some sort of angst-fueled hormonal fallout for the two of you? Because if so, it's a *little* over the top."

Heat flashes across my cheeks like a slap. "This is not hormonal fallout! What is wrong with you guys? I get that we're not friends, but you know me. At least you know *of* me. In what universe do you see me involved with *anything* like this?"

"In what universe would we have predicted something like this?" Jude holds up his wrist, and I try not to look at the letters scrawled across his skin.

"I didn't do this!" I'm getting louder. I can't help it. "It was done to us. To me!"

"OK," Emily says, but she looks so uneasy. I'm pretty sure she just wants me to stop screaming. "I believe you. Let's just… do this."

I press my lips together. Jude says nothing. Lucas watches me until his gray eyes turn to flint. He pulls his bottom lip between his teeth like he's thinking, but my stomach flips all the same. I still can't look at him without it turning into that. I guess my mom's DNA is always going to be there, swimming around in my blood, ready to make me a complete idiot.

"Do you want to hand everyone stage directions, Spielberg?" Lucas asks. "Or can we just go?"

I shake my head and swallow back the argument stinging my lips. I can't afford to care about this right now. We have to find Ms. Brighton, and we have to get out of here. That's all that matters. I wipe my hands down the front of my shorts and move out of the tree line.

We're back at the top of the clearing. No rain now, but the river is a swollen artery, pumping mud-brown water and chunks of debris through the forest valley. Half the bridge is gone, sunk deep into the stream. The rest of it sticks out like a mangled ramp, metal supports twisted like bits of aluminum.

No one used that bridge or crossed this river. Not at this spot anyway.

We fan out along the outcropping above the riverbank. No one talks about the claw marks left in the mud from our escape yesterday. No one talks about the fact that we can't hear or see anybody. We just stand there and stare.

The quiet presses at my ears, but no one moves to break it. We're all watching with blank faces like storm survivors, stumbling along, looking for someone in a Red Cross shirt to save the day. I spot the word on Jude's arm, and I can't help but press my fingers over the black letters on my own wrist. I wish I could scrub it off, but it's Sharpie, so I know better. I sported black *x*'s on my hands for a couple of weeks after a summer concert.

"There," Lucas says, pointing up at a ridge above the water.

I shift closer to him, and I can't see anything at first. Trees. Patches of blue sky. Then I spot it—a sliver of brown canvas between two trunks. Another swath of green that's too bright to match the foliage. That's where they put their tents. The camp is on a rise maybe fifty yards back and twenty feet above the river. It's behind a small cluster of trees, but it's definitely their tents.

43

Lucas calls out, his voice rough but loud. The silence that answers is like a wet towel in my throat. A dragonfly hums past my shoulder, buzzing over the murky water. Jude tries next.

"Ms. Brighton!" he shouts. "Madison! Hayley!"

I hear a rustling from up near what I'm sure is their tent, and I droop with relief. Thank God. I nudge Emily's shoulder, and she looks up, hope in her gaze. But then it's quiet again. I wait one beat and then another. Nothing.

"Where are they? Do you see them?" Jude asks, shoulders hunched.

I open my mouth, just waiting to spot a streak of blond hair or Ms. Brighton's dark braid. Instead, there are just leaves waving softly and an occasional bird flitting through the canopy. A noise rustles, and I tense again.

"It's not them," Lucas says, sounding strained. "Whatever that was wasn't big enough."

Sure enough, the sound of skittering leaves drifts away from the tents, and then we hear something scrabble behind the tree. A passing thought of our ghost stories sends icy fingers up my spine. I should know better, but still.

"We should go back," Jude says. "Check later."

"Where the hell are they?" Lucas says it so softly, I'm not sure who he's asking.

I twist my hands together. "Maybe they went for help like you said. If they called and we didn't answer…"

"But they just left their tents up like that?" Lucas asks. He doesn't look convinced. "They might try to go back to our starting point, but that's a two-day hike."

"Maybe whoever came for us came for them too. Maybe they're still sleeping," Emily says.

"Someone would be up," Lucas says, sounding grim. "At least one of them, right?"

Jude takes a step backward and releases a shuddery breath. "Let's just go. I want to go."

Lucas whirls and lifts his chin, looking at Jude. "Why?"

He lifts his hands, eyes too wide. "Because this is pointless! Obviously!"

"It doesn't feel pointless to look for the rest of our group," I say.

"Not unless there's something we shouldn't see," Lucas says. "Do *you* know something about what's going on here, Rich Boy?"

Jude's lips thin. "What the hell are you talking about?"

Lucas takes a step. "You. I'm talking about you. Tried to paint Sera as the problem, but suddenly, you're twitching around like you've got a secret. If you do, you should know I will break every single one of your talented little fingers to find out what it is."

Jude's lips twitch, his gaze flicking toward Lucas's arm. "And just like that, you make it crystal clear why your particular label was assigned."

"You have *Deceptive* written on your wrist," I say, chin jutting. "Why would that be?"

"Because he's hiding something," Emily says, accusation in her soft voice lending a chill to the air.

"It's an interesting point," Lucas says, smirking. "Until now, I figured that was because of the ridiculous 'is he or isn't he' crap."

"Is he or isn't he *what*?" Jude practically snarls the words, but no one answers. I think it's a rhetorical question. He's good-looking, talented, and super tight-lipped about his romantic preferences. He can't think that girls and boys all over Chevington High don't wonder.

Last year, my friend Sophie wanted to send him a letter pledging her support to his coming out, but I told her that was totally weird since (a) they aren't friends, and (b) we have zero idea if he's gay.

"Oh, come on," Lucas says. "Are you going to pretend that not one person has asked the boy with two dads if he's gay?"

Jude's eyes narrow, and his voice drops. "What the hell do you think you know about me? What could you *possibly* know about me?"

Lucas laughs and throws up his hands. "Well, since we're going daytime TV here—"

"Lucas, don't," I say.

"Don't what?" He shakes his head at Jude. "This isn't a controversy in our school, Jude. Do you not get that? No one's going to beat your ass or write shit on your locker. But maybe that's why you want to keep it so hush-hush. Hoping to amp up the drama?"

Jude lunges without warning, and Lucas lowers his chin. The look in his eyes is a threat. In a fraction of a second, I know how this will end. Jude is a brilliant cellist with a chip on his shoulder. Lucas is in the office so much for his temper, it's a miracle he hasn't been expelled. He will eat Jude alive.

Jude lands one punch to Lucas's jaw before I shove my way

between them. Emily yelps and ducks away. The guys pull back, but Lucas has long enough arms to go right around me. I hear his palm connect with the side of Jude's head in a hard slap.

"My hand stays open once," Lucas says. "*Once.* Next time, you lose one of those perfect teeth of yours."

"Stop it!" I shout, plowing both hands into Lucas's chest. It's like pushing a truck, but he relents, stepping back with a confused look at me.

"What is wrong with you?" I ask.

Jude shakes his curls out of his eyes. "Nothing we can fix. I think it's genetic."

Lucas goes red. "You mother—"

I push at him again. "Hey! We have bigger crap to deal with right now!"

Emily whimpers softly, and Lucas takes a step back, running long fingers through his hair.

"You're right," he says, then nods at Emily. "Sorry."

"You're apologizing to *her*?" Jude starts turning toward him, and I can practically see the next fight starting. But then it's gone. The anger, the violence—it disappears as his mouth falls open, pupils shrinking to pricks of black. "Holy shit." He breathes the words quietly, backing up so fast that he slams my shoulder into a tree.

I protest, but Lucas follows his line of sight, and then his face goes sour too. His soft mouth goes as thin as I've ever seen it. "What the hell…"

I scoot sideways to see what they're looking at, but there isn't anything. Just trees and branches and—is that something over the river? Something hanging in one of the trees?

It is. Something's dangling there. Hard to see in the sunlight.

"Don't, Sera," Jude warns me. "Don't look."

But I look. Though every instinct in me tells me not to, I can't tear my eyes from whatever thing is dangling. It's swaying at the end of a string, swinging gently, fifteen feet above the muddy water. Dark at one end and a strange purpling gray. Like a lonely plum-colored wind chime, long and thin and—

My thoughts flatten to a static hiss when I make out the shape, when I spot the little flash of bright lavender at the top.

No.

My stomach shrinks into a fist and squeezes. I want to look away, but I can't. I want it to be something else—*anything else*—but it isn't.

It's Ms. Brighton's finger.

CHAPTER 6

We run and scream, like there's somewhere to go or someone to hear. Come to think of it, there might be someone. And if there is, we probably don't want them to hear us.

An image forms in my mind, a stage scene with low lights, all filtered blue. I'm curled in the muted spotlight as something enters, stage left. In real life, I'm still running, but in my mind, I'm frozen in the spotlight, and that something is edging into my ring of light. A long arm reaches for me. Spidery fingers ink a *D* onto my upturned wrist, then raise a knife to the base of my finger.

My cheek smacks a branch, my eyes tearing as pain flashes through me. I ignore it. Move faster until the fire in my lungs and the pain in my face burn the images away.

Thornbushes scratch at my arms, and something snarls in my hair. I'm off the path. Am I alone? Am I even going the right way? I run harder. Harder.

Stop.

I don't know if I hear the word or feel it, but I don't stop. Not even close.

"Sera, stop!"

This time, it clears the fog in my head. Someone's calling me. My feet stutter-step, and someone grabs me by the arm. I jerk myself loose, stumbling back until my head smacks a tree. My tongue goes slick and coppery. Lights dance in front of my eyes.

"Freeze!" Lucas says. "Just everybody freeze!"

My outsides are stopped, but my insides are running wild. I grip a tree and hold on. If I don't, I'm not sure I'll stay still. I look around, spotting the others. Jude, shoulders heaving. Emily, sweaty hair plastered to her temples. Lucas, breathing hard and hair in his eyes.

"What happened?" Emily pants. "Is someone following us? Did you see someone?"

The three of us who are not Emily look at each other.

She doesn't know.

She didn't see the finger.

None of us needed the seven-letter word on her wrist to tell us she's got anxiety issues, so what do we do? What will *she* do if we tell her what we saw? Sob? Panic? We can't deal with either of those. We can't even deal with what we've already got.

Lucas takes a slow breath. "I think we ought to get back to the path. We'll stick together. Talk about it in a bit."

"Agreed," Jude says, looking sick again.

"No," Emily says. "Not until you tell me. You saw something."

Lucas's sigh blows any chance at a cover-up.

Emily crosses her arms. Stares us down one by one.

How do you say this? There is no way that feels right, and the boys are looking at their feet. What the hell? Does *explaining things* default to me because I have ovaries?

Fine. *Fine*, but where do I start? I exhale hard. There's no way to pretty this up, so I lift my hand in an awkward gesture and get on with it. "There was a severed finger hanging over the creek. Purple nail polish."

"It was Ms. Brighton's finger," Jude adds in case she didn't get my reference.

Emily's brow puckers briefly before it goes glass smooth and pale. She looks at Lucas with a doll's frown.

"Someone cut Ms. Brighton's finger off?" she asks like she's just clarifying a weather report or maybe a homework assignment.

Instead of answering, he looks away. Real master of communication that one.

Emily is completely still, but I can see her nostrils flaring, can hear the way her breath shudders in and out. In and out.

"We can't stand around here," Jude says. "We need to run. Right now."

His words prod at me, clearing the fog of Emily's shock. "Wait, we can't!" I point back at the river. "Madison and Hayley could still be over there."

"Uh, whoever strung up Ms. Brighton's finger like a pagan sacrifice could *also* be over there," Lucas says.

"It was only her finger. She could just be hurt," I say because I really want to believe it. "Madison and Hayley could be trying to find help for her."

"The kind of help *we* can't give." Lucas looks around, eyes darting. "We need to save our own asses here. We can send help back for them."

"They're not over there," Emily says. Something cold shapes every word, pulls the end of her sentence into a point. "We would hear them if they were over there."

"You think they're dead, right?" Jude asks. "I mean, that's what we're all thinking, isn't it? We're assuming they're dead."

I hope no one answers. Emily looks down. I think she *wants* us to say no. She wants all three of them to be OK, but she saw the number three in the ground and the abandoned tents. She heard the silence. Emily's quiet because she knows better. And my stomach sinks because I know better too.

"I think we're back to my plan of running," Lucas says.

Jude nods. "I'm in. But it's three more days on the trail, right? We've got zero supplies. We won't make it."

"We cut north," Lucas says.

"Why north?"

He points through the trees. "There's a state route north of here. It's the road we took when we dropped off Ms. Brighton's car at the end point. The trail we're on runs in the same general east-west direction, but we're way south of the road now. If we stay on the trail, we'll head even farther south to hit that waterfall Mr. Walker was talking about. But if we cut north through the forest, we'll get back to the road faster."

"Is anyone here remembering that there is a fifth member to our group? One who isn't up for cutting north or walking at all?" My voice is too loud, so we all fall silent. I shift my feet and hear wind in the leaves and birds chittering in the scatter of branches overhead. After a minute of nothing that sounds like a serial killer approaching, I lick my lips and continue. "Mr. Walker is still sick. We can't leave him."

"We'll send help when we're safe," Jude says. "If someone's out here cutting off fingers, I'm not going to sacrifice myself for a guy who goes out of his way to avoid touching my desk."

I tense at that, trying to think back to the class we share. Does Mr. Walker do that? I don't think I ever paid attention. Jude was a blur in a seat behind me. That prodigy kid from Columbus with perfect skin, solid grades, and two well-dressed fathers.

"OK, but he knows this land better than anyone," I say. "He's the one who got the permits for us to hike this old trail, right?"

Jude says, "Yeah, the remote factor he sold us on feels *really* helpful right now."

"We should have just done the Appalachian Trail," Lucas says. "This shit would not be going down there. There'd be other hikers."

"It doesn't matter what we should have done," Emily says. "What matters is what we did do and what we do now."

"If we run, we could get lost," I point out. "Plus, won't there be rescue groups coming? In the event of an emergency, Mr. Walker and Ms. Brighton both told us to stay put."

"They also said to put out a distress call on one of our phones or the GPS," Jude says. "We can't do that because we were robbed and attacked. This *isn't* what they had in mind when we talked emergencies, Sera."

"But if we don't check in, they'll come looking for us," I reason.

"When, Sera?" Lucas asks. "How many hours until that happens? How many more until they manage to find us?"

Jude pushes his hair back from his forehead. "And how do we know that whoever this is didn't take our GPS? They could be checking in, pretending everything's right as rain."

I swallow, and it burns all the way down.

"I see three options." Lucas lifts his chin. He looks like he's trying to be older than he is, and I'm annoyed. "The river is still too high to cross without the bridge. We could walk along the water, hoping to find a bridge or a shallow spot, something to get us back on the other side, then we could follow the trail back to where we left Mr. Walker's van. We'd have water at least."

"It's at least a two-day walk. And unfiltered river water?" Jude looks like Lucas offered him a bowl of maggots. "Next option?"

"We stay on the path and hike like hell toward the finish line. Ms. Brighton left her hippy-mobile there, right?"

"Yes," I say, remembering my ride down in the passenger seat. The backseat was littered with spirituality books, and a dream catcher dangled from the rearview mirror, but she had the greatest playlist of indie music, stuff I'd never heard. My next breath is harder to pull.

"It's supposed to be three more days of hiking to our end point," Jude says. "And we don't have water. I'm thirsty as hell."

"Me too," I admit, hoping option three is to head back to camp.

Lucas scuffs the ground with his boot. "Option three is to cut through the woods like I said. It's a fairly straight road. I'm not a Boy Scout or whatever, but I know how to find north. I saw it on the map, so I know it can't be that far. We'll intersect it."

"And I should trust you on this *why*?" Jude asks, stepping forward. "Because of your exemplary academic record?"

"Look at how many shits I don't give about who you decide to trust," Lucas says. "The road and the trail both head east to west. I don't know exactly how far apart they are, but the road is north, and cutting through the woods means we aren't getting sidetracked on the trail for sightseeing stuff. It looked close on the map."

Jude scoffs.

"I think we should go back to camp," Emily says. "Help will come."

"She's right," I say, shoulders hunched. "My dad…" I swallow back a sudden push of tears. God, my dad. It was hard for him to even sign the permission slip. I'm sure he's watching every check-in. No way would he sit by for eight or ten hours with no word. "My dad would call for help. I'm all he's got."

Lucas sighs. "And every police officer worth his badge will write him off until we've been gone a hell of a lot longer than this. This whole trip was supposed to be off grid, so no one's going to realize we're in danger. Plus, Jude's right. Whoever trashed our stuff might have kept the GPS to send check-in messages."

"But there are supplies in camp," I say, sounding weak. Almost desperate. I'm losing the fight, but I can't let go.

"*Destroyed* supplies," Jude says. "Wake up, Sera. We know this isn't a prank now. Even Lucas is thinking smarter than you are right now. We need to get ourselves out of here. We can send help. Anything else is stupid."

"Agreed." Lucas ignores Jude's derision this time. "So, north until we hit the highway."

I laugh. "I'm sorry, did I miss the part where someone voted you two rulers supreme?"

Lucas whirls on me. "What the hell do you want us to do? Leave you here?"

"I want you to respect the fact that *you* don't get to decide for us."

Lucas stalks forward. The hair at his temples is damp, and his chest is heaving. "You know damn well I respect you. But if your choice is to sit here and wait for someone to come lop off a finger or two, I *don't* respect that. I won't make you go, but I won't stay here with you."

"But Mr. Walker—" Emily starts.

"Mr. Walker needs a doctor," Jude says. "Among other things."

"Since I haven't seen any doctors around…" Lucas trails off as if that's all that needs to be said on the matter.

"Then let's go back to camp and talk about it," I say. "We can check on him."

"You mean go back to camp so you can talk us out of leaving." Jude's chin is looking extra sharp again. "No way. Whoever took Ms. Brighton's finger could be taking Mr. Walker's right now."

I rub the back of my sticky neck, my whole head set on a

continuous throb. "Maybe we could rig some of the phone pieces together from the supply pile."

"Are you even hearing yourself right now?" Lucas scoffs. "There is a psycho out here. You want to waste time trying to build a phone out of busted microchips and bird shit?"

"Maybe she wants us to go back for another reason," Jude says, eyes narrowing.

My fists clench. "Stop trying to pin this on me!"

"Whatever you say, *Darling*," he fires back.

Lucas laughs. I think he aims for cruel, but tired is closer to the mark. He pushes his sweaty hair off his forehead, and his eyes go half-mast.

"She didn't do this. No chance," he says.

I let out a little disbelieving huff. Maybe I should thank him, but I know when he opens his mouth, he'll ruin it.

And he does. "She's nowhere near ballsy enough to pull something like this off."

My fists clench. "I'm not going anywhere with either of you."

"I'm staying too," Emily says softly.

Lucas's mouth opens, but he doesn't fire anything back. I see the briefest flash of pink tongue, and then it looks like he's going to smirk. But then his eyes go sad. "Hell of a risk just to stay away from me, Sera."

"I can't leave Mr. Walker," I say.

"We're better off together," he says, and when I don't respond, he shrugs. "Suit yourselves. Can't say we didn't try. We'll send help."

They walk away, and I stand there, fists clenched and face red. We can't see them for long, but we can hear them. Voices and crashing footsteps. Then just the footsteps. Then nothing.

That's when I realize Emily and I are on our own.

CHAPTER 7

"D o you think they're right?" Emily asks me when we're back in camp. "Do you think whoever…do you think they'll come back for us?"

"I don't know, but hopefully, Mr. Walker will wake up soon." I look up at the sunshine glinting through broad leaves. It makes the forest look charming. Harmless. It's not either of those things anymore. "If they wanted to hurt us, they kind of had their chance, right? I mean, they drugged us and wrote on us, but that's it." Except that's *not* it. When I close my eyes, I can still see that awful discolored *thing* that was Ms. Brighton's finger.

Emily shrugs. "They say some murderers have a type. Maybe we don't fit?"

I glance at Emily's smooth-lidded eyes and then down at my own coppery arms. She could have a point. Madison and Hayley fall on the opposite side of the human color wheel.

Emily cocks her head. "Ms. Brighton isn't blond though. Maybe it doesn't make as much sense as I thought."

I sigh. "Truthfully, none of this makes sense. If it's the other three they want, why bother with us at all? We weren't even on the same side of the river. I still don't know how they got across for that matter."

"Not easily. That's why I don't think it's over."

I hold back a cold shudder. "What do you mean?"

She sits down by Mr. Walker's head and checks his pulse, looking perfectly composed. "I think Ms. Brighton and Madison and Hayley—maybe they were just the start. The first three."

Our eyes drag to the number three beside Mr. Walker's tent.

"The only one we know was hurt was Ms. Brighton though," I say, trying to hope.

Emily frowns. "It's weird. Ms. Brighton wasn't even going to do this. It was supposed to be Ms. Appleton, but something changed. Maybe Mr. Walker requested her? It was kind of eleventh hour, but I know he was in charge of the whole thing."

"How do you know it changed?"

Her head ducks, and the tips of her ears go pink. It looks like there's a tiny short spot of hair behind her ear. Like she's cut off a lock for someone. Creepy.

"I was in the counselor's office," she says. "They were reprinting the assignment sheet in the hallway."

Counselor's office. Questions burn on the tip of my tongue, about the word on her arm or maybe the gray-black bruises, even about the little missing chunk of her hair. Everything about her posture says closed book though. I take a breath and look around instead. "Maybe we should just get started."

"Not much else to do."

Emily keeps vigil over Mr. Walker while I go through the heap of ruined supplies, trying not to dwell on the visual of someone cutting our packs apart, busting our phones. I force myself to treat it like a trip to a thrift store for costume supplies. It's all about potential.

Easier said than done. Everything is wrecked. Cell phones and notebooks and a leather bracelet I remember my fingers tracing around Lucas's wrist at Sophie's. I drop that like a cockroach and move on.

Jude's top-of-the-line phone is painful to look at now, shiny white pieces scattered all through the pile. I try to imagine someone slipping it out of his pocket, try to picture the fingers plucking his earphone cord out and leaving it dangle. Why leave the cord?

Then again, why write on our arms? Why cut off a finger?

Why only one finger?

Or *was* it just one?

Every answer I can think of leads me to a scarier question, so I stop thinking. I should focus on getting home to my dad and on trying to find anything in this heap of crap that might help me do that. Like this sock. A sock could come in handy.

This is depressing.

I work anyway, finding bits of electronic stuff here and there. The pile is overwhelming, so I make smaller piles: trash, maybe useful, definitely useful. That one's the smallest. I found a corner of the map, the size of a deck of cards, but it's on the river. I also have some rope and a couple of empty water bottles that make me painfully aware that my tongue feels like a giant sand-coated raisin.

I'm careful with the electronics, separating them into

several tiny stacks of similar-looking items. Maybe if I organize it enough, I'll suddenly develop a competency for computer engineering?

Who am I kidding?

I have zero idea what any of this is. The only thing I know for sure is that I haven't found a single bit of yellow plastic. As far as I know, Mr. Walker's GPS is still intact, sending out signal after signal to tell the world we are A-OK.

I abandon my engineering project and do another pass through ripped bits of backpacks. I manage to score a couple of breakfast bars in a side pocket, so I offer one to Emily and sit beside her at Mr. Walker's tent entrance. It's like eating sand. I'd do anything for a bottle of water.

"Doesn't look like you found much," she says.

"Nope. Not one trace of Mr. Walker's GPS, so that's not great. Has he changed?"

"No." Then she frowns. "If anything, he seems worse than before. I've tried to move him a little, but he doesn't even groan. He's out cold."

We trail into silence because there isn't much to talk about. All I can think about is how thirsty I am, but I doubt she wants to hear it. I'm going to have to come up with something. It's not like Emily's going to—

"What happened between you?" she asks, then lifts one shoulder. "You and Lucas, I mean."

"Nothing." I press my hands to my cheeks and find them just as hot as I'd suspect after a lie like that. "Nothing."

She wrinkles her nose. "But everybody—You know what? Forget it. It's not my business."

"It's not that," I say, but where do I go from there? If it isn't that, what is it? "It's just stupid. Not worth talking about."

"*Oh.*" Her tone implies things that never happened, but I can't exactly correct her either because something *did* happen, even if it's not what she's thinking.

I close my eyes and push my sneakers into the dirt, and just like that, I'm back at school, helping Lucas carry the set up the stage stairs.

"Don't break anything," he says when I grunt under the weight of our load.

I huff. "I'm not made of glass."

His laugh does something to my insides. "I'm aware. Just trying to be polite."

We set it down on the empty stage and join the new piece to the other half. It's a metal mess of angry lines and dark shadows—an abstract version of a fire escape. Now that I've seen it, I can't imagine any West Side Story *without it.*

"It's crazy good," I say, gesturing at the set. "You'll be working Broadway one day."

He laughs. "I'll be welding on a construction site. Nobody pays for shit like this."

"I would." I run a thumb along a seam in two metal sheets, heat rolling up my neck. "Learn to take a chance on something, Lucas."

"You're one to talk." His gaze drops to my mouth, and it isn't the first time.

Sometimes, I wish he didn't stand so close to me. And sometimes, I wish he'd stand closer.

Emily's laugh drags me out of the memory. She's shaking her head, like my face is telling secrets. It probably is.

"Whatever you're thinking, you can stop," I say. "I'm pretty sure you're wrong."

"I'm sorry," she says, looking amused. "But I think I might be a little right."

My lip quirks into half a smile. It's as close as I've ever come to admitting anything. Knowing what happened myself is enough. Maybe I went stupid for a while with Lucas—I know I lost my mind completely on Sophie's back deck—but that's not who I really am. That's my mother.

Everything swoony in me died the morning my mother curled her long, pretty hair just a little too carefully, the same morning she gave me a hug that lingered more than usual.

"You are just like me," she'd said. "I hope you'll trust your heart too. No matter where it leads."

I should have known something was up, but I was fourteen years old, and my mother was north on the compass of my heart. Now, she is a cautionary tale. And I'm smart enough to listen.

"So you were never actually dating though?" she asks.

"I don't really date." I shrug. "Not seriously. It seems a little ridiculous, doesn't it?"

"Sometimes," Emily says. "To some of us. But I've seen you at dances and out with groups. I guess I thought…"

"Casual stuff," I say. "I just don't see a point in losing yourself in some person you'll probably never see again after graduation."

"Did you lose yourself in Lucas?"

"No." *But I could have.* "So, what about you?" I smile wide, ready to deflect. "You have your eye on anyone?"

"My family wouldn't like that." She says it like it's not weird, so I nod and play along.

A dragonfly whirs past on shimmering wings, hovering briefly over Mr. Walker's tent. He's still out cold, stretched flat beside his tent door. He hasn't moved, which is odd.

"It doesn't make sense," I say, nodding at him. "He should be getting better."

"Unless he was drugged again," Emily says with a soft snort.

I gasp. "Oh my God."

"What?"

"If he woke up while we were gone, he might have had more to drink. Did we check his tent? Did he have any extra bottles?"

Emily doesn't answer, but she gets up. She slips easily over Mr. Walker's body and into the tent. There's a soft rustle, then a silence that starts too quickly and stretches too long. My ribs clamp down like someone's tightened a screw.

"I found something," Emily says, but I already knew that.

Emily's steps are soft when she returns. I don't need to ask what she's found because she's carrying it. Six gleaming plastic bottles that make my tongue scrape like a hunk of sandpaper across the roof of my mouth.

Water. Big bottles too.

Our eyes meet, and her hands shake when she sets them down. We need it badly. I've only peed once, before we started rummaging. It wasn't much. And I'm not sweating anymore, even though it's still hot.

"That's not all," she says, ducking inside the tent to grab something. "His old bottle *was* empty," she offers, then holds up the old bottle. It's not empty now. There's about half an inch of water in it, but it looks weird.

"There's something in that," I say. "It looks cloudy."

"Yes," Emily says. "But the other bottles seem fine. The plastic overwrap is still intact."

"Great. Except that we don't know where they came from."

She doesn't answer for a while because we *do* know. And if they drugged us once, why on earth would we think they won't do it again? My eyes drag to the cloudy water in Mr. Walker's bottle. They already *have* done it again.

"I'm thirsty." Emily's voice is small and desperate.

I nod, my tongue moving again inside my tacky mouth. "But we know who brought that water. It could be drugged. Or worse." I force myself to say it because if I don't say it—don't think about it—I will tear off the cap and suck down that entire bottle. Looking at it makes the thought of it almost painful, cool and sweet on my mouth. I could drink two bottles. Maybe three. No, no, I can't. There are five of us and only six bottles, so I have to—

"There are six more bottles inside," she says.

I swallow and my throat clicks. "It could be drugged. It's probably drugged."

"Maybe it's not," she says, sounding young. Emily always seems young, though I know that's not fair. I barely knew her before we started sharing a tent, and it isn't like we spent the first two days bonding out here.

"Emily…"

I don't know what to tell her. We're both staring at each other because we could drink this and end up like Mr. Walker. Or we could take our chances with whatever biological nightmare is cooking up in the river. Either way, water is a roll of the dice we can't avoid much longer. I don't need a medical degree to know we have to drink, and we have to do it soon.

"Would the river be better?" she asks.

I open my mouth and then hear something snap and crack in the woods. It's a ways off. Could be nothing. My ears strain, catching bits of birdsong and the *hush-hush* of leaves rustling. And then another snap. Maybe a grunt.

Emily lets out a shaky breath. Her knuckles go white on the water. Another crack, and we both flinch. I stand up.

Someone's coming.

CHAPTER 8

Rescuers? No, they'd call for us. We'd hear them. Besides, even if no one's using the check-in function on the GPS, we only sent a message once or twice a day. We're not late enough for anyone to be here yet.

I flex my hands, look around as adrenaline tries to kick-start my limbs. We need to do something. Run.

The footsteps are coming closer, and I catch sight of the *Damaged* on Emily's arm. Whoever wrote that could be coming for us. Maybe the water is drugged and they are hoping we already drank it—that we're passed out again right now.

A flash of Ms. Brighton's severed finger washes through my mind. We can't be here. We're like sitting ducks.

I wrap my hand around Emily's wrist and start walking, finger to my lips. She doesn't need to be told twice to follow, slipping past Mr. Walker and to the edge of our campsite clearing. I still hear the footsteps. The grunts.

My eyes drag over the trees. Better cover there, but we'll be noisy as hell. Our chance is better on the path. We'll head back toward the river.

Back toward the finger?

My limbs go heavy. More noise, stomping. It's like a herd of elephants. They won't hear us over their own racket. We step back into the trees, my finger at my lips to remind Emily to stay quiet. She's better at this than me. Her steps whisper quiet as we edge into the trees.

Whoever's coming is close now.

"Sera! Emily!" The shout is loud, coming from the woods on the other side of camp. I start moving faster backward, my heart tripping like my feet. "Hey! Sera!"

I deflate. It's Lucas. I turn back, shoulders dropping in relief. They hunch when he calls my name again with a grunt. Why isn't Jude calling for us? Where is Jude?

Emily's already striding back for the camp before I say anything. We see Lucas as soon as we come closer. Jude's there too, one arm slung over Lucas's shoulder and head lolling.

Lucas takes another step, and Jude's feet drag-thump along, his knees bending too deeply. He's only on his feet because Lucas is holding him up. He looks awful, hollow eyes and sunken cheeks. His skin has a strange ashy tinge. His lips are cracked and bleeding.

"What happened?" I ask.

"No idea. He said his head hurt. A little later, he collapsed. He's barely making any sense."

"Dehydration," Emily says decisively. "He was vomiting, so he's worse than us. We found water. I'll get it."

"Emily, you can't!" I turn to look between them. "Someone *left* that here. It's not ours."

"Someone left it?" Lucas asks. "Who?"

"The same someone who we think drugged Mr. Walker again."

Lucas's expression turns dark. Emily ignores my protests and retrieves the water. She's back with it before I can form a new argument. A plastic crack pierces the quiet when she twists off the cap. My throat bobs at the fat drop of water that rolls down the side of the bottle. I know I had something to drink last night, but it's probably dinnertime. Maybe later. Maybe it's only been twelve or fourteen hours, but it feels like it's been a week.

"We can't give him that," Lucas says, but his gray eyes are tracking that bottle like a predator. "No way it's safe."

"He's sick. It's only going to get worse," Emily reasons.

"Then we get some water from the river," I say. "They make antibiotics for whatever's floating around in that, right?"

"Hell no," Jude croaks.

His eyes are half-open, and I feel a pang of worry. I'm thinking of his dads, especially Thomas, who's always nice, even when people aren't nice back. If he saw me handing Jude this water…

I shake my head and turn for the path that leads to the river.

"No," Jude says, reading my mind. "Not drinking fish piss. Give me the bottle."

My brow furrows. "It could be drugged."

"Drugged is better than this."

"Could be poisoned," Lucas adds. "This was probably left by the psycho who cut off Ms. Brighton's finger."

"I'll take that chance."

Jude makes a clumsy grab and bumps the bottle, sloshing water out and down to the ground. My tongue burns. Aches. It's Emily who brings it to Jude's lips. Emily who also pulls it back after a few swallows.

"More," he says.

"Not yet. You'll puke again."

She's all quiet focus, feeding him half the bottle sip by sip. He sinks to the ground, and we watch him like he's a lit fuse. He's mostly sleepy, waking up to take drinks. Whining about his head. I feel a sting and smack at the mosquito on my leg as Emily cracks open a second bottle.

Maybe it's my imagination, but within a few minutes, Jude looks better. Not good by a long shot, but better. He's eventually strong enough to hold the bottle and sit up against an oak. His curls are wild and his lips are still a mess, but his eyes don't look as sunken when he opens them.

"How do we know if it's poison?" Lucas asks.

No one answers, but Jude chuckles. "I guess you wait to see if I die."

He hasn't died so far, but how long has it been? Ten minutes? An hour? No way to know, but I'm pretty sure I should wait a little longer. The problem is, I don't know if I can. I dig my fingers into the dirt and feel like my mouth is turning itself inside out. All I can see is that bottle at Jude's lips. All I can think about is ripping it out of his hands and pouring it down my own blistered throat.

"Screw it," Lucas says, caving with a quick swipe of one of the bottles near Emily's lap.

"Go slow," she warns him, but she grabs her own bottle.

I fumble for one too, cracking it open with clumsy fingers.

"Slow," she says again.

I try. I really do. The first sip turns me into an animal. I'm sure I've never known thirst like this, never understood the way a few swallows of water can taste like the best thing I've ever had. My throat soaks it up like a desert. I'm sure it doesn't even hit my belly, just soaks into all the parched places on the way down. Another swallow and another, and I will never think of water the same again. I will never take this for granted—

It's ripped from my hands, and I gasp. I'm winded. Queasy.

Lucas's face looms in front of me, worry creasing his brows. "Easy."

I reach to snag my bottle back, but it's half-gone. My stomach rolls. Emily was right. I close my eyes and wait for the sloshing to settle.

"OK," I say, opening my eyes when Lucas doesn't give my water back. He raises his brow, and I glare. "I'm *fine*."

I'm actually nauseated as all hell, but I snag the water back and take a sip to spite him. I go slower now, feeling my cramped joints go loose, that dull ache that's spread through my head relenting.

I don't pass out midway through my second bottle. Neither does Lucas, who's had two, or Jude, who is starting his third.

No one talks about the fact that it's getting darker. Maybe two hours of daylight left, and it will be night. The last night carried more than darkness on its shoulders, but we don't talk about it. We just sit around Mr. Walker's tent, stinking to high heaven and looking at each other like one of us is a rabid dog and we're just waiting to see who lunges first.

But if someone's going to lunge, it isn't going to be one of us. My eyes drag to the trees, where trunks, thick and thin, smooth and rough, rise up from the forest floor in lazy rows. Limbs twist toward the sun, reaching here and there overhead. I see things move out of the corner of my eye. Leaves. Squirrels.

A killer maybe.

A sudden, awful thought blooms: What if Madison and Hayley and Ms. Brighton *aren't* dead? What if they are over there, alone and terrified but not able to make noise? Did someone leave them water too?

My heart pinches. I think of my dad helping me drop off lemon chicken soup at the downtown church. We used to go as a family. I refuse to let my mother take that from us too, and Dad refuses to let me drive down there alone. The soup is easy, and the drive is short. It's the rest of the experience that makes me flinch.

"How do you put up with this?" I look at the women who watch us too closely as we pass, smiles tight enough to tell me they're more interested in where he was born than who he is. "You have to see how those women look at you, like you're dangerous. I'm sick of it."

"I see very well. Well enough to see my daughter feeding hungry people."

"Dad." I form the word with my lips, and my throat feels thick. Dark eyes, brown skin, the lilt of his accent that turns my name into a song—did I ever say anything that mattered to him? Did I thank him for staying? After my mom left, he could have gone home to Beirut. Did he want to?

"My parents would freak if they saw me like this," Jude says, so I must have said it out loud, picked at his worries too.

I don't know what he calls them. Are they both Dad? Maybe I ask that out loud too because he swirls the water in his bottle and nods. "Tom is Dad. Brady is Pop."

Pop. The word makes me smile, but I'm not sure Jude would appreciate that, so I hide it behind my hand. "My dad's a worrier," I say. "Probably because it's just me."

"Divorced?" Emily asks softly.

I laugh, but it's not funny. "Very."

When Mom left us for Charlie, Dad got a set of divorce papers and I got pneumonia. He didn't talk about it, and I was too sick to push. Instead, he brought me endless bowls of oversalted soup and cups of undersweetened tea. A week later, I climbed out of bed and brushed the worst of the tangles out of my waist-length hair.

He asked me if I knew how much I looked like my mother. And then I asked him if I could cut my hair.

"What are you staring at?" Jude asks.

I shake my head, jarred back to our ugly reality. "Sorry. Thinking of when I had pneumonia when I was younger."

"I don't have pneumonia," he snaps.

"I know that. I just—"

"I'm *not* sick."

"Unless asshole is a disease," Emily mutters, but I smile, hoping to disarm him.

It doesn't work.

"What is your problem with me?" he asks me. "You think it's charming I have two dads? Does it make you feel more *evolved* to know me?"

"Um, am I missing something?" I ask, stunned at the sudden outburst.

"She didn't do anything to you," Emily tells him.

"I can see the look on her face!" Jude says. "It's patronizing."

My cheeks go hot. "I wasn't patronizing you! I was missing my dad!"

"Stop being a tool sack," Lucas tells him. "Believe it or not, we mere mortals do think about other things."

Jude crosses his arms and scoots back against the tree. The sun is closer to the top of the branches now. I frown, and Lucas follows my line of vision.

"It's getting dark," I say, thinking of last night's events and all those stupid stories. Ghosts running men off cliffs. Dead girl parts being dragged off, *eaten*, by bears. "What should we do?"

"We keep watch in shifts," Jude says. "If whoever this guy is comes back, we should be ready to run."

Lucas shakes his head. "Screw that. I say we run now. We take the water and one of the tents—"

"Take them where?" I scoff. "I doubt any of us are up for a hiking trip. Jude was half-dead an hour ago. And what, we just leave Mr. Walker to fend for himself?"

"At night?" Emily looks scandalized at the idea.

Lucas cocks his head. "Would you rather snuggle up beside him and maybe wake up with nine fingers?"

"I'm starting to think leaving won't help," Jude says. "Especially if it's too dark to see."

I feel my brow quirk. "Why the change of heart?"

His eyes lock onto mine. "I had some time to think about it. Look at our wrists. This isn't random. Whoever did this isn't going to just wander off and hope we stay put—they're watching us. How else would they have known to leave the water while we were away from the camp?"

"For God's sake, Jude," Lucas says. "Do you want us to just sit here and wait for the lunatic to show up again? We have no idea who this is."

That's it. I stand up, a little edgy. "I agree. And two hours ago, you were all set to follow Lucas into the great beyond. Now you're acting like we might as well stay put and not even bother trying? Tell me again why we should all be sure *you* aren't the guy behind this."

Jude's eyes are cold slits. "Because I don't think you're a darling."

Can't argue with that.

"Enough," Lucas says. "First off, nobody here could have crossed that river, and second, let's stop pretending Sera got the lucky word in this mess."

A chill runs up my arms. Jude looks at his shoes, so I turn to Lucas.

"What are you talking about?"

"Nothing," Lucas says.

I whirl on him. "It's not *nothing*. What are you talking about with the lucky word?"

Lucas points at everyone but me. "The rest of our words are problems, Sera. We're dismissed or defective. Whatever you want to call it."

"I don't—"

"*Deceptive, Damaged, Dangerous.*" He shakes his longish hair out of his eyes. "The three of us were found *lacking*, but you weren't. Your word makes it sound like you're chosen. Or special."

"It's true," Emily says, but she doesn't look at me. She looks right past us, her eyes so cloudy, I can't tell if she's seeing anything at all.

"These could be random," I say. "Think about it. Everyone's damaged, right? Everyone lies now and then."

"So someone just happened upon us and spent God knows how long destroying our crap and inking these words onto our wrists?" Jude asks, obviously not buying it. "No. The words fit. This isn't random."

"Why not?" I ask because I don't want to be chosen or special. I still want to believe it's nonsense. "Because you have a secret? Who doesn't?"

His face shutters. "Don't start with me."

"Don't bite my head off! I'm just asking."

Lucas rolls his eyes. "Ignore him. He obviously wants the damn primetime interview about it. Like anyone gives two craps."

"For people who don't care, you're all pretty obsessed with figuring me out," Jude says.

"We're *not* obsessed," Emily says. Her focus is sharp now, slicing away at the attitude Jude's wearing like a second skin.

"Please," Jude says. "People watch me constantly. They've *always* watched."

Lucas throws up his hands. "*What* people?"

"Don't be obtuse." Jude bumps his chin. "A black kid with two white dads and you think people don't ask questions? Everybody has always wondered about me. I couldn't pick between a pink or blue crayon in preschool without someone making a tick mark in a book somewhere."

I furrow my brow. "What book?"

Lucas scoffs. "What does any of that have to do with whether or not you're gay? You *do* realize you go to an art magnet school, right? Nobody cares, Jude!" Then he leans in, eyes going wide. "Unless you care. If we're still wondering, you're still interesting, right?"

Jude's gaze could leave frostbite in its wake. His voice is deadly low when he speaks. "I don't give a shit what you find interesting."

"You are such—"

I touch Lucas, and he goes silent, his gaze moving to me before I can pretend it was an accidental brush. It should have been an accident. I shouldn't touch him at all.

"Please stop," I say.

"Protecting him now?" Lucas asks me softly, but it feels like he's asking me something else. He's staring so hard, and I'm staring right back, and I can feel all the things that happened before simmering in the smell of moss and dirt and wood. God, is this what I'm still about? When you peel back my layers, is it still my mother hiding in the center?

"Let's just drop it. Leave him alone," Emily says.

That grabs my attention. Emily's been pretty cool toward Jude since we started this trip. The sudden switch is weird.

"Don't tell me you're playing into his pity party," Lucas says, but he's not angry now.

"I'm not," Emily says. "But this isn't the time. And it isn't our business."

Jude lifts his head, watching Emily with an expression I can't read.

The breeze has gone cooler, and the sun is below the tops of the trees. It's later than I thought.

"We need to decide what we're doing," Lucas says.

"I don't think I can walk," Jude admits. "Not far."

And then I get it. All this crap he's starting. All the anger. It isn't about what he's hiding or even who's after us. It's just that he can't leave. He's afraid of being left behind.

"Me either," I lie. I could walk now. If it meant getting out of here, I could probably fly. But if I'm not leaving Mr. Walker, I'm not leaving Jude either.

"I can barely stand up," Emily says.

"I have two granola bars left," Jude offers. An olive branch if I've ever seen one.

"Good idea," Lucas says. "Let's divvy up snacks while the serial killer closes in."

I glare at Lucas. "Enough!"

He points at the remaining three bottles of water. "Someone is out there, Sera. Yeah, they left water, but they drugged us last night. Probably after they *killed* the other half of our group."

I storm toward him. "We don't know that! We haven't even checked on them, and they might be like Mr. Walker. Maybe the drugs affected them worse. Maybe they're over there right now, alone and scared, while you sit here having a pissing contest with anyone who'll listen."

Lucas pushes his hair back, and his smile is predatory. "Fine. Let's check that river. Right now. Because if you're right, then maybe they need help. And if *I'm* right, we're going to find dead bodies, and maybe then you'll agree it's time to get the hell out of here."

"Stop talking like this. Can we just try to hope for something good to happen?" I ask. "Maybe we'll find them and help them."

Lucas sighs. "The only thing that can help any of us is a way out of this hellhole or a phone to call for help."

"They might still have their phones on the other side of the river!"

Lucas stalls at the argument, his eyes flashing with interest. "All right. We'll check the river."

I laugh. "Just like that?"

"The phones are a decent point. We'll check. You two stay here with Mr. Walker."

Before I can ask which two, Lucas nudges past me, plucking at the edge of my sleeve. I take a breath I swear smells like Sophie's yard and makes my stomach fall like a Ferris wheel going over the top. God, that night was so long ago. And still not long enough.

CHAPTER 9

At the river, the finger is gone. My stomach tries to stuff itself into my throat as soon as I see it. Or don't see it, I guess. There are flies buzzing by the string but nothing else.

"Did he come back for it?" I ask.

Lucas shakes his head. "Birds probably."

Birds. I hear them in the trees up on the rise, big heavy things with dark bodies and talons that scrape at the bark on the branches. My eyes pick out a few individuals. One bobbing its head, another fanning its dark wings wide. A third turns its head, and I spot something stringy dangling from its beak. I turn away with the sting of bile in my mouth.

"What are they?" I ask.

"Turkey vultures."

Scavengers. And obviously, they've found something to pick clean. *Someone?*

Lucas is waiting for me to say something, but I'm not going to. I can't. I look down at the stream, and my head swims like the river below, brown and slick and moving fast.

"OK," I say. It's not OK. I take a step, and the world tilts.

My hand catches on a tree, and there's a weird, gray humming behind my ears. I hold on tight. Breathe slower.

"Hey, you all right?"

Lucas. He's closer. I catch a whiff of something earthy, but I think of spiked punch and that night this summer when his eyes held me hostage at the cast after-party.

He is not what I'm supposed to want. He is long hair and ripped jeans, and none of it matters when his smile curls above the rim of his plastic cup.

I can't just stand here staring. I should thank him, as the director, because he did his job.

Lucas lowers his drink to his thigh when I get there. Condensation rolls down the side, right into a hole in his jeans, just above his knee. I have the ridiculous urge—

Stop it! Just…I have to stop this.

I raise my Coke. "The set was amazing, Lucas. You outdid yourself."

"You didn't give me much of an option, did you?"

I bite back a smile. "A good director gets what the show needs."

"What about what you need?"

My chest and neck go from warm to hot. I look to my friends, who are too busy with an impromptu sing-along to look back. "I should go."

Before I can, his hand is around mine, fingers at my wrist. I've been thinking of this more than I want to admit. His hands are even bigger and rougher than I thought. Better too.

"Sera?"

His look rises up through me like steam from a shower. He crooks his head toward the kitchen, toward the back door. And I follow because even I know what this means.

"We can just go back," he says, dragging me back to the present. But we can't go back. Not from that night at the party and not from this either.

I open my eyes and look up at him. He is not conventionally pretty, but I'm not the only girl who can't seem to help looking.

"I'm sorry." My voice cracks on both words.

Lucas sighs. "Let's just head back. We can go up the path, maybe make double time."

"No, we have to check on them," I say. "If Ms. Brighton is dead, then they're alone. Probably terrified. We have to try."

"That river is still dangerous," he says, voice low and gentle. "And those birds are telling us everything we need to know about what's going on over there."

My stomach constricts as I think about the stringy bit I saw dangling. "We can't be sure unless we go. I'll never forgive myself if—"

"Sera, be serious."

"I am serious. If one of them is hurt, if they can't talk and we just—we can't just—" A sharp breath severs my words. Tears smear my vision, but I refuse to even acknowledge them with a swipe of my hand.

"Shit." He swallows hard and throws up his hand, mouth going thin. "OK. We'll try. Be heroes or whatever."

Something swims up through my chest. I'm not sure if it's relief or terror or something else. I swallow it down.

"But I don't trust that current," he says, "and the bridge is out of the question."

"So what do we do?"

He looks around, hand at the back of his neck. "All right, I'll loop my belt around that tree. I'm going to keep a hold on that, and you're going to hold on to me. If the water goes over either of our knees, we're done. If it's freakishly shallow, we'll…"

"Let go?"

He looks like he hates the idea but shrugs. "I guess that's the only way to do it, yeah?"

I nod and try not to watch as he shucks his belt, briefly revealing one hipbone and the hollow in front of it. He finds a tree right on the edge of the river and secures the belt through the buckle around the trunk. One hand on the leather strap, he steps into the water.

"We're not going to get close enough to the halfway point," he says. "We'll have to go back for the other two to help us."

"Let's just see how bad it is," I say because I can't leave here without doing something. Without trying. Maybe the water will be lower than it looks. I hope so because something tells me Emily won't cross this again. I'm not sure Jude would do it either, not with the vultures hovering or that weird noise that's drumming at my ears.

What *is* that anyway? I didn't notice it before, a tinny droning that skates along the sound of the rushing water. The drone rises and falls a little, and when I look up, I see a black mist clinging above some of the underbrush.

Flies. It's flies.

Don't think about why they're there. Don't.

But it's hard not to think about it when the smell suddenly hits me, so pungent, I cover my nose and eyes at once. The scent is unfamiliar and unmistakable at the same time. Death is on the other side of this river. I'm sure of it.

"Let's head back," Lucas says. "Let's get the others."

I want to go back more than anything, but if it were me over there, I'd want someone to try. I step farther into the water. It's maybe ten inches deep here, but it's dragging at my ankles. The current is a shock, and instinct sends my hands flailing. Lucas catches one, and I lock my gaze onto his.

"Don't you dare let go," he says.

I won't. I inch my way deeper, the current rushing up my calves, not quite to my knees but close.

Really close.

"Too deep," Lucas says. "You're not even a fourth of the way across. Look."

"It's not that deep," I say, and it's not. Still below my knees. And all I can think is that they could be over there. Bears could eat them. Carry their parts away just like Madison's story. "Just another couple of steps so I can get a good look up the ridge toward the tents."

"Then switch with me. I'm taller."

Something we should have thought of before. Still, I strain on tiptoe to peek at the other side of the bank. There's something behind the shrubs but a good twenty yards from the tents. There are too many leaves to be sure of much, but I can tell it's dark and large. Maybe wet.

That's what the smell is coming from, what the flies are after.

I stop dead in the water, feeling the blood drain out of my face.

"Lucas, something's up there. Can you see it?"

He pauses, looking, I guess, and then he tugs my hand. "I can't. Switch with me."

My heel hits something slick when I turn. My foot flies wild, and the current takes it. Everything is twisting, my knee, my ankle, the sharp thing that bites into my leg, carving a hot line into my cold flesh. Lucas pulls my arm with a jerk that makes my shoulder pop. I'm up. Standing like a newborn giraffe, but it's better than hurtling downstream. Lucas has one hand twisted in mine, another curled into the side of my shorts. We're both dripping and panting.

"You hurt?"

"No," I lie, but I don't think he'll buy it. The water is shallower here, and streaks of red are swirling into the brown around us. I can't tell how bad it is. My joints feel OK. I'm sore but intact.

Lucas swears, and I'm sure he's seen the bloody water, but he hasn't.

He's looking at the shore, at the place where I saw the dark thing. One glance and I can see it again, a shadowy lump behind the green. The flies are the only thing moving. The only thing alive on that ridge.

Lucas groans like he might be sick. "Go back," he says, gagging a little.

I don't argue. I limp my way to the shore and try to see what he's seen. I can only see the cloud of flies from here, a hungry web shifting and darting. *Feeding.*

I turn away, and Lucas gags again. I don't know if he brings anything up, but his fingers go around my arm, and he starts walking fast.

"We're done." His voice is rough. "We can't help them."

"We—"

"Sera, we can't help them. Do you understand?"

I close my mouth so I won't scream, close my eyes so he won't see how close I am to crying.

"OK," he says softly, and somehow, I can tell he knows I understand. They're dead. There was a body on that hill. Ms. Brighton's probably. And something else by the tents, where the birds are hovering. It's them. It can't be anything else, can it?

He moves back toward the path, and I follow. We're ascending when my cut brushes a tree. I yelp, and Lucas startles, turning back.

"What is it?"

"My leg. I cut it."

I turn my leg so we can see. It's not tragic, a diagonal slice just above my boot line, so it won't rub the edge at least. It should be fine as long as it's clean. A sinking through my middle reminds me that water isn't even *close* to clean, and I don't have a thing back at camp that can bandage it. No way I'm wasting bottled water either.

"Do you want me to carry you?" Lucas asks.

"I'm fine." I bristle at myself as soon as I say it. Maybe I don't want to be falling all over him, but I don't want to be nasty either. Why can't I ever find a happy medium with Lucas?

We head back through the woods toward camp without talking.

I can just see the shape of my tent through the trees when Lucas stops suddenly, his hand coming up to slow me down. I open my mouth to ask, but Lucas shakes his head.

He's listening to something. I cock my head. Voices inside the camp. Emily and Jude.

My fingers snag the side of his shirt, twist in a stranglehold. Are they in danger? Is there someone else there?

"I'm telling you, *Darling* means something." Jude. Definitely Jude.

My fingers move to the word on my arm, nails scraping at the *G*.

"She didn't do this," Emily says softly. Gratitude blooms through my middle.

"But she wants Lucas," he says. "Which means you can't trust her either."

Fire roars up my chest and neck even as my face goes cold. I move to storm up the path, to argue, but Lucas grabs me, squeezes my wrist, just a little. He's still listening.

I can't hear the first part of what Emily says, but the last few words are clearer.

"…really think he did this?"

"I think he could be involved. They wrote *Dangerous* on his arm because that's what he is. He's violent. Probably desperate. I think he did something to me when we tried to leave. I didn't pass out for no reason."

Emily's muttering too low to hear again. I make out "Tyler" and "in three places," but everything else is a jumble. I watch Lucas while I try to listen. His jaw clenches until I hear his teeth grind, but he is as still as stone. Waiting for the rest, I guess.

"I don't know," Jude says. "I'm just saying be careful."

Quiet falls over the forest again. I expect Lucas to start walking, but the minutes stretch on, and my ears ache for some sort of noise. There's nothing but wind and forest sound and, here and there, a long, shaky breath that belongs to the tall boy next to me.

I sigh and start to move forward, but Lucas leans in until his hair brushes my cheek and breathing becomes a thing I cannot do. His chin scrapes my cheek, and then he's talking, so low I have trouble pulling the words apart.

"Tell me you don't think I did this." Every word is ice lit on fire over my ear and neck.

I nod without thinking about it, swallowing hard.

"Jude tried to blame you at first," he says. "Now he's moved on to me. Something's going on with that. I don't trust him."

I nod again, and he leans back a few inches. Thank God. Everything feels spinny, and my face tingles.

I don't know what to think. I don't trust Jude either, but that's not saying much. I don't trust anyone here. My gaze drifts to Lucas's mouth, reminding me I don't trust myself either.

"We need to get back," I whisper. "We need to tell them what we found."

"Don't be alone with him, Sera."

I nod, though I can't imagine a scenario where I would. But I'm alone with Lucas right now, aren't I?

The letters on his arm catch my eye. *Dangerous.* It fits in more ways than one. If I'm afraid to be alone with any of them, it's him.

CHAPTER 10

We go to bed in shifts, and I lie awake for hours, imagining the phantom buzz of flies. I didn't enjoy our happy little camping adventure before bodies were left to rot by the river while we were violated in our tents. Now? Well, it isn't really camping anymore, is it?

Emily rolls over. She was pretty quiet once we got into the tent, but I don't know if she's asleep. I thought things were better between us. Earlier today, we talked, even laughed a little. Then again, that was before she talked to Jude.

Is that why she's gone quiet again? Is she afraid of me?

Neither she nor Jude said much when we told them about the bodies. But I caught them exchanging a careful look. Maybe they don't believe us, or maybe they really think we're involved. Whatever. We're all getting paranoid, and Lucas *is* the biggest and scariest of the bunch, I guess.

Plus, I'm the one with the Lucas history here. I'm also the one who went with him earlier.

I try to push out my memories from the river, squeezing my eyes shut for the millionth time. My mind supplies images of vulture talons and a gooey bit dangling from a black beak. OK. No more closing my eyes. Maybe ever again.

The cold returned with the sunset, so I zipped myself tight into my sleeping bag. The fabric is sticking to my cut, which feels icky and probably looks even worse, but since I have all my fingers, I guess I shouldn't gripe.

I turn to stare at Emily's dark hair. I'm sure I can still hear the flies. Impossible. I know the buzz isn't audible from here. I catalog other sounds to distract myself. Crickets and the low hoot of an owl. A branch snaps outside, and I jerk to attention. Is that the murderer?

Is this when the real nightmare starts?

No one comes, and the noises continue. Eventually, they all fade together: coyote howls and frog songs and the occasional repositioning of whoever is on watch—Lucas now because Jude just finished.

Is that why I didn't sleep? Because it was Jude guarding us, and I don't trust him? Maybe. But I'm not sleeping now either, and it's Lucas outside. I don't think he'd hurt me.

My cheeks warm because it's not something I think. I *know* Lucas wouldn't hurt me. I at least owe myself that much honesty after everything. After the party…

Outside, Lucas clears his throat, and with absolutely no warning, the memory I pushed so hard to hold back rolls me under. It was hotter that night, and the cicadas were much louder in Sophie's yard than the crickets are here. I let my gaze drift to Lucas's faint shadow through the tent wall. But even with my eyes wide open, I remember.

My heart is pounding in my ears, in my fingertips. My hands tremble when I try to push my hair away from my face. Lucas is no stranger to this back deck dance of waiting, but I am.

He cocks his head. "Are you afraid of me, Sera?"

"Yes."

"After all this time?" His smile makes me shiver. "You don't need to be."

I give a half laugh that ends on a shuddery breath. He moves closer, and I look up, finally less nervous, finally feeling a real smile curve my lips. "You're so tall. It's ridiculous."

"I've heard that once or twice." He bites his bottom lip, looking younger than usual. "I've got an idea. Ready?"

"OK—whoa!"

His hands are on my hips, gripping tight, and then the decking beneath my feet is gone. He lifts me up, up, up—sets me on the wide wooden plank on top of the deck railing. He waits for me to wrap an arm around the post beside me. My head swims at the change in height.

Maybe I should be afraid of falling, but I'm not. I'm afraid of myself because I don't do things like this. I don't, but my mother does.

A *crack* jerks me back to the forest. The sound is different. It's less of a snapping and more of a ruckus of branches and sticks. There's a soft, low noise that goes with the shuffle-crunch. My eyes pop open, ears straining. Outside, Lucas isn't moving.

Was it him? Or did I drift off? Dream it?

It comes again, a strange whirring—almost like a far-off engine—humming and whining until it dips into a grumble. No, not a grumble. A *growl.* My breath freezes into a solid mass in my chest.

That's not far away. It's close. And it might be a bear.

That stupid story of Madison's flashes through my head. The bear dragging that girl's arm to the edge of the woods. *Oh God.* I scan the dark tent, finding Emily and nothing else. My heart thuds painfully, every beat tapping at my collarbone, the hollow of my throat. I'm panicking. I'm definitely—

OK, stop. Think of Mr. Walker. What were the bear safety rules?

We don't have any food. We haven't cooked. I haven't seen any poop or scat or whatever Mr. Walker called it.

We're supposed to make noise if they attack. Is this an attack? I crawl out of my sleeping bag and cross the tent on my knees. Emily snores softly, and the growling comes again. Goose bumps erupt on my arms. My ears strain by the door, and my eyes follow the dark shapes moving somewhere beyond the front wall of our tent.

There's no noise. Nothing.

Nothing.

Grunt, grunt, huff, huff, huff.

Something scrapes along the ground like it's being dragged. My throat goes dry. Tight. Where's Lucas? I can't see *anything*. Everything is lost in dark smudges beyond the canvas. I push my palm into my chin, trying to hold my chattering teeth still.

I won't be able to see unless I unzip the tent. Lucas is still out there. If he fell asleep out in the open, I don't know what the bear will do. I shiver. I can't think about what the bear will do. I just have to stop it. We're supposed to make a racket, right?

I don't want to though. It sounded good then, but now I don't know what else is in these woods. If the bears are real, are the ghosts real too? I shake my head, trying to rattle some sense back into myself. I can't dwell on stories; I need to focus. I hold my breath and listen again, catching no sound beyond my own heart, a bass drum trapped in the closet of my ribs.

Another *grunt, huff, grunt.* Farther away now. Past Jude's tent, I think.

This is my chance. I pinch the zipper between my thumb and forefinger and hold my breath for one beat. Another. I hear nothing. Unzipping the tent is the loudest thing I've done in my life.

No way did that go unnoticed. Bears in other *counties* probably heard that zipper.

It's done now though. I close my eyes and finish the job, then breathe in the cool air rushing into the tent through the gaping flap.

Huff, huff, huff. I freeze, scanning the camp through the crack. God, it's so dark. I see flashes of movement that melt into blackness. It's making other sounds. Somewhere on the other side of camp, behind the tents across from ours. Scraping, pushing, short bellows that send the hair up on the back of my neck.

Where is Lucas? He should be here. I step out, and a warm hand covers my mouth from behind. I bite and scream at the same time. Lucas yelps, and I whirl. There's huffing again. Oh God, it's close. So close I swear I can feel the heat of the bear's breath.

It's not the bear. It's Lucas. He clamps his hands onto my

arms and turns me, and I can finally see it. Not a shadow or a smear of darkness. A bear.

It's across from us. Mr. Walker said black bears are small, but it's not. Maybe for a bear, he's right, but it's not even thirty feet away from me, looking like a mass of fur and teeth that could tear me into bits and pieces like our pile of stuff.

I think of the vultures I saw earlier, the sinewy something in its beak. My mouth opens, a scream tearing its way up my throat. But then Lucas's hands squeeze my biceps again, and I stuff it down deep.

"There are three of them," he whispers.

"Three?" That's why I'm hearing it everywhere.

"Mom and two cubs. Just stay still." I try to duck my head, but he gives me a little shake. "Keep your eyes on her. Don't look away."

The bear snuffles. I see another splash of black, smaller than the first. And then another. They are scampering over in an area behind Mr. Walker's tent now, noses rooting through the grass like we left something over there. But we didn't. There wasn't anything to leave.

"Go back inside the tent," he says.

And sit there in the dark listening and wondering? Sure. I shake my head violently.

Lucas reaches down and zips my tent tight. It's not much defense for Emily, but I'm glad he's trying.

"Should we wake the others?" I ask.

"Not unless we have to."

A barking grunt rips through the air, and I cringe. Mama bear raises up on her haunches, and my whole body quakes. She sees us. I'm sure she sees us.

"Don't look away," Lucas whispers. "Keep your eyes on her."

My knees shake, but I do it, eyes open and bladder on the verge of total failure. She lifts her long brown nose high, testing the air around her. I clench my teeth and pray I don't smell like food.

Finally, she's down to all fours again. My shoulders droop.

"Do you think—"

Another growl cuts me off, this time near Mr. Walker's tent. We step sideways around the camp to put distance between ourselves and the bear. Inside the tent, he groans. I turn, staring so hard at the tent, I half expect it to move an inch from the pressure of my eyes. There's nothing. Quiet. Maybe I imagined it.

Then another very human groan. It sounds like *Hello?*

"Mr. Walker," I whisper.

"*No*, Sera."

A shrill cry comes from my right. One of the cubs is wandering our way. No, no, no.

Lucas swears softly under his breath, but I loop my arm through his and start walking backward out of camp.

"Go slow. Don't run," he says.

I pause, looking at our teacher's tent, my voice dropped to a whisper. "I heard Mr. Walker."

"You probably heard one of the bears," he replies just as softly.

Something rustles inside Mr. Walker's tent. A groan and a thud. The bear hears him, scuttles back and then forward, with lots of loud, angry chuffs. She's agitated, I think. Mr. Walker goes quiet in his tent. He must hear the bear, right?

I start to edge closer. The mother bear lopes behind Mr. Walker's tent, and the cub we saw patters closer to us. Lucas snags my arm.

"We have to get out of here," he says. "That cub is too close. If the mother sees us…"

He doesn't need to explain. Every sound those animals make is ratcheting my shoulders closer to my ears. Still…

"What do we do about the others?"

"Hope to God they're smart enough to stay in their tents if they wake up."

It's the slowest version of running away I've ever known. One step. Another. The cub moves closer to us. Another few steps back. I can't see Mr. Walker's tent now. Or Jude and Lucas's. I can only see mine and Emily's, dark and silent in the night.

We stop by a large oak, listening to the bears moving around the camp. Somewhere in the distance, I can hear the soft hush of the river. We're caught between two terrors, and I don't think I'll ever stop shaking.

My vision's gone smeary. The darkness swirls dead leaves into monsters, the ground into a living carpet. I stay close to Lucas and try not to think of what happened earlier at the river. But when I close my eyes, it's all I see.

"The bears could come back this way," I whisper.

"We'll wait and listen." Lucas isn't shaking. He's warm and calm. Everything I am not.

"If anyone wakes up—"

"It's better if we stay away and don't scare them. Black bears aren't normally violent."

He's right. It's probably more dangerous for us to go back, but the guilt still sits around my neck, heavy as a noose.

The bears take their time. Of course, what feels like ten hours could be ten minutes. I don't have a phone, a watch, any real indicator of time passing—unless I start counting the beats of my heart. Or Lucas's heart, I guess. Sometimes, I can hear it too.

We wind up sitting shoulder to shoulder with our backs against the rough trunk of the oak. After a while, I open my eyes. I didn't know I'd closed them. The moon is maybe half-full, but I can make out the shapes of trees, the shadow a couple hundred yards ahead that must be my tent. We can hear the bears now sometimes. Soft grunts and snuffles. They sound farther away. No one sounds terribly aggressive or agitated. I guess that's good.

"How long will they stay?" I ask, my whisper sudden and sharp in the long quiet.

"Until they're full."

"They found food?" I ask.

Moonlight sends gray-blue shadows over Lucas's jaw. I see it tighten and jump, like he's furious. "I'd bet money on it. Whoever left that water might have lured the bears to us, hoping to scare us."

"But just scare us, right? Black bears don't usually eat humans, do they?"

"Well, mothers with cubs are up for anything," he says. "But we're safe enough here, so try to relax."

"It's my watch," I say. "You were on watch when they came."

"I'm not tired," he says.

I mean to argue that I'm not either, but I've told enough lies today. I force my eyes open, but it's like fighting gravity.

It isn't comfortable. Bark is digging into my back, and I'm smelling my own stink and maybe a bit of Lucas's too, but my body is nudging me hard for sleep, and I can feel it will win. I will sleep soon, right here, with bears in the camp and the cold air chilling me to the bone and the stupid cut on my leg throbbing like one of the club anthems Sophie blares when she drives. I can still picture her behind the wheel, long brown hair and flared eyeliner. Liv's in the back with her constant laugh and shiny braids. I drag in a deep breath and try to roll my shoulders.

Lucas swallows and plows his feet through the dead leaves on the ground. Little sounds of nothing, and they lull me like a siren song. I don't realize I'm asleep until I open my eyes again. The forest is different now. The black sky is replaced with gray haze, mist clinging to the ground and trees around us. Everything is still, so I do not move.

"You snore," Lucas says beside me.

"I don't," I say automatically, but then I frown, pulling my head up. It wasn't on his shoulder, but I've got grooves in my cheek from the bark. Reasonable trade, I guess. Except I think I'd feel better if I wrestled a tow truck.

"Just giving you shit," Lucas says, lumbering to his feet and pulling an ugly face.

"Where are the bears?" I ask.

"They wandered off east about an hour ago? Hell, I don't know. They're long gone though."

"Why didn't you wake me? It was my shift to watch."

"I don't know much about keeping watch, but I'm pretty sure consciousness is required for the job."

My cheeks go hot, and I swipe them with my hands, feel those bark grooves again. "I'm sorry. I can't believe I fell asleep."

He shrugs. "We're wasted. I fell asleep with *Jude* watching my back."

"Scary thought," I say.

"Yeah," he says with a laugh.

Out here, in the misty trees and cool predawn air, it's easy to admit how much I like looking at him, at his hard face and sleepy eyes. Mom used to tell Dad it's not a sin to look. Maybe she's right on that one, but she did a hell of a lot more than look.

I pull my fingers through my shorter hair and remind myself that this is not the same. Lucas is not Charlie. I'm not breaking any vows looking at him, and I'm not falling head over heels or getting stupid. This isn't going to hurt anyone.

But then he smiles, and I'm not so sure.

CHAPTER 11

Lucas walks me to the camp but then leaves me, claiming a need for a tree. I'm pretty sure he's trying to find the food that brought the bears closer, but I don't argue. I spot Emily first, just outside of our tent. She doesn't ask where I've been, and I can tell by the rings under her eyes she didn't have the most restful night.

"Did you hear the bear last night?" I guess.

"Yes. I'm glad you're all right."

"The bears spotted Lucas and me, so we backed out of camp. We thought we'd be less likely to piss them off."

She nods and pushes her hair behind her ears. "I heard you guys leave. Thanks for zipping the tent closed for me."

"That was Lucas." I pause. Let it sink in before I go on. "Did you hear Mr. Walker?"

She nods slowly, lips thin. "I was excited at first. I thought he was coming to check on us. I almost opened the tent, but then I heard the bears again, so I stayed quiet."

"I almost thought I'd imagined hearing him," I say. "I heard him say 'hello,' but then the bears walked close to his tent. That's when Lucas and I ran. The cub was getting close to us too."

She shakes her head, lips downturned. "No."

"No?"

"I heard all that, but I heard him after you left. He came outside."

Something slithers in my belly. "Wait a minute. He came outside of his tent? Are you sure?"

"I *heard* his tent unzip. It was loud. As loud as ours was when you left. I thought I heard footsteps, so I figured it was him, but then the bears were sniffing all around." She flushes, like she's embarrassed to continue. "It freaked me out, so I didn't leave. But his tent is zipped back up now, so he must have gone back to sleep."

"Or maybe you just imagined it. Maybe it was the bears making noise."

Her eyes lock onto mine. "I *know* what I heard."

I can barely muster a nod before I'm back up on my feet and heading out of our tent. If Mr. Walker was awake enough to walk, he was awake enough to help. He'll know what to do, how to get us out of here. I'm fizzy with hope as I make my way across our camp.

Jude opens his tent and sticks his head out. His eyes are squinty, and his hair is mashed on one side. "What's going on?"

"There were bears in camp last night," I say.

He startles and looks around, then scrubs a hand over his face. "I didn't even hear them."

I don't answer. I just stop in front of Mr. Walker's tent, listening to the quiet.

Jude is stretching, and birds are waking up in the trees. They chitter softly in the murky canopy. I clench my fists and swallow my fear.

"Mr. Walker?" I call out. No answer. I say his name again, louder.

By now, Jude is with me, brow arched. "Did you hit your head last night? Mr. Walker is in a coma, remember?"

My mouth thins to a hard line when I look at him. "He woke up last night. We heard him moving around and talking."

"We? You mean Lucas and you?" He quirks his lips in a way that insinuates loads of filthy things.

My eyes narrow. "Everyone here *but* you, actually."

His expression shifts at once, gaze drifting to Mr. Walker's tent. He calls his name next, and I stare at the *Deceptive* on his arm. Well, I know one of his secrets. As cool and collected as he acts, Jude isn't any different from the rest of us. He's scared, and he wants the teacher back in charge. He wants someone else making the decisions.

I lean in and start tugging the zipper up to open the tent. It's still dark inside, and the smell wafting out nearly knocks me over. Vomit. Jude backs away cursing, but I try to push that odor into a teeny-tiny corner of my mind. I have to wake Mr. Walker up. If he was awake last night, he can be awake again.

He's in the corner, slumped over sideways, but he was conscious at some point. Long enough to pull on a black long-sleeved shirt and to be sick all over his sleeping bag. My eyes drift to another mostly empty bottle of water I know I didn't leave inside this tent. It's not one of the new water bottles. It's like the old ones.

He was awake long enough to get drugged again too.

"The son of a bitch came back," Jude says. "He was here again, wasn't he? He did something to him."

I cover my nose with my sleeve and ignore Jude, calling Mr. Walker's name. I move close enough to nudge him. Nothing. His breathing seems fine, but when I prod at his neck, it's hard to find his pulse. I'm not a doctor, and it's dark in here, but I don't think his color is good.

Emily slips in next with zero reaction to the potpourri of sweat and puke that's about to make my eyes bleed. It must not bother her the way it does us. After a fleeting glance at the mess on the sleeping bag, she moves much closer.

"That bottle wasn't here," she says simply, indicating an empty water bottle next to him. "I zipped his tent closed last night. It wasn't in here, unless it was stuffed down inside his sleeping bag."

"Seems more likely someone decided to pay another visit," I say.

Emily holds up the bottle and frowns, trying to examine the dregs of water left.

"So they drugged him again and just left?" I ask. "In the middle of a bear visit? What is the point of this?"

My hands are shaking, and I have too much saliva in my mouth. The smell is getting to me. I tip my head up, but there's no fresh air to be found, just the cool musty tent smell.

"We should look for bottles or pill casings," Emily says. "Maybe we can figure out what he's taking or what they're giving him. And we obviously can't leave him alone again."

"Right. OK."

Emily nods and goes right for the sleeping bag to search. She doesn't even flinch. God, I don't know what that girl is used to cleaning, but it's got to be bad if she can handle this. Maybe she's got a future in medicine.

I wimp out, checking around the edges of the tent closest to the door. I'm grateful for something to do though. Panicking isn't helping. I find parchment-dry leaves, his boots, and—*gross*—a dead daddy longlegs.

"I'm going to check outside," I say, hoping Lucas is back so he can…I don't really know. I'd just feel a little better knowing he hadn't wandered off a cliff. Or been eaten.

Emily doesn't call me on my quick exit, but one more second in there, and I would have added to Mr. Walker's mess. Jude wanders off to his tent, so I'm not the only wimp. Outside, dawn is finally breaking in full, turning everything pink-yellow happy and burning the mist from the sky.

Lucas still isn't back. What the hell is he looking for? Should I try to find him?

Jude emerges from his tent with his T-shirt on and something slim and white in his mouth. I pull in a sharp breath.

"What's in your mouth?" I ask.

"What?"

"What is that?" I point at the white thing. "There were bears in the camp, Jude! They can smell food, and you've had that in your tent the whole time?"

"It's not food!"

I cock my head. "Then what is it?"

"It's…" Jude sighs and reaches into his pocket, pulling out a small Ziploc bag of—glory Jesus hallelujah. Are those toothbrushes?

"Are those what I think they are?"

Jude wrinkles his nose. "Practically worthless travel brushes? Yes."

"Worthless?" I laugh a little breathlessly, already imagining the idea of slick, minty teeth. I think I'd give a kidney for *anything* resembling a toothbrush. "Can I please have one?" He looks at me like he has to think it over, and I scoff. "Really? You have, like, a dozen."

"Eight," he corrects, handing me two. My heart soars at the tiny dot of blue in the center of the white brush. "I have eight. Six now."

I laugh. "I can't believe you have any. I mean, who *has* these?"

"Pop's a dentist." He cuts his gaze to Mr. Walker's tent. "Is she finding anything in there?"

I shake my head, bringing myself back. "Don't think so. I'm still looking for some sort of evidence of what they're putting in the water."

He shrugs. "Roofies probably." He opens his mouth again but doesn't say anything more. Instead, his eyes drag over the camp with purpose. "Where's Lucas?"

"Bathroom," I say because I know Lucas doesn't trust Jude. Everything about Jude's narrowed eyes tells me he's not buying it, even if it's the only thing I'm selling. I relent with a sigh. "I think he's trying to find out what the bears were after. He thinks somebody might have left food to lure them, so he's looking for whatever was left, hoping to find some sort of clue as to what the hell is happening to us."

Jude's nod comes a second too late, but he doesn't ask more

questions, and when I resume my search, he looks too. The only thing I find is bear tracks. It's hard to miss the claw punctures in the muddy ground around the back side of the tent.

"I found something," Emily says inside the tent. She emerges, and the three of us convene at the entrance. Her word arm is outstretched. I notice the *Damaged* before I see that she's cupping something in her hand. It's tiny. Like a bit of bone or a chipped tooth. Please let it *not* be either of those.

"What is it?" I ask.

She tilts her palm so I can see better. Not a bone. Thank God. The chip is flat and bluish and sort of oval on one side—definitely a pill. So that settles the drug question once and for all.

"Do you recognize it?" she asks.

Recognize it? The extent of my medicinal experimentation would be trying three Advil on a brutal headache day. I shrug and look at Jude, who's studying the pill carefully. His eyes narrow as he leans closer.

"There's an *HA*," he says. "It's not familiar to me."

"Let me see it." Lucas's voice booms from the other side of the camp, jarring us all. Emily turns, and Lucas crosses the camp in three long strides. He's holding something too, but I can't tell what from this angle. Whatever it is, it's behind Jude.

Lucas flips his hair out of his face and looks at the pill for a few seconds, checking the lettering. "That's Halcion."

"It's what?" I ask.

"Halcion," he says. "It's a sleeping pill."

Jude arches a brow. "Watch me not be shocked you know this."

"As much as I'd love to go toe to toe with you again, we've got bigger fish to fry," Lucas says. He shifts to show us his hidden hand, where I find five crumpled protein bar wrappers.

"What is that?" I ask.

"Bear bait," he says. "Also known as the granola bars in Madison's backpack. I found them scattered all around the woods south of our tents."

"How are you sure they're Madison's?" Emily asks.

Jude nods, looking grim. "Same cheap brand. Crap ingredients."

"Don't worry. I don't think the bears minded," Lucas says. "And I'm betting your special people food will turn up too, Jude."

"What do you mean mine will turn up?"

Lucas points off in the woods. "There was a section of ground that had trampled plants. The ground was all torn up and smeared too, like someone tried to cover tracks. It was almost directly opposite of the bars and, if I had to guess, upwind."

"Was it one of us?" I ask.

"Don't think so. I'm not a tracker, but it looked like someone was waiting there. Every time we leave, we head toward the path or the river, to the east, right?" He points again, and I shiver because he's right. And if he found a spot where someone was just standing around…

Jude tenses. "Are you saying you think somebody was watching the camp last night?"

"After they baited the bears closer with Madison's stuff," Lucas says. "I imagine they have your bars too and any other food from our packs."

"Well, whoever it was, they snuck into camp in the middle of a *bear encounter*," I say. "Mr. Walker was drugged *again*. There was a new bottle of cloudy water, and Emily found that pill."

Lucas narrows his eyes, scanning the horizon, maybe looking in the direction he found the footprints? "That's ballsy as hell."

"Sneaking in while there are *bears* here?" I say. Then I laugh because ballsy doesn't quite cover it. "I mean, you'd have to *really* know your way around animals, right?"

Lucas shrugs. "Or you'd have to be batshit insane."

Emily rubs her temples. "All of this is insane. I still don't understand how someone could hurt Ms. Brighton and then get over here to us. How did they cross the river?"

We all turn like we're not sure what she's asking, but we are. We just don't have any answers.

"Maybe there's another bridge," I say.

Lucas nods. "There's some way across obviously."

Jude looks off in the direction of the river, like maybe he'll spot it through the trees. "We should find that way."

Lucas groans and shakes his hair out of his eyes. "We have no idea how far that way might be or in which direction. It's a wild-goose chase, and being close to the river ups our chances of running into the bears again. Feels like a bad plan."

He's right. I remember Mr. Walker's warning about camping too close to the river. Hiking along it feels dangerous.

Lucas straightens. "We should head north to the road like we planned."

"What about Mr. Walker?" I ask.

Jude points at me. "Are you planning on carrying him, *Darling*?"

"Obviously not, but we're not leaving him."

"I agree," Emily says.

Lucas swears softly. "I don't have time for this fight again. If you want to bring him, we need to build a sled or something, and we need to do it now."

Jude nods. "All right, then we need two long sturdy branches and a bunch of shorter ones and then some rope or tough vine. We can steal some rope from the tents."

I feel my brows lift in shock. I'm not alone. Emily covers her mouth, but I can still hear the chuckle she tries to hold back.

"What?" Jude asks.

"Uh, nothing," I say.

Emily laughs harder, and Jude crosses his arms.

"Is it so funny that I'd know something you find useful?"

"No, no, of course not," Lucas says too brightly. "We just didn't know you had a Boy Scout badge in search and rescue. Or is it a first aid certification?"

"Shut up," he says. "And it was Civil Air Patrol."

Lucas bites his lip, but I can see the smile in his eyes. Closest thing to civility I've seen between them. Lucas claps his hands together, a sudden *pop* against the bubble of quiet.

"All right, let's invent some shit. I want out of here before the next *visitation*."

It takes a ridiculous amount of time to build the sled. On TV shows, a plane crashes on an island and *boom*, they have tents and rafts set up on the double. In reality, we have to tear two of the three tents down to get enough rope, and then Jude, for all his Civil Air Patrol training, is useless with knots. So Lucas does it, shirt off and fingers nimble with the string. He's good at it, but he's even better at strutting around like a peacock so God and everyone knows we're all *so* lucky he's here to save us.

I really want to hate him. For being shirtless and annoying and most of all because he's right. We *are* lucky he's here because I don't think we could have gotten Mr. Walker out of camp without him.

Emily and I disassemble the final tent while the boys work to secure Mr. Walker to the sled. It's all a sloppy mess. We're not good at this survival crap. We don't have backpacks, and we're running low on water again. The only thing that's going right is that the cut on my leg is managing to *not* get infected. Still, I can't shake the feeling we're not alone.

As we're heading out, I hear something snap behind us. I've been hearing breaking branches and crackling leaves all day long. But then a bird flies overhead, shrieking an alarm—a blue jay warning us that something is out there. The jay is gone soon enough, but the tingling at the base of my skull remains.

"Come on," Lucas says, leading the way out of camp with the awkward, heavy sled behind him.

It's Jude who finds the number first, maybe forty feet outside of our tents, forty feet from the place where we've talked and laughed and tied knots all day. Lucas starts swearing when he sees it; Jude too. But I don't scream because if I do, I'm not sure I'll stop.

A dead tree stands, a skeleton sentry with no arms or flesh left to cover the bleached white core of its trunk. Is this what the jay was warning me about? That someone was here, right here, carving a number two into this tree while we worked on, oblivious?

I swallow the rock that has grown in my throat. It scrapes its way down as Lucas clenches his jaw and marches on.

No one says a word. We all know what this means. Yesterday, it was three, but now it is two. It is a countdown.

We are running out of time.

CHAPTER 12

There is no easy way to drag a two-hundred-pound man up a hill. We'd probably make better time climbing this mountain on greased roller skates than we are with this sled. Lucas and Jude aren't bad at it, but they're taller and stronger, and I can still see the dark sweat stains between their shoulder blades.

I'm pretty sure they expect to have to handle it the entire time, but we're all shaky and hungry, so after maybe half a mile heading north, Emily and I offer to take a turn. Lucas doesn't seem inclined to drop the heavy work on two exhausted girls, but Jude is ready for a break. They watch in quiet disapproval as we shift back and forth, trying to find a way to hold the branches that form the sled's handles. Emily's lucky. Her half has a piece broken off, a nub she can hook her thumb over. For me, it's just sheer force of will. I'm sure my hands will burn for days from gripping this stupid thing.

We start out dragging it behind us. At the first hill, we try a few ways before deciding we'll have better leverage climbing backward. Bent over, we inch our way slowly, slowly up, pulling the sled as we go.

"I can help," Lucas offers.

"We'll at least get him up the hill," I say.

Four steps later, Lucas staggers left and then snorts. "This is ridiculous. I could fireman carry him faster than this."

"Lay off," Jude says. "They're helping."

"I'll be sure to get their participation medals ready."

I'd like nothing more than to kill him really dead, but all four of my limbs are shaking so badly, I can't expend the energy to even snap at him. I'm going to collapse or maybe burst into flames because my muscles are burning hotter with every foot we climb. And my hands—I can't even think about them.

The forest around us mocks my misery on every level. It's like the whole place has gone Disney. Birds trill softly, and sunbeams slant through leaves just this side of golden. Everything smells fresh and earthy and warm. Well, everything but us. I've met hockey bags that smell better than we do.

I glance over my shoulder. Oh thank God. We're almost there. This was bad enough on the straight path, but we've been heading uphill for four hundred miles. Or forty feet. Whatever. My hands slip on my handle, so I tighten my grip, even though my left palm is scraped raw. It feels way worse than the cut on my leg, and it hasn't had a day to really get nasty.

We reach a clearing at the top, and sweat trickles down my brow, stinging my eyes. I blink and keep pulling until the sled is on level ground. Then we ease Mr. Walker down, and I look at Emily. I think she might want to cry. If she does, I'm joining in.

"We need a break," I say.

I'm surprised when Lucas doesn't taunt us. He just takes the sled and hands me my half-empty water bottle. We move into the shade of an enormous maple. There's a gnarled root jutting up from the ground. Lucas leans the sled against it so Mr. Walker isn't flat on his back.

We split up the last bottles of the water, which worries me.

"We're low on water," I say. "How long until we hit the road?"

"Hard to tell," Lucas says. "I know we'll cross the intersection way before we reach the end point on the trail. But we're obviously not at full speed."

"We're not leaving him," I say.

"No one's saying that," Jude says, his eyes moving over Mr. Walker's prone form. "Do you think…"

He trails into silence, his gaze still fixed on our teacher's face like he might wake up and join in the conversation at any second.

"We should try to wake him up again," I finally say.

The statement falls like a gauntlet. We all nod and look at each other because no one wants to get too close to Mr. Walker. He peed himself while the boys were carrying him. I saw the thin trail of liquid seeping out of one of his pant legs and onto the trail. I'd sucked in my breath, hard and fast, completely appalled, but Emily just stepped over the trickle with a shrug. So it doesn't surprise me when it's Emily who strides forward. She calls his name three times and then shakes his shoulder a bit. I think his brow furrows.

"Mr. Walker, we need you to wake up now," she says. Firm, not angry.

"Tell him I'm going to kiss him if he doesn't wake up," Jude says, and Lucas smirks.

Mr. Walker's face is definitely moving, his eyebrows and this time his mouth.

I step forward, feeling woozy. "Mr. Walker?"

"Mr. Walker, can you hear me?" Emily asks.

I stop where I am because he doesn't smell good, but she scoots really close and squeezes his hand. His eyes flutter.

"Holy shit." Lucas sounds awed.

When Emily says his name again, Mr. Walker's eyes open. His pupils shrink tight, trying to adjust to the brightness, but he can't seem to hold his focus.

And then he does. He licks his chapped lips and looks at the girl in front of him.

"Emily?"

He's really awake.

Or was awake.

He's out as suddenly as he woke, head drooped to the side and thin lips parted.

Emily keeps trying, but after a few groans and a few more slurred attempts at our names, he's out cold.

"He's still really druggy," she says. "How long does Halcion last?"

"Like four hours," Lucas says. "I can see it knocking him out but not keeping him out like this. My mom takes something else with it or she'll wake up."

"Then why use it at all?" I ask. "Seems like something else would be better."

Lucas shrugs. "It's strong. It'd knock him out. Maybe he was taking something else anyway. Or maybe whoever is doing this wanted him out longer and gave him something else."

"He was taking pills when we woke up the first day," I say. "For allergies, I think. But something prescription too, I thought."

Emily nods. "If it's a heavy-duty antihistamine, it might cause this kind of sedation, right? I mean, an over-the-counter allergy pill can knock me out cold."

"Or whoever did this could have just given him a cocktail of sedatives," Lucas says. "Or roofies. It's probably a miracle he's still breathing." Lucas drops into a crouch, scoffing.

"Any ideas on how long a mix like that might last?"

"I think it should wear off if he doesn't get more," Emily says.

My head pulses with the promise of a ripping headache. "He was drugged last sometime before dawn, right? When the bear was there."

"Yeah, and why the hell is that?" Jude asks.

Lucas tilts his head. "I'm not following."

"I mean, I can't figure out why Mr. Walker's the only one getting drugged. Why are we being left alone now?"

"Because whatever crazy thing this is, it's about us. He's not part of it." Emily tucks her hair behind her ears, her expression blank.

"He doesn't have a word," I say. I run my thumb beneath the *Darling* on my arm and look at Emily's *Damaged*.

Jude tsks. "Since you brought it up, doesn't it seem strange?"

Lucas brandishes his *Dangerous*. "Tell me the strange factor isn't *just* occurring to you."

"Yeah, but everything is about the four of us," Jude says. "Why? What the hell do the four of us have in common? We might as well be strangers on a street."

"We aren't *all* strangers," Emily says.

My gaze moves to Lucas, and he's already watching me. I think of the first scene in *The Phantom of the Opera*—all those curtains pulling back, back, back. That's what Lucas's eyes do to me.

"But we really aren't strangers," I say. "We live in the same town, go to the same school. We obviously have things in common. Maybe we need to figure out what other things that includes."

"Apparently, someone thinks we're all messed up in some way," Jude says. "Well, except you, princess."

Lucas stands up. "All right, let's think. Did the four of us ever share a class?"

We didn't. We go down the line, offering every possible connection we can think of. Nothing matches. Not where we live, who we hang out with, where we're thinking of going to college. There are connections but nothing that carries all the way through. Emily and Lucas frequent the Last Drop, but Jude and I hate coffee. Emily and Jude and I share Mr. Walker's math class, but Lucas is on the other side of the school during that period.

The threat of a headache is culminating in a splintering throb behind my left eye. *Please don't be a migraine. Please.* I lean back against the tree and try to take deep, slow breaths. Yoga breathing.

Mom's face materializes in my mind's eye, long black lashes and a wide, perfect smile. She'd position her mat across from mine and sit there like an older version of my own reflection. Mirror images of each other, she always said. She talked a lot about finding my balance and releasing negative energy. Of course, she didn't seem to care about energy when she took off with Charlie, leaving a metric ton of negativity behind.

Something drags in the dirt. I search for the noise, seeing Emily tuck her legs closer, her chin settled on her knees.

"The sun's dropping. That's west. It'll be dark again in a few hours."

"We lost a day building that sled," I say, my voice wobbly. "An entire day."

And we only have one left. But one left until what? I don't ask because I know I don't want that answer.

"Nothing else has happened today," Emily says. "Maybe it's over."

"Pretty sure our little carved messages are an indicator that this isn't over," Lucas says. "Somebody didn't go through all this just to change their mind. We should keep moving. It's not dark yet."

"I agree," I say. "I just wish it wasn't so…mountain-y."

"It's going to get worse," Lucas warns, nodding north where we can all see the shadows of mountains rising higher.

"Perfect," Jude says.

I sigh. "I just wish we knew how far the road is."

Lucas opens his mouth to respond, but the words never come. I can tell he's heard something by the look that crosses his face. Emily lifts her head, and Jude cocks his chin. Then I hear it too. A faint whir whines through the air to the east.

It fades away, and Jude starts to speak, but we hush him, straining to hear. It couldn't have been our imagination. We all heard it. Unless the water drugs are coming complete with mass auditory hallucinations.

After a tense silence, it comes again, rising in pitch and then falling off. It's definitely east, and it's not an animal. It's too steady and even, more machine than beast. I look up, feeling a hard swell of hope rush into my chest.

It sounds like an engine.

CHAPTER 13

Dirt bikes. We thought quads at first, but Lucas was sure that wasn't right. He'd ridden both and said this engine was higher in pitch. Either one could make it through the tangles of ferns and moss-covered rocks around here.

"We need to head that way," Jude says. "If they have dirt bikes, then they have a truck. A trailer. They came from a *road* somewhere or at least a path that leads to a road."

"I agree," Emily says.

I nod because I agree too, even if I'm not sure how I'll actually stay upright to head anywhere. I pull myself up using the maple tree behind me for support. The bark digs into my raw palm, but it's OK. The pain gives me something to hold on to.

"Maybe I'm a cynic, but I don't trust it." Lucas stretches his arms wide, pointing in opposite directions. "The road is north, and whatever we're hearing is southeast. How do we know it isn't a trap? We've probably only made it a couple of miles at this point. Following that noise could erase what little we've done."

"Seems like a pretty poor trap to me," Jude says. "We could just as easily ignore it."

The engine grows a bit louder, and we all look up. I can

feel myself leaning toward the sound, the idea of vehicles. People. Civilization. Home. It pulls me like a june bug to a porch light.

"Ignore it, huh?" Lucas's voice stiffens my spine. He's shaking his head at all of us. "If I weren't here, the three of you would be tearing through those woods."

"Because it makes sense to tear through those woods," I say. "There are people over there. Probably people with *phones*. We would be insane not to try."

"I agree," Jude says. "That sounds like a way out of here."

"Sound travels weird in the mountains. We could be wrong. Mishearing it. Or worse, they could be long gone by the time we get there," Lucas says. "And then what? How much time will we have lost? How much longer can we go?"

"We're going," Jude says. "Well, *I'm* going."

"I'm with you," Emily says.

"Be smarter than this," Lucas says, but he isn't talking to Jude or Emily. He's given up on them, and that searching look he's wearing? It's for me.

In the distance, the engine starts again. Emily shifts on her feet, waiting for me. How am I supposed to make a choice like this? We can't move Mr. Walker without Lucas, and everything about the way he's crossing his arms tells me he knows it.

Do they think I can talk him into it? The *Darling* on my arm itches. I run my thumb over the letters and bite my lip.

"We'll just give you two a minute to decide," Jude says, and somehow, he's woven a smirk into his tone. I suck in a breath to snap at him, but he holds up a hand. "Emily and I are going on ahead. We'll stay in shouting range."

Emily won't look at my eyes, but she's edging closer to Jude. My mind goes back to their conversation last night. I thought things had changed between us, but maybe I was wrong. Maybe they still think Lucas is in on this, that he's trying to keep them from getting help.

"Maybe Lucas has a point." I'm not sure I agree with his points, but they're making choices about Lucas's character that are just wrong. He isn't the bad guy here. Lucas is notorious for a smart mouth and a quick punch, but I can't imagine him behind something like this.

"Yeah, you two talk all you want about those points," Jude says.

"Emily?" I ask.

She looks up at me, chin trembling. "I want to get help, Sera. He needs help. We all do."

They disappear into the trees without another word. When I hear them break into a jog, my eyes drag up to Lucas's face. He's watching me with a blank expression, arms open and shoulders relaxed.

"It's up to you, Spielberg," he says, and I know from his tone he means it. I'm in control. I have been since we stood on that deck two months ago.

Lucas isn't moving closer or touching my hair. He isn't convincing me. He's waiting.

Is this why my stomach is tumbling end over end? Is this why I don't back away from the choice I know my mother would make? I swore to never be this girl, but here I am, so swept up in this boy that my insides are coiling tighter with every breath.

Lucas is all that I am not, shoulders relaxed and a smile in his eyes as he asks, quite suddenly, "Do you want to kiss me, Sera?"

The words sling into me like hot bullets. I swallow, and he touches me—just his hands on my hands, leading them to his shoulders.

"Because you can *kiss me." His eyes bind me to this moment. "And you can* not *kiss me. You're in charge here."*

I shake my head. I'm just like her right now—all impulse, no thought. I'm not in charge of anything. And kissing him is an inevitability.

Lucas calls my name and drags me back. Nothing that happened on that deck should matter here. Hormones rage. Hearts lie. And I'm not stupid enough to fall for it because I am *not* my mother. Not even out here.

But what if here and now is all you have left?

"I don't know what to do," I say. Not about the engine we're hearing or the kiss we shared or any of the rest of it. I never know with Lucas, do I? He blurs my world.

"We should go north," he says. The tone that snapped and bit at me before is all softness now, like the time he taught me how to weld. Or tried. "We're running out of water, and even if these people could help us, if they leave before we find them—"

"We can scream for help," I say because even if I don't know what's best, I *want* to go to those engines. I want to sprint after Jude and Emily and find someone. I want to go home. "If we can hear them, they'll hear us soon too."

"It feels too easy," he says. "Doesn't it?"

I can't read his tone or his expression, so I sigh and drop my head.

"You want to go," he says. "Chase the noise."

"Yes," I say. What I don't say is that I won't go without him and Mr. Walker, but he knows it. He has to know, or I wouldn't still be standing here.

He blows out a sigh and picks up the sled. I don't wait for him to change his mind. I move out, and he follows, dragging our fallen teacher behind. We follow the noise and catch up to Emily and Jude sooner than I would have guessed. But I'm rushing. God, I'm rushing.

When the engine noise comes again, Jude and Emily shift direction, following the sound. It's not hard because it never moves left or right. The rumble just keeps coming, dead ahead.

The forest is thicker here, thin saplings growing in clusters and tall, prickly plants sprouting up instead of the broad, sweet-smelling ferns around our campsite. The three of us push back the bushes we can't avoid so Lucas can duck through. One branch whacks Mr. Walker in the face, and he groans, offering a slurred curse word before he's out again.

My arms are scraped and my throat is dry, and none of that compares to the waves of dizziness rolling through me. I'm hungry, I think. My mouth waters at the idea of food. An image of Madison's granola bar wrappers flashes through my mind, and it *hurts*.

We start calling for help when we catch snatches of other sounds between the engines. They're indistinct, but they might be voices. So I lick my parched lips and join the others.

"Help! Can anyone hear us?"

"Hello!" Jude adds. "We need help!"

Mr. Walker groans again when we descend over a bumpy ridge. His eyes roll, and he slurs out something. Maybe, "Careful. Careful."

"Just rest." Lucas is panting hard, even though Jude is helping him again.

Mr. Walker groans after another awful jostle, and Emily looks back at him. "We're going to get help now. It won't be long."

Mr. Walker tries to nod, but his head just rolls to the side, and I stare at the crimson thread of blood the bush left on his cheek. Red like strawberries. Cherries. My stomach gurgles. God, I'm so messed up.

"He's getting better," I say to Emily, mostly to distract myself. "Mr. Walker. He doesn't seem so…out of it."

She nods but keeps her focus ahead. I can't blame her. The engine is clear as day now, but the sky is growing darker. We don't have much light left. We're getting closer though. Another murmur filters in through the drone of the engine.

I touch Lucas's sleeve. "Did you hear that?"

"I hear it." Emily this time. She looks at me, eyes bright and lips quirked. "Voices."

That's exactly what it is—a rambling murmur that pulls up at the end like a question sometimes. Other times, there's a short sound that might be a laugh. My fingers curve over Lucas's slightly sticky wrist.

"There are people," I say, bubble-light with hope. "I can *hear* them."

"I smell fire," Jude says. "Am I crazy? Is that crazy?"

I take a deep breath through my nose, closing my eyes. No, it's not crazy. It's there—a faint hint of smoke that makes me think of hot dogs and cheeseburgers, a bratwurst so juicy it bursts, blistering hot against my lip. I barely hold in my groan.

Lucas inhales deeply, and his face lights up. He readjusts his grip on the sled and nods forward. "What are we waiting for? Let's go."

Hope gives us strength. Even the forest seems to turn in our favor, the trees thinning and the grade trending downward, the miserable thorns giving way to soft ferns and patches of moss. Soon enough, the smoke is easier to follow than the engine noise. I'm surprised we didn't notice it before. Maybe they just built it? Maybe it's time for dinner?

I don't care. I don't care. I just want to get there.

I don't know who starts shouting for help again first. We should be close enough now, but they might not be able to hear us over the dirt bikes. Or is it one dirt bike? It sounds the same. And it still doesn't seem like it's moving much.

Emily and I are ahead of the boys now, but I can't make myself stop. I stumble toward the smoke as fast as my legs will go, shouting out with a voice that sticks in my throat and cracks on my teeth.

No one answers, but I can hear the voices between the engine more clearly now. They are laughing. Whooping. *Happy.*

"Help! Help us please!" I scream it over and over, but they don't answer. They have to hear us. They have to by now!

My lungs are burning when I see the first orange glow of the fire. I break into a run anyway, half tripping, half racing. Emily has already seen it, and she's ahead of me. I'm dizzy again, so dizzy that my vision's going gray and everything is spinning, but the smoke is right there. The fire.

We're here.

We made it.

I spin around and around, looking for the dirt bike, the people, for the source of all this noise and laughter and fun. It's so noisy. Even with my heart still thumping wildly behind my ears, I know we should see them. They have to be right here, so what am I missing?

Where is everyone?

Wait—

The next laugh is like a scream, and when the engine rises, the sound slices through the air and drills into my ears. My hands clamp over them instinctively, head ducking. It's too loud. It's far louder than it should be.

I hear my own breath better with my ears plugged, ragged and fast.

My eyes drag to the fire, a small, fresh-looking deal with three logs, and a dirty plastic-wrapped box of bottled water behind it. There's a small green cooler too. It might be dirtier than the water.

So where are the people?

I suck in breath after breath until the next laugh comes, a witch's cackle on a Halloween sound track. I hold my next breath in. That laugh is the same. *Exactly* the same.

The engine rises again, and I recognize the same hooting cheer. Next will come the low whoop. And it does. It's a pattern.

A squirmy, awful feeling worms through my chest. And then my stomach drops away. This isn't real. It's a recording, one track playing over and over. Which means there's a speaker. Somewhere.

I try to take a step, but my foot lands all wrong. My knees bend too far or maybe not far enough. I don't even know. A smooth-barked beech catches my stumble. I right myself on its pale trunk and look around. Emily is sobbing, head covered. Jude's eyes are wide.

Lucas finally emerges from the thicker part of the trees, hair damp with sweat and face red. I can see Mr. Walker squirming on the sled behind him, looking bleary. Lucas looks at the fire, the water, me. Whatever he finds in my expression drains the color from his face.

"We need to find the speaker," I say, but I don't know if anyone hears me. I can barely hear myself.

The speaker isn't hidden. It's sitting on a fallen tree maybe twenty feet to the right of the fire, a little black box that scares me more than the letters on my arm.

I bend forward so I don't fall over, propping my hands on my knees for a second. I'm the only one who seems able to move, so I force myself to keep going. When I reach it, my hands tremble around the plastic box. Wireless. I turn it this way and that. Find the switch on the back and flip it off. We are plunged into silence.

My chest curls in tight, a flower closing out the night. The quiet is much worse than the noise. I drop to my butt and listen to my fast breathing and roaring blood. Emily is still sobbing, soft hitches of her shoulders that shake me to the bone.

I look at the fire like it's under the spotlight. The rest of the stage is set—the water, the cooler, finally the speaker. Lucas was right. This is a trap, a carefully constructed production. And we played our parts to perfection.

CHAPTER 14

When I was ten, I had a hamster in one of those big cages with the tubes that led to different levels and little play areas. My dad was so proud when he set that thing up. I used to spend hours watching the hamster scamper down the curving slides and up the brightly colored ladders. Mom called it Plastic Alcatraz. Dad and I argued that the hamster wouldn't survive on its own, but Mom always said dead is better than caged. At least it would be free.

Mom loved saying *freedom* almost as much as she loved to say *follow your heart*. I probably should have had some sort of spidey tingle, some internal alarm when Mr. Walker peppered the word *freedom* into every speech about this camping trip.

"Someone should check the cooler," Jude says without moving to do it himself.

Lucas's nostrils flare, the sudden friendliness between them straining. "Were you expecting one of us to play support staff for you?"

"I was just putting it out there," Jude says, but apparently, he can't resist either because his smile tightens. "Though support staff is a job title you should get used to."

I lumber to my feet, feeling shaky. "Don't start up again. I'll check the cooler."

"Sera…" Emily's cheeks are pale.

She's afraid of what's inside, and suddenly, I am too. I catch a glimpse of the black letters on Jude's arm and think of Ms. Brighton's detached finger. I really don't want to find the rest of her in here.

"I can check it," Lucas offers.

"I'm fine. Just give me a second."

I press my fingers to the top of the cooler and wait, assessing. I've seen coolers like this at garage sales and picnics. It's older, olive green with a yellowed plastic handle. Nothing special or particularly ominous.

OK. On with it. I pull my chin back even as I push the lid open.

My shoulders relax instantly. "No fingers, so that's a plus."

"What's in it?" Jude asks.

"Cups of grapefruit. Greek yogurt." My hands shake as I move the tubs aside, then my spine stiffens. "Packets of SunButter and crackers. It's food."

"What the hell is SunButter?" Lucas asks.

"Sunflower seed butter," Jude says. "People with nut allergies use it."

I stare at the packets, at the little tubs lined up, exactly like the ones in my fridge at home. I tip back a familiar-looking Greek yogurt. Blueberry. I snap the cooler lid closed with a shudder.

Emily shifts on the ground. "You're allergic to nuts, right, Sera?"

"Yes." I pick at a cuticle on my thumbnail and feel the weight of three gazes settling on my shoulders like a yoke. The seven letters on my arm feel like the numbers underneath a mugshot. I'm guilty. Guilty because I'm *Darling*. Which means I'm somehow chosen. Trouble is, I don't know what I'm chosen for.

"The SunButter is for you," Emily says softly.

I shrug. "Anyone can eat it." It sounds pathetic, even to me. This was left for me like an offering. A present. The hunger pangs that have haunted me all day vanish.

"Shit," Jude says softly.

"Don't," Lucas warns. "Sera?"

I can't look at him. I can't look at any of them. I shove to my feet because sitting here isn't possible now.

"I need to use the restroom." I say it like we're in the middle of chemistry class and not lost in Notown, Nowhere, with a psycho stalker cutting off fingers and packing me custom-made lunches.

"Alone?" Emily asks. "It's dark."

"It's not that dark." My voice cracks. I'm going to cry. I shake my head.

I don't wait for anyone to answer. I storm off through the trees, even though the shadows are stretching long. I break into a run, which is so stupid. So incredibly stupid because there's nowhere to go and I might not find my way back. I'm still half-starved and shaky and a little dehydrated, and my best chance, maybe my *only* chance, is to stay with the group.

I find a small stream, some little offshoot of the river probably, and force myself to stop at the muddy edge, where clouds of gnats hover like patchy fog. The sun has set, but I spot streaks of red and purple through the web of branches that cross the sky like bars. Bark and wood and sap that lock me away from my world.

I only cry a little. I hold the worst of it in, pressing my fist to my mouth and praying silently, though I'm not sure God will listen to a girl with an absentee mother and a D in biology.

"Sera?"

My shoulders hitch in surprise, and they shouldn't. I knew he would come. I open my eyes and search my pockets for a used tissue, coming up dry.

"Here," Lucas says, shoving something cool and damp into my hand.

It smells like baby powder, and wiping my nose is suddenly a diary-worthy moment. It's a diaper wipe. I find a clean corner and wipe my forehead and nose, which have never felt greasier. Then my chin and cheeks. I'm moving down to my neck when I hear him chuckle.

"I have more," he says, offering a small plastic packet. "I should have thought of it earlier when you cut your ankle."

I start in on that cut now, but it's scabbed over and not nearly so tender. "How long have you had these?"

"The whole trip. I kept them tucked down in my sleeping bag," he says, then he smirks, tapping the bubbly letters and cartoon pacifier at the edge. "I asked Mom to pick up hand wipes from the dollar store, and this is what I got."

"Real men bring diaper wipes?" I ask.

He laughs. "Real men have pothead mothers who don't pay attention, I guess."

I take another wipe instead of trying to figure out what to say. He follows my lead. It isn't soap and water, but it's close. And it's *amazing.* I scrub my neck, my arms. When Lucas turns his back to me, I use one inside my shirt, swiping my armpits and the valley between my breasts.

It isn't great, but man, it's better. So much better.

I rummage through my pockets for the little toothbrushes, handing one to Lucas. He groans the second he pops it between his teeth, and I couldn't agree more. It's even better than the wipes. I brush every single millimeter of my mouth, sucking the minty drop of toothpaste in the center until it's long gone.

When we're done, we have a wad of used things neither of us wants to look at. I can't believe that much filth came off me. I leave my pile on a rock, figuring I'll carry it back to… well, to somewhere.

"So, why'd you freak out?" he asks. "Was it because of the butter stuff?"

"SunButter."

"SunButter. That's why you took off, right?" he asks.

I nod, my gaze pulling to the little stream. Water gurgles around rocks and under mossy outcroppings. "It's not just the SunButter. That cooler could have been packed out of my refrigerator at home. Every single thing in there is something I eat, down to the flavor of the yogurt. Someone picked all my favorites."

"Does being away from it help?"

"Yes. No." I take a shaky breath and look up at him.

"It's cool. Take your time."

I chuckle. Take my time? What happened to the guy who was

breathing down my neck to keep me moving faster across the river? The snapping, the dirty looks from earlier—they're gone. I mean, there's a comment here and there, but mostly, he's back to the Lucas from months ago. The one I flirted with and kissed… and then totally ignored.

"Why are you being so nice to me?" I ask.

He lowers his eyelids and drops into his dirty tone. "I'm *always* nice, Sera."

"No, you're not, and that's not the kind of nice I'm talking about." His smile disappears, but I force myself to go on. "When we first got out here, you seemed pretty pissed."

He toes the mud at the edge of the stream with his boot, his jaw clenched. "Pissed?"

"You going to deny it?" I ask. "I mean, I get it. I do. But the first couple of days—before everything went to hell—you seemed determined to either pick me apart or load every single conversation with innuendo."

His smirk chills his whole face. "I can't help it if you read sex into everything, can I?"

"That's *exactly* what I mean. I'm not complaining about the change, mind you. I guess I just expected…" I don't know what I expected, so I trail off into weird silence. Did I think he'd confront me? Hate me? Act like we didn't kiss or I didn't ignore him after? Not likely. I've been fricking awkward as hell in school this year, trying to avoid him.

He tilts his head, and the shadows on his face turn long. "Did you think I'd pretend it never happened? I mean, *you've* done a nice job of it, right? Walking around like you're too good to even breathe my air for the past two months."

He steps forward, and I take a breath that feels hot and tight. He's staring down at me, looking even more hollowed out and dangerous than usual in the low light.

"Don't." The word comes out of me soap-opera breathy, and the shame of it warms my cheeks. I sound like a victim, and I'm not.

"Don't what?" he asks, tilting his head. Too-long hair slides to cover one gray eye, but the other holds me hostage. "What do you think I'd do?"

My throat clicks when I swallow, but I don't respond. Because he wouldn't do anything I didn't ask him to do, and I know it. I walked into this conversation with my eyes wide open, just like I walked onto Sophie's deck this summer. He's waiting now. He waited then too.

We've been half an inch apart for a year. A century maybe. Lucas chuckles, and I feel it on my lips like electricity.

"I'm taking forever to do this," I say, laughing. "Can you do it?"

"Yeah." Then his hands are on my jaw, cradling my face like I'm made of something expensive. His voice drops low. "Hell, yeah."

Lucas leans in, and I try to do everything my friends talked about, but he isn't pressing as hard as me or using tongue or doing anything they said. Maybe I'm doing it wrong. It's not like I have a reference for comparison, but it's not what I thought kissing would be.

I ease back and feel him smile against my mouth. And then it's magic. Lucas goes so slow, a brush at my top lip. My bottom. He tilts his head and threads his fingers into my hair, and my hands finally unclench when he grazes both lips at the same time.

"This OK?" he asks.

I nod, though OK doesn't even touch what this is. After a second or a minute or a lifetime, his mouth shifts. He makes a sound that I will hold in my memory forever. It feels perfect, all of it, and that's how I know it's wrong.

Because when you're chasing a perfect moment—losing yourself in the perfect guy—before you know it, you're throwing the rest of your life away.

His mouth is every bit as pretty as it was that night, but he's frowning now.

"I'm sorry," I blurt out. He knows why.

"You didn't say one damn word to me after we kissed."

I don't know what to say, so I nod. I bolted half a minute after, lipstick smeared and knees wobbling. I confessed to Sophie on the drive home, but that wasn't what I expected either. I didn't feel giddy; I felt wrecked. No, worse than that. I felt as foolish as my mother.

I still remember flipping down Sophie's passenger-seat visor, staring at my smeared, traitorous reflection in the tiny mirror. My hair was shorter, my makeup was lighter, and my acting days were traded in forever. I had changed *everything* that made me like her.

It didn't matter, and it still doesn't. No matter what I change, when I look in the mirror, I will always see my mother looking back.

Is that who my father still sees?

Is that who I really am?

"What are you thinking?" Lucas asks.

"I don't know," I lie.

Lies are part of the game I play with Lucas, and my heart told the prettiest ones of all. All those weeks that led up to kissing him, I inched my way from one flirtation to the next, convincing myself nothing would come of it. Until it did.

I guess I lied to him too. I made one silent promise after another, knowing I'd break every one. God, that's so not fair to him.

"So what was it, Sera? Get tired of slumming it with the white trash boy from—"

My heart snags like a hooked fish. "Lucas, *no*."

"Or is that just your act—the virginal, never-been-kissed bullshit."

"It wasn't an act."

He steps forward and tilts his chin. My heart is climbing so high and beating so hard, I'm sure it will fly right out of me. God, I hate this feeling. Even the steady pulse of my body— inhale and exhale and over again we go—it's all affected by him. I can't think straight, and I want to. I don't want to follow my heart—I want to be *so* different from my mother that one day, she disappears from my head. Just like she did from my life.

"What am I supposed to think, Sera? You came to my shop every day for three weeks. And every time, we talked a little longer, and you sat a little closer."

"Stop." My face is going hot.

"Stop what? Stop rehashing the fact that you *literally* asked me to kiss you, and now I feel like I misinterpreted or—I don't even know! I feel like I wronged you on that deck."

"You didn't! I never, *ever* felt wronged!"

He throws up his hands, looking twice as big as usual. "Then what the hell was with the silent treatment? What did I do wrong?"

Nothing. My insides are breaking apart. My mother is winning, isn't she? I push my hands into the center of my chest and beg my ribs to hold true. "Can we just let it go? It was *one* kiss. One night."

He moves in until I can see lighter flecks in his irises. "You made it clear that kiss was a really big damn deal for you, that whatever it was between us was *worth* that deal."

Shame burns up my throat like acid. "I know that."

"And the second you walked away, you acted like you didn't know my name."

"I did, and I'm sorry."

"Why? Why did you do it?"

Because after I walked off that porch, I *knew.* Lucas wasn't just some guy to hang out with on a Friday night. And all that fluttering in my middle wasn't just a lethal cocktail of teenage hormones and postwrap high either. It was different. *More.*

It wasn't going to end on Sophie's deck. I knew I could *fall* for him. Get swept away. Follow my heart until I changed. Until he changed me the way Charlie changed my mother.

How can I explain *any* of that? Answer: I can't.

"I'm so sorry I hurt you," I say instead.

"Don't tell me you're sorry. Tell me why."

My eyes fall to the *Dangerous* on his arm. Feels about right. "Because I'm afraid."

"Afraid because we kissed?" he asks.

"Afraid because you're *you*."

He steps closer, and my breath catches. Another step and I'm not sure I'll be able to pull air at all. He lowers his head until I can see the prominent line of his nose, the wide, heavy-lidded set of his eyes.

"You wishing you could undo what happened?" he asks.

My heart double-thumps because I know that look. He wants to kiss me again. Or still. I don't know which word applies. I only know I want it too. And I can't.

I step back, foot wobbling over a root, finding harder ground. Another step and I'm turning, trees stretching up around me like walls. I can't be here anymore. The real world is out there some-where, with my dad and my senior year and all those little stupid things I worked hard to keep under control. My room is out there, my yellowing quilt and the window air conditioner that smells like a cheap hotel and drips cold water onto my carpet. I want to go home.

Lucas catches me a hundred yards down the stream. I'm already breathless and stiff-legged, and mosquitoes are flitting around my head and neck. But he's not winded, steady hands clamped on my arms and voice even when he says my name. Of course he's steady. He takes one step for every three of mine.

"Let me go," I say.

"It's dark, Sera," he says.

"Let go!" I push against his grip with a keening sound that should embarrass me. It doesn't. Pushing doesn't work, so I pull hard. I'm free but not for long.

Lucas grabs me again, gently, but I'm lurching like a dog on a chain. He hauls me back against him, and I take a breath. He doesn't smell great, but he's so solid and warm and making all the right soft, hushing noises.

"You're smarter than this," he says. "Think for just one damn minute here. We don't have to talk. Just don't run."

"I can't stay here," I say around a hiccup. "I have to get out of here."

"You will."

I swallow hard, eyes jumping from tree to tree.

Lucas's hands tighten on my arms. "*Sera.* You *will* get out of here, OK?"

"You can't promise me that." I hiccup over a sob. "You can't rescue us."

His smile softens all his sharp places. "Hell, what are you talking about? I'm planning on *you* rescuing me, Spielberg. Figured you could piggyback me back to town."

A laugh finds its way through my sob, but I'm still shaky.

"I didn't mean to make you run," he says.

"You didn't." Which is why I can't keep ignoring his questions. I don't want to talk about us any more than I want to talk about the food in that cooler or look at the letters on his arm. But I have to.

I take a slow breath and look at him. "I don't regret what happened, but it wasn't supposed to happen. I can't go to that place, you know? It's just not something I can do."

It's a weird explanation, one that hints at rules he can't possibly understand and wreckage from my mom he can't possibly see. I wait for him to sigh, maybe to let go. But he doesn't. He just accepts it.

Forest sounds stretch between us, and weird, twitchy energy hums beneath my skin like I'm an amplifier. I'm buzzing with too much power, primed to pop at the slightest provocation. Lucas's hands spread over my shoulder blades, and I go still. The humming slows. I can feel the press of every finger. The heat of his chest.

Something stirs low in my belly, and I think of a dozen afternoons in the shop, his welding mask propped up on his head and his face streaked with sweat and grime. I always sat on the edge of a bench, swinging my legs and watching him work. Feeling as frenetic and confused as the sparks scattering on the concrete floor by his boots.

I feel like those sparks now, but it's familiar. Almost comforting.

His thumb grazes my spine, and my stomach dips low. He does it again, and my whole world shrinks down to that single touch. The repetition of it crawls under my skin, bringing back all the times I turned the other way when I saw him, hand on my chest, trying to press my pulse back to something normal.

Regret turns bitter on the back of my tongue. Someone is hunting us, someone who thinks I'm a *Darling*, but I'm not. I haven't been darling at all.

I've been a liar. I've been cruel to him. He is better than that, and so am I.

"Lucas." His name is full of all the things I don't have words for.

My arms go around his waist, so shaky it's like I'm ill. His thumb pauses at the change, lifts away. An ache unfurls in the place he touched, spreading out through my middle.

I burrow closer and feel him take a sharp breath. Looking at him like this pushes confidence into me. For the first time since I woke up with this word on my arm, I'm in charge. This decision—this reckless, crazy choice—is all on me.

His hands slide down my back, and I'm pulling at the front of his shirt because I can't stretch up any further on my toes, and this kiss is not like before. There's no finesse to either of us this time. It's too hard and hungry to be sweet, but I don't want sweet out here. I want the scrape of his scratchy chin and the burn of losing my breath.

Lucas makes that certain sound again, and heat and adrenaline race neck and neck through my veins. Is this still wrong? Do my rules apply out here, with my whole world gone to hell and this thing between us gluing me back together?

He breaks off, sighs my name against my lips. I lean my forehead into his chest and take a breath that smells like moss and woods and dark, rotting things. I don't know what this means. I don't know what happens next.

And then I hear the screams.

CHAPTER 15

It's Emily, and there's blood. That's all I can sort out at first when we stumble back to the fire. My brain flips through images like a slide show in fast-forward. A charred, still-smoking log rolled away from the fire. A hunk of dark hair hanging over Emily's left eye. A smear of blood on her chin. On her hands. But she doesn't look injured.

Is it Jude's blood?

My focus widens, and the scene unfolds, making no more sense as a whole than it did in pieces. Jude's shoulders are tensed, and Mr. Walker is sleeping again, head lolled on one shoulder. Emily is a trembling mess.

The cooler is pushed out, cockeyed from where it was. I can see that there's a rectangular hole in the soil beneath it. A hole one of us was bound to find.

It was right there, waiting for us. A raw ache in my gut tells me whoever dug that hole was counting on us finding it.

I don't want to look at what's inside, the thing that has Jude and Emily so pale. The thing that left blood spatters on Emily's fingers.

My first glance doesn't tell me much. The hole is maybe ten inches deep and wet at the bottom. My insides shrivel up. Please don't let it be a part of Ms. Brighton inside that dirty hole.

I lean closer, spotting the bundles of sticks. I think they're tied together. Like they're supposed to be something.

"What is that?" I ask. Sticks and blood? What kind of art and craft from hell is this? Then I see it. They're arranged and bound into torsos and limbs, little heads and scraps that might be clothing. Like voodoo dolls made from bits of trees.

There are four of them. Three dolls are standing or sitting, and one is sleeping. My eyes catch on a scrap of red fabric on the biggest doll. Red like Lucas's shirt. There are curling leaves on the head of the doll beside it—poplar leaves, I think. They remind me of Jude's hair, and I don't think that's accidental, especially when I see the black moss and sharply slanted eyes on the doll that's supposed to be Emily.

These dolls are supposed to be us.

That means the sleeping doll must be Mr. Walker. And I'm… missing? Hidden? I inch forward, my belly a sack of eels and every one of Emily's hitching sobs making it worse. The doll in the middle has dark hair. There's a jut of sticks—a pointy chin— dark eyes, and a pool of black liquid underneath it. Ink?

And then it all comes together. That's not Mr. Walker; it's me. It's a me-doll, and it's lying in a pool of blood.

A wave of vertigo rolls over me. I want to look away, but I can't.

"Where did you find these?" Lucas asks. "Were they here?"

"The whole time," Jude says, sounding broken.

My vision's gone blurry. I can't focus.

"Sera." Lucas's voice is low. He means to be soothing. Because I'm standing here, mouth gaping and eyes wide like a crazy person, and I'm probably scaring the fricking crap out of him. I should say something.

"Why is there blood?" I ask stupidly, and Emily just cries louder.

"Knock it off!" Lucas snaps at her. "You're not helping."

Emily doesn't knock it off, and Lucas is too keyed up to handle it. He stomps forward, and Jude launches to his feet. "Back off!"

"Then calm her the hell down!"

"We're all freaked," he says, "so get your little Neanderthal power trip in check, and let her cry if she wants."

"Neanderthal power trip? What the hell are you talking about?"

Jude's eyes narrow to slits. "Do you need me to spell the big words?"

"*Why is there blood everywhere?*" It's more scream than question, and it shuts everyone up. Even Emily. She's got tears smeared down her face and snot running over her upper lip, and she's looking at me.

"Is that supposed to be me?" I already know. I don't know why I'm playing stupid.

No one will meet my eyes.

"I'm sorry, Sera," Emily says. "I'm so sorry."

She didn't do anything to be sorry for, but that's not the point. I know why she's sorry. It's what decent people feel when something bad happens to you. Or when something bad is *going* to happen.

I force myself to look at the dolls again, to make some sort of sense of this. My doll is definitely not sleeping. The eyes are still open. And there's a section of hair that's shiny and stuck together. A head wound. So there it is. In this scene, I'm the dead girl.

Another flare of dizziness hits, so I close my eyes and take a breath. Slow and steady, my chest opens wide, but it does nothing to soothe me.

I'm supposed to be dead. Or I'm going to be dead.

The other dolls look alive. Lucas is standing. Emily and Jude are seated. No one else's doll is stretched out in a pool of blood. None of the other dolls are bloody at all.

Wait.

No, they do have blood. I lean in a little because even the last bits of purpling sky are going black. Even in the low light, I can see the dark stains at the ends of the other dolls' arms.

"So I'm dead and someone's cutting off your hands?" I ask. I sound like someone else, someone who is asking about something that does not matter.

Emily wipes her snotty nose on her sleeve. She still won't look at me.

"I mean, that's what the blood is about," I say. "Whoever he is, whoever left this—they want your fingers or hands or whatever. Like Ms. Brighton. But you lucked out because they only want me dead. The *Darling*."

Someone laughs. Is that me? I think it is. The *Darling* is amused. That makes me laugh again because it's ridiculous. Every last bit of it.

"Sera, this isn't going to happen," Lucas says.

Something hot rolls over me. I push back at it, but it curls around my edges. It will swallow me, this feeling. I'll snap.

"We *won't* let that happen," Lucas says, misreading my quiet.

"How the hell do you think you'll be able to stop it?" My volume startles me. "I know you want to help, but how can you? We don't even know what this is. Is it a psychopath? That dead girl's ghost? A serial killer? You should worry about yourselves. About your hands."

"I don't think the hands are cut off," Jude says. He's studying the dolls with a strange expression, eyes narrowed and thumb at his chin, his *Deceptive* lost in shadows.

Lucas scoffs. "Why's that? Because your special hands play such beautiful music?"

"They do, but that's not why. Do those dolls look injured to you?"

I don't know. I can't look anymore. My ears are ringing, and I can't beat back the image of that sticky pool underneath the doll with my hair. My face.

Lucas's boots crunch as he walks closer. "No. They look like they're worried about Sera. Because she's the victim."

"I don't think we're supposed to look worried," Jude says.

Emily sniffs into her arms. "Me either."

"Holy shit." Lucas sounds faintly sick. "We're supposed to look like the killers."

My face goes numb, but I shake my head. "That's stupid. There's no weapon. No motive. The only thing we can see is that I'm dead. Lying in a pool of blood."

"And that same blood is on our hands," Jude says. "Think like a director, Sera. Look at the scene. We're lording over you, looking down at you. Your blood is on our hands."

My hands ball up. Jude's right. Whoever put these dolls together didn't do anything unintentionally. Doll-Jude and Doll-Lucas are looking down on my body. Doll-Emily is watching like it's a movie. My mind swims with masking tape x's and a dozen light checks. If this is a scene set, then I've been murdered.

All three dolls have my blood on their hands. As if they are my killers.

CHAPTER 16

An owl calls softly in the distance—deep, hollow hoots that warble into a low trill. It sends goose bumps up on my arms, but I still can't tear my gaze away from the dolls.

I shake my head because it doesn't make sense. This makes it look like one of us is responsible for killing me, but what about Ms. Brighton and Madison and Hayley? And what about the words on our arms? If this whole stupid thing is some sort of elaborate warning, who the hell would bother?

Why wouldn't they just save me?

I bite my lip and look at the four people in camp. It doesn't fit. None of it. They don't have a reason, and they couldn't pull this off. Jude was vomiting that first day. Emily was asleep beside me. Lucas was—Lucas just wouldn't. No way. And Mr. Walker is half dead. Plus, I don't know who would have access to serious drugs.

Except that Lucas's mom takes Halcion. And Jude has enough money to buy whatever he wants. And I don't know anything about Emily.

I push my hands into my hair. None of those facts change anything. Even at a record-breaking level of paranoia, I can't buy any of them doing this. Period. They're being framed.

In the weirdest possible way I've ever seen.

Lucas and Jude are watching me like I'm an injured animal they desperately want to rescue. My mouth goes dry, and I swallow hard. I'd like to rescue them back. I'd like to rescue all of us, but we need someone who actually has some damn clue how to survive out here.

My shoulders jerk. That's why Mr. Walker is drugged. Someone who plants food and speakers and writes words on people's arms… someone who would plan something this elaborate wouldn't want us to outsmart them. With Mr. Walker's help, we would.

It makes sense. He doesn't have a word on his arm or a doll made of sticks. He's not part of this like us. They're keeping him drugged because he's the one person who could get us out of here before that countdown is done and I wind up dead.

Someone brushes my arm, and I jerk, my heart pushing out an extra beat.

"Hey," Lucas says.

He's using his soft voice, the one he uses when he's finishing a piece. I remember bringing him a cup of coffee one morning—since I can barely stand the smell, this should have been a clear sign of how bad I had it—and he offered me a velvet-soft *thank you* that turned my insides liquid warm. He stayed quiet and gentle until it was done. Ten minutes later, there was a new sheet of steel—a new thing to fold and cut and weld. And Lucas was back to standard volume, his laughs echoing off the high ceiling.

"You all right?" he asks.

"I won't be for long apparently. And neither will you."

Jude shakes his head. "I told you, I don't think we're hurt."

"I know you're not." I point at my doll, ignoring the way my finger shakes. "Victim." Then I point at the other three. "Killers. It's pretty obvious."

"But it's not going to happen," Lucas says.

"You're damn right it's not," I say, walking closer to the sled. Mr. Walker's head lolls to the left, and his mouth is slack. There are fresh stains on his T-shirt. I frown. "Why is he out again? He was coming to when we got here. When the speaker was playing. What happened?"

"I'm not sure," Emily says. "He didn't wake up when I screamed."

"Oh, he did. Long enough to throw up again," Jude says. "That's about it."

Emily nods. "Maybe he's working it out of his system."

"Well, he needs to work it out quicker," I mutter.

I walk around him, assessing. Which is ridiculous because I don't know anything medically helpful. But I know it's time to wake him up. If Mr. Walker has been drugged to keep him out of the way, then we need to fix that. It's time to change the game.

My muscles are sluggish and achy, and my stomach hurts, but I square my shoulders like I'm giving final instructions before opening night.

"I think we need to stop reacting," I say.

"What do you mean?"

"We're responding to everything this asshole does. We find water—we all talk about whether or not to drink it. We hear noise—we chase it."

"We get food, and we all sit around wondering if we should eat it," Lucas says, nodding at the cooler with a look of disgust.

I smile. "*Exactly.* We are feeding into this game like rats in a maze. We need to stop trying to solve his little riddles. We need to remember what he did to Ms. Brighton and Hayley and Madison. He's going to do that to me. And he's going to try to pin it on you somehow."

We all go quiet at the mention of their names. It's easier when we pretend to forget.

"So, what then?" Emily finally asks.

Jude and Lucas nod, and I straighten my back.

"We change the game," I say. "Wreck his plan."

"I'm in," Jude says. "But how?"

"First, we wake up our teacher. He's been asleep the whole time, and we haven't. That's *not* an accident. He knows more than us, right? He could get us out of here."

"She's right." There's an energy in Jude's expression I'm not sure I've ever seen. "Asshole or not, he *could* get us out of here. He knows all this crap."

"Yes," I say. "The drugs have to wear off. We haven't left him alone, so we know he hasn't gotten any today. He's come around a little, right?"

"Some," Emily agrees. "Here and there."

"So we keep trying to wake him up."

Lucas nods. "OK, what else?"

"We eat. We're all out of energy, and it's slowing us down too much."

Emily arches a brow. "How do we know it's safe?"

"We don't," Jude says, arms crossing under his chest.

Lucas's mouth twitches. "The blood around those dolls tells me it isn't poison we need to be worried about."

"But logically, it's a risk, right?" Emily asks.

"Logic isn't working out here," I say. "Believe me, I prefer to have both a method and a plan, but I have to go with my gut here. I don't think the food will hurt us."

"You could just be hungry," Jude says.

"I'm ravenous. But those foods are all my favorites," I admit. "You could have packed that whole cooler at my house."

"Since you're the one who winds up dead, that isn't comforting," Jude says. "No offense."

I wave it off. "It's fine. It's a valid point, but I think this is part of the plan. It's my last meal or whatever or at least that's his plan."

"Whose plan?" Emily asks.

"Whoever wrote on us and made these creepy-ass dolls," Lucas says. Then he bumps his chin at me, and I can see the smile in his eyes, hear the affection in his tone. "The same freak who thinks this walking pistol over here is a *Darling*."

"That freak could kill us *all* instead," Emily says.

Anger, white-hot and knife-sharp, runs along my skull. I scoop the dolls out and toss them, sending them scattering. "That freak isn't counting on how hard we're about to fight back."

CHAPTER 17

The food doesn't kill us, but Mr. Walker's stench might. I don't think there's a bodily function he hasn't experienced on our sled, and as bad as I feel for him, he smells vile enough to melt my skin right off my face. Emily's the only one who can get within six feet, and every time she ventures into the hot zone, I wonder a little more about what things are like at her house.

Jude catches me watching and gives me a calculating look. What the hell gives with that? Two days ago, Jude and Emily were virtually strangers—and not overly friendly ones at that. Now they're so buddy-buddy, he gives me the stink eye for looking at her wrong?

Then again, two days ago, I would have said I'd sooner grow a pair of wings than kiss Lucas. Again.

My lips tingle with the memory. I press them together hard and turn back to the task at hand. Mr. Walker is rousing. *Finally.* We've been chattering at him nonstop, and at first, we didn't get much—just nonsense noises and head movements, a little kid rolling away from the light in the middle of the night. We all go still when it changes.

He groans out something closer to a word and lifts his head. Then he smacks his lips together, and my shoulders hunch. Is he going to throw up again? God, I hate watching people vomit. His shirt makes me queasy enough.

He jerks his head back a few times like he might, and then his eyes flutter and finally open. He looks at Emily, then Jude, then Lucas. Finally, he looks at me, and his lips stretch into a strained smile. Cue the rising music—we've got a live one.

"You all look pretty freaked out." His laugh splinters like dead wood. "I don't know what I got in to, but it messed me up plenty. Did we run into bad water?"

I tilt my head. "You could say that."

"It's all right," he says. "I'm alive, so you can stop with the long faces."

None of us can seem to manage a response to that. Because it's clear he doesn't remember the bits we've told him. He doesn't know what's happened to us.

Mr. Walker gives an awkward laugh, but I can't force myself to smile back at him. No one says anything, and I have zero idea where to start, but we have to tell him. Because right now, he thinks the extent of our problem is a teacher with a nasty stomach bug.

My heart twists, imagining what he's going to feel when we fill him in on Ms. Brighton.

"Well, don't everyone talk at once. What time is it? How long was I out?" he asks, and then he looks around, forehead furrowing. "Wait, where are Ms. Brighton and Madison and Hayley? Are they still on the other side of the river?"

"What do you remember, Mr. Walker?" I ask.

I can tell his brain is prodding at his foggy memory, pushing for answers. His expression turns grave before he speaks again. "Where are the tents? Where are we right now?"

Emily tries to reply, but the words catch and snag on her tears.

I'm done crying for now, so I take the lead. "Things are bad. You've been asleep for a couple of days. Do you remember anything? Do you remember us moving you on the sled?"

His brow scrunches, creases forming so fast that I think of one of Mom's scarves sliding off her dresser, folding over and over, an accordion of silk against the bedroom wall.

"No," he says. "What's happened?"

"There is a murderer out here," I say. It's the first time I've said the word, and I have to fight off a shudder. "We think Ms. Brighton has been killed. We don't know about Madison and Hayley, but we called for them. They didn't answer. There were—" I think of the birds, the swarms of flies buzzing. "I don't think they made it. We haven't been hurt, but we were all drugged. You most of all. We think they used sleeping pills or some other sedatives. They put it in our water."

He struggles like he wants to argue, but I hold up a hand and fill him in on the rest, bit by bit. The destroyed supplies, the words on our arms, the numbers we've found, building the sled, our plans to head north, and the noise that led us here. When I finish, Mr. Walker's eyes search the area.

"Where exactly is here?" he asks. "Does anyone have a compass? Anything useful?"

"No on all counts," Lucas says.

"How far are we from where we started? From where we left the girls?"

"Maybe three or four miles?" Lucas guesses. "I've been trying to cut north for the road."

"You shouldn't be too far off it. Maybe a day's hike, six or seven miles? But we need to head back to the river first. That bridge is out, but there should be another a mile to the west. Or there will be places where the water may be low by now."

We prickle so fast at the idea, it's like we're turning into cacti. Lucas picks up on it and leans forward.

"We're not going back to the river. It was a hard hike, there were bears baited to our camp…and we think we're being followed."

Mr. Walker's expression twitches. It's like he's holding himself in check. Forcing himself not to sigh or roll his eyes. I can see it written all over his face—he's in denial.

He doesn't believe us. He doesn't believe us because he can't handle this.

"I know it sounds crazy," I say. "But someone is out here, and they aren't hunting deer. They are hunting *us*."

Mr. Walker shakes his head, making a sound that's somewhere between a laugh and a groan and a complete dismissal. He does this in school sometimes when a kid makes a joke. He tries to play along, but then he'll make a sound—just like this one. It's his version of a fade-out. Yes, the joke was funny, so *har-har-har*, but could we all turn to page sixty-nine and get serious about these polynomials?

He makes the sound again, eyes going a little wide when no

one laughs or opens a textbook. I feel so bad for him when I lift my arm to show him the word again. Lucas shuffles to my doll and holds it in the air with a tight smirk.

Mr. Walker's eyes fix on that mess of twigs, and I see the realization sliding down over every feature. Just as fast, his guard slams back up. I can't blame him. None of this is easy to swallow.

"Let's try to stick with the facts here and save the boogeyman talks for later." He licks his lips, obviously determined to hold on to his disbelief.

I get it. If I could cling to the world where camping trips mean mosquito bites and leaking tents and maybe a sprained ankle, I would.

Ms. Brighton would have been better at this. God knows she would have bastardized bits and pieces of half a dozen religions to explain it, but I'm pretty sure she could handle mystery words and voodoo dolls better than Mr. Walker.

Jude sighs. "It doesn't matter if you believe us. We just need you to help us get out of here before our neighborhood psychopath figures out you're awake and comes back for us."

Mr. Walker holds up a hand that looks pale and shaky. "Something's going on—that's clear—but murder? We're in the middle of nowhere. Now, you saw something. I believe that, but we can't just—"

"I saw a body," I say softly, interrupting him. "I think it was Ms. Brighton. It was—" I pull a breath that feels like spun glass, thinking of the dark, wet thing behind the bushes. "Someone cut off her finger, Mr. Walker. Hung it from a tree. There were flies. Vultures."

"I saw it too," Lucas says. "Looked like there might have been more than one body."

"That's just that damn rumor talking," Mr. Walker says. "It's messing with your heads."

Lucas moves forward. "That stupid ghost story? That's real?"

"It's not a ghost story!" Mr. Walker seems incensed. "It's a terrible tragedy. It took days to find that girl, and her family was grief stricken. No one should have ever started using her death as some sort of cheap fireside entertainment."

Days to find that girl.

"What are you talking about?" Jude snaps. "You're telling us the girl was real? The one who was eaten? I thought that was an urban myth."

Mr. Walker turns away from him.

"I knew it was real but not like that," Emily says. "And it happened here in these woods?"

"No, not *right* here," Mr. Walker says, but I can see the way his eyes shift. He's skirting the truth. "And it was nothing like Madison told it, Emily. It's tragic, and she treated it like a joke."

"She treated it like a ghost story," Jude says. "And that's what we all *thought* it was!"

Goose bumps bloom on the backs of my arms. "Why are we even out here if there was a *murder*?"

"It wasn't a murder!" Mr. Walker goes pale. Or more pale. He's already looking like death eating a saltine cracker, but I can tell something changes. He drops his voice to a soft mutter. "Look, when bad things happen, people talk. They want someone to blame."

Emily stiffens. "My dad said no one really knows what happened to her."

"Yeah, I remember hearing that too. Back when we all thought it was a *ghost story*." Jude scowls at Mr. Walker. "Tell me, were our parents aware you planned to have us camping at an old crime scene?"

"I already told you it wasn't a murder!" Mr. Walker looks at Jude like a glass of curdled milk. Maybe Jude was telling the truth about Mr. Walker avoiding his desk.

"There was a camping trip," Mr. Walker continues. "Not organized like this. Just four kids who planned a party in the woods. They weren't prepared, and one of them didn't make it back. These things happen in the wilderness."

"And then a bear eats your body," Lucas says.

"It's all about preparation." Mr. Walker says. "Careless people die in the woods all the time."

"Maybe," Lucas admits. "But I'm pretty sure they don't wake up with words on their arms and dollies dressed in their clothes. If you're wrong and that girl was killed, her killer could still be out here!"

Mr. Walker's face mottles, and I stiffen. He looks like he wants to hand out detentions. Or worse. Does he really think we're pushing his authority here? Or that this is some senior live murder-mystery prank gone horribly wrong?

"If I find out this is all someone's sick idea of a—" He stops abruptly, eyes lolling and breath gone raspy. Emily approaches with quiet detachment, and the rest of us wait. In a moment, he opens his eyes and struggles against the sled. His expression is still surly. "We'll discuss this more as soon as you help me out of this."

Lucas tilts his head, and something cold zips through me. He doesn't untie him right away, and if Jude's expression is any indicator, he'd just as soon leave him to rot in his own filth. Eventually, it's Emily who unfastens the ropes.

My heart clenches when Mr. Walker stumbles awkwardly to his feet, but I don't reach to help him. I stand there like a pillar of stone.

He disappears in a clump of trees and brush, and we can hear him groan. Fumble with his belt buckle. Before I can think too long about that or about what will inevitably follow, I move away, and the rest come with me.

We cluster together by a hemlock, heads bowed and fists clenched. Lucas budges in close to me and takes a slow breath.

"OK, am I the only one who's suddenly thinking about the fact that it was *Mr. Walker* who gave us the drugged water first? It was in his pack."

My stomach sloshes, a boat bumping over a rock at the bottom of a stream. "What are you saying? He's our teacher."

"I'm saying I don't trust him," Lucas whispers. "I mean, *come on*. He planned this trip intending to take us to the exact forest where a girl mysteriously died?"

"He was *drugged*," I whisper.

"Drugging can be faked," Lucas says. "He was asleep, not foaming at the mouth. He knows too much about that dead girl."

Jude nods at him, a strange camaraderie in the look they exchange. His voice is also low when he responds. "I'm with Lucas. That makes two of us."

"Three," Emily says. Her eyes are dark smudges in the shadows.

In the distance, Mr. Walker gives a gurgling groan that wrings my insides out. I press my sweat-slick hands together, my pulse going thready. "So, what now? What do we do?"

Jude shuffles closer, whispering even lower. "We watch him like a hawk, and we watch out for each other."

"But he's going to try to take charge," I say. "That's what teachers do."

"He's too sick to take charge," Emily says. "Whatever else is true, he's not faking that. He has a fever."

"Which means he can't be a part of any of this," I say, hating how desperate I sound to believe it. "Sick people can't carry out crazy elaborate plans."

"Maybe that's why nothing's happening right now," Jude says.

"Maybe he's not as sick as you think," Lucas says. "He could be a good actor."

Emily shakes her head. "No, he's got a fever. You can't fake that sort of thing."

"Can't fake what sort of thing?"

The hair on the back of my neck rises as I turn, but we all know who's asking. It's Mr. Walker. He's standing maybe twenty feet away, and I have no idea how he finished up and got this close without us hearing him. But I know he must have been moving quietly.

And I know he might have heard more than any of us want.

A little-girl scream shrieks through the air. I cringe, arms lifting to protect my head, but there's nothing. I can't see a thing, and the scream is—*there*. Again. Another rasping wail that scrapes at my ears and needles up my spine.

It fades away, but I'm not crazy. We're all looking around. Everyone's terrified.

Everyone but Mr. Walker.

"It's just a barn owl," he says. His eyes are glassy beads beneath his brow. "You're letting all the wrong things scare you."

Is he thinking of things that should scare us? Because the way he's watching makes me wonder if he's enjoying this. Enjoying our fear.

CHAPTER 18

Mr. Walker doesn't press when we don't tell him what sort of thing you can't fake. Maybe he figures the owl scared us out of talking. Maybe he doesn't care because he's got creepy, murderous plans to carry out now that his "pretend I'm drugged" act is out of the bag.

I bite my lip because I'm still not sure I buy it. Would a killer really do that? Just lie there in his own filth so he could watch us freak out until his countdown runs out? You'd have to be pretty committed to wait that long to kill someone in the end.

Unless you've got some sort of very specific time line in mind. I think of the number two we saw earlier. Tomorrow, will we find a one? The day after that, do I die?

I watch Mr. Walker limp toward the tree near his sled. He doesn't look like a killer when he slouches into a heap. Emily offers him water, playing her unconcerned caretaker role beautifully. After a few crackers, he pushes the water away and gives us a big "everything is all right" smile.

Sure it is.

Mr. Walker takes the lead, just like we hoped he would. Of course, that was before. Now it chills me when he orders us to stay close. He makes us repeat what we've already told him about waking up with the words on our wrists and finding Ms. Brighton's finger, even about the bears and the food we spotted around camp.

Emily does most of the talking, while the rest of us watch him like something under a microscope. He's too weak and sweaty to look dangerous. I've gone completely paranoid though because I'm convinced all his active listening is a scripted performance. He's making all the right noises, but the director in me wants to tell him to dig a little deeper. Every frown and furrowed glance feels like too much or not enough or just...*false*.

Emily's right about the sick thing though. That's no act. Mr. Walker is shivering and pale, and if we go by Emily's hand-to-the-forehead thermometer, he's rocking a hell of a fever.

But is he sick enough to not hurt us? Does he even want to? Because why would he?

I rub my forehead and roll my shoulders, the bark of the hickory behind me digging hard into the space between my shoulder blades. The whole thing is crazy making. How could he have set up the dolls and the speaker? He hasn't been out of our sight, so what gives? Did he set all this up before?

Does he have a partner?

It's too scary to even consider.

I look down at the mostly eaten yogurt cup in my lap and finish it off. Thank God for the food. I'm nowhere near as shaky, and even Jude's starting to lose the death pallor he's been wearing since getting dehydrated. Of course, for all I know, we're just fattening ourselves up for the soup pot or whatever.

The thought materializes in my mind, and nausea rolls through me. We aren't any closer to getting out of here. My plan isn't working. We were supposed to get Mr. Walker awake and healed enough to help, and now he might be the very person we're running from. How in the hell did my turn-the-tables plan come to this?

I stand up because I can't just sit here. Everyone's looking at me. Emily, lips pursed; Lucas, hair flopped into his face; and Mr. Walker, his dark eyes shiny in his sweat-slick face.

"You headed somewhere?" Mr. Walker asks.

"Bathroom." I sound frantic. About the bathroom. Great.

"Alone?" Emily asks.

Jude frowns. "It's dark."

"You shouldn't go alone," Mr. Walker says, but he's too slow, I think. It's like living in a badly dubbed film. Everything's half a beat off, and it's making me seasick to watch. Or am I imagining it? Am I that crazy?

His eyes sweep me up and down, a quick assessment. My skin tingles and then crawls.

Lucas stands up between us. For once, I'm grateful for his size. "I'll go with her," he says, taking my arm and moving off into the trees.

I don't even think about arguing. My heart is skipping like a scratched record. Jude comes too, claiming his own need for a break. This is way too obvious. Two boys do not accompany a girl to pee behind a tree. He'll know we're talking about him.

Or think something *entirely* different is going on out here.

Jude and I slow at a cluster of river birches, the bark peeling off in sheets and clumps, but Lucas holds up a hand before we can

173

speak. He moves back a few paces toward the camp, shoulders back and wide hands balling into fists over and over. I can't quit looking at his fingers, thinking of them curved over my waist. Threaded into my hair.

This is so stupid.

"It's not stupid," Jude says.

My cheeks burn when I realize I said it out loud. Maybe he won't get what I'm referring to, but when he shrugs and nods at Lucas, I'm pretty sure he does. Lucas takes a few more steps away from us, and Jude drops his voice to a murmur. "It's a survival thing, completely physiological. I've read about it. Hormones go crazy in life-and-death situations."

My hands squeeze into fists, and pain stabs through my left palm. It's starting to look like raw hamburger, and it feels just as raunchy.

"We shouldn't have left Emily," I say, looking in the direction of the camp.

"I don't think he's after her. Plus, she'll bolt if he even moves in her direction. He's definitely too slow to catch her off guard."

I nod, relieved. "So, what's going on with you and Emily?"

"Nothing is going on with me and Emily." His tone is sharp enough to cut.

I look up, shocked at the return of his frosty expression. I hold up my hands. "I just noticed you were getting along better. I wasn't trying to imply…whatever."

"Maybe I'm smart enough to play nice with the one person who knows something about first aid," he says with a sniff.

I don't buy it, and I'm tired of backing down, so I shake my head. "Are you that desperate to be elusive? So you're friendly with Emily—what does it matter?"

"What does what matter?" Lucas asks, returning to us.

Jude's jaw clicks. "She thinks I'm boning Emily because she wants to bone you."

Heat scorches my cheeks, but Lucas cocks his head. "Wait, I thought we established earlier that you're gay."

"No, the only thing we established is that I'm not going to help you find a label for me."

"Someone already found a label for you," Lucas says, winking at the *Deceptive* on Jude's arm.

"Don't," I say.

"Yes, *do* keep the redneck in check," Jude says, but it's different now. Neither one of them seems as riled up. Guess we know who the enemy isn't at least.

"Well, we're all labeled," I say to Jude. "And for the record, I'm sorry if…" I trail off because I can't put my finger on why I'm sorry, but I feel it, a slow burn in my gut. I *am* sorry.

Am I sorry because of the assholes who weren't nice to his dads? Or maybe because I was curious or insensitive or some other thing I can't figure out? Finally, I sigh. "I'm just sorry for…well, whatever."

He tsks. "When you figure out what *whatever* means, you let me know."

Lucas coughs or laughs—I honestly can't tell which. "Can we maybe set aside this group therapy moment to discuss whether or not our teacher is trying to kill us?"

"He seemed completely false to me," I said. "I know he's sick, but it was like watching a bad understudy botch a lead role." I rub my temples. "I don't know. Maybe that's me."

Lucas holds the back of his neck. "No, no, I picked up on that. He's being weird as shit."

Jude frowns. "He's always weird. I'm still trying to wrap my head around him being intelligent enough to plan something like this. It's intricate."

I nod. "I can't wrap my head around why *anyone* would do this. What's the point?"

"Serial killers do pointless things all the time, right?" Jude asks. "Rituals and trophies or whatnot. I just want to know what he did with my hair."

A chill runs up my arms. "Your hair?"

"There's a piece missing. I didn't think anything of it until I saw Emily's a bit ago. Check yours," he says, pulling up some of his wiry curls to tap at the nape of his neck.

I see the small short piece. My fingers worry at the same spot underneath my hair, just below and behind my ear. I freeze when my fingers brush freshly cut strands, making me shudder.

"Well, that's plenty creepy," Lucas says, finding his own piece in front of his ears where his bangs are longer. "So the question is, is Mr. Walker the type to do something like this?"

"I think we just need to ask her about the doll," Jude says, and then they exchange a dark look. They want to ask *me* something?

My heart thumps too slow and then double-beats to catch up. "What about the doll?"

Lucas frowns. "There is no classy way to ask this."

"*Please*. She came back from that river sporting your stubble burn, so I doubt either of you are concerned with classy." Jude turns to me. "Are you wearing blue panties?"

My cheeks could melt glaciers. "I…what?"

"Panties. You know, *underwear*."

"I know *what* panties are. I just don't have a clue why you're asking."

"Your doll had on blue panties," Lucas says. He takes two steps and lands right in front of me, so close I have to look up to see him. "And Mr. Walker was checking you out back there, so I showed Jude. Look, I know this sucks, but does he watch you in class? Give you good grades? Special attention?"

There's a funny buzzing in my ears, like I've got a mouthful of hornets. I shake my head, trying to clear my mind. "I don't…no. I mean, I do all right in class but nothing noteworthy. And I don't even think I own blue underwear. When did you guys even talk about this?"

"We didn't. But after he showed me, I thought we should ask. Maybe the color doesn't matter," Jude says. "Do you have an outfit like this? A shirt/skirt combo he might love? Or maybe you just laugh at his bad jokes. It wouldn't take much for a guy like that."

I flinch because I do laugh at his jokes. Everyone else rolls their eyes, and I feel bad, so I—

Someone's sharp breath cuts my thoughts short. I look around, but it wasn't someone else. It was me. My hands are going tingly. I'm breathing too fast.

"Sera." Lucas's hands drop, feather-light, onto my shoulders. Tears are filling me up, blurring my vision and drowning out anything I might say.

"Just breathe," Lucas says with a sigh. "It's all right."

"The hell it is," Jude says.

Lucas's grip tightens on my shoulders, and I can see his jaw clench when he turns to Jude. "No, but freaking out won't help, right?"

"No." I square my shoulders and pull my crap together. "It won't."

"So, what do we do?" Jude asks.

I turn to him. "You could run. You and Emily and Lucas. You guys could go because if our guess about the dolls is right, he's not after you. If this is just about me, you could get away."

"And in this plan, you'd stay here with Mr. Manson?" Lucas asks.

"You could try to send help," I say because I have to pretend I'm brave. I can fall apart when they're gone and safe.

"We're not leaving you," Jude says, surprising me. "We stand a better shot together."

"And *we're not leaving you*," Lucas repeats. Hurt flashes over his features. He's surprised I'd think he'd consider it.

"Look at us," Jude says. "Living all that happy, dreamy team-work stuff."

The joke bolsters me. "OK, then we leave when he falls asleep. Together, right?"

"We need to do it closer to dawn," Jude says, searching the trees with a frown. "No damn way am I wandering the woods at night."

"It's a fair point. We're getting closer to where there might be cliffs," Lucas says. "Mr. Walker mentioned drop-offs and a rim trail in this area. So, daylight?"

"A little before," I say. "We should bring most of the water, but we have to leave some for Mr. Walker. Some food too. All we have is a hunch here. He *could* be entirely innocent."

"He's a homophobic survival junkie," Jude says. "I bet he has a stockpile of rations and weapons in his basement. *Entirely innocent* is probably a stretch."

"I hear that," Lucas agrees.

"That doesn't mean he's a killer. We're not judge and jury, OK? We're leaving him water and food, and that's that."

Jude opens his mouth, but Lucas shoots him a look and speaks first. "Fine. Whatever you need to do. But no one breathes a *word* to him. We'll head north hard and fast. Mr. Walker said a day's hike."

"What about Emily?" I ask. "She's taking care of him. How will we tell her? Will she even come with us?"

"She'll come," Jude says.

"But she's doing everything for Mr. Walker. She's practically a nurse out here."

"She's stronger than you think, and she's a survivor. She'll come," he says. "I'll go back and find a way to talk to her."

We move to follow him, but he shakes his head. "Wait a bit. I'll try to convince him that you two really are out here pawing at each other and that we're not plotting against him."

His laugh follows him through the trees, but when it fades, the forest seems too loud and too quiet at the same time. Crickets hum, and that same rasping cry—barn owl, I guess—tears through the quiet. It's farther away this time but no less haunting.

I close my eyes, and an image of the doll forms in my mind. The hair, sticky red, and then the panties beneath the skirt, the ones I didn't see. I wipe my hands down my jeans and jerk back with a hiss. The left one is screaming. I hold it up, and suddenly, I remember something.

"I don't wear skirts," I say, hope catching in my throat.

Lucas chews on the corner of his lip, like he's biting back an argument.

"I wear dresses," I say. "I hate skirts, but I own a ton of dresses because they're easy and lightweight and—"

"Hot as hell."

Warmth curls up through my chest as he smirks. I look down because he'd know. I wore every last one I own around him.

"Sorry," he says, rubbing the back of his neck. "You were saying. Dresses?"

I clear my throat and my mind. "Dresses. The doll was wearing a skirt and a different color shirt, right? That's not me. I wear dresses. And even if I did own blue underwear, I wouldn't be flashing skivvies in math class, for God's sake."

"What are you getting at?"

"I'm saying…what if it's not me? The doll. What if it's someone else?"

He lets out a slow breath, looking unconvinced. "I don't know, Sera. You've got *Darling* on your freaking arm."

My shoulders slump. "I know."

"I know for girls it's all different, but guys don't know the difference between a dress or a skirt. At the very least, they don't care. They're just going to notice…"

It's his turn to flush, and it turns my stomach fizzy. All those butterflies and fluttery feelings, all the obsessive thinking and lip-glossing my mother thought I should live for. Lucas brings that out in me.

I bite my lip hard enough to sting. Lucas is watching me with interest I wish I didn't want. When he looks away, swearing, I flinch.

"I hate this," he says.

"Hate what?"

"I can't even say that you look good in a dress without feeling like I'm being an asshole."

Words flood my mouth, but I bite them back. Study my feet instead. My heart is beating so hard because he's in knots, and I know it's over me. Some part of me is eating this up. God, that's so sick.

Maybe it's genetic. Maybe that selfish streak that let my mother ruin us is in me too. I can cut my hair, change my life. But how do I cut *that* part out?

I must be quiet too long because Lucas laughs a little desperately. "Look, I've got a lot of things wrong with me, but I'm not *that* guy."

"I know."

"Do you, Sera?"

My shoulders hunch when he looks at me. I feel like the river birch behind me. My bark is peeling away, stripping bare things I should cover. He'll see everything underneath if I let him, and I'm afraid I *will* let him. I'm afraid I want to.

Trust your heart.

Right. Because my heart would never lead me wrong.

"So, you said you can't go there," Lucas says. "Is that with all guys or…"

He's waiting for me to fill in the blank, and the lie is ready on my lips. Just say it. Tell him it's everyone. It's some Lebanese thing, a cultural deal. That'll shut him up, and I won't even look like a jerk.

But it won't be true.

"I haven't run into anything quite like this before," I say instead.

What I mean is, I haven't run into anyone quite like him.

"But I've seen you go out with people," he says. His expression turns stony. "I'm different though? Because we kissed? Or is it because of the fights? Because of Tyler?"

It probably should be the fights. Last year, I saw him in the office with Jamie Peterson, sporting swollen knuckles and busted lips. Seems like a good reason. Too bad it's not *my* reason.

"Do you believe this?" he asks when I take too long to respond. He turns up his hand until I can see *Dangerous* scrawled onto his pale skin. "Do you believe I'm violent?"

"Is it still up for debate? How much trouble have you been in this year?"

He shakes his head and stalks forward, his expression cooling.

It scares me. "Tell you what, Sera. You want me to tell you all about how dangerous I am? I'll do that. Let's play that game."

I'm not sure I want to play anymore, but when I take a step back, my shoulder blades bump into a tree trunk. And he's right there, frowning at me.

"That Tyler thing? It was one of my first soccer games in Marietta. Mom and Dad move a lot. All part of their free-spirit stoner ways. Soccer was something I could do in any town, so I did." He drops his chin, deepening the shadows on his face. "That hit on Tyler was clean. Just a chance collision, but some hits go bad, and this one did. He broke his leg in three different places. Did you know that?"

"Yes."

"His teammates came after me for months. Did you know that part too?"

I swallow hard.

"I let them go at me in the beginning," he says. "Couple of black eyes. Bruised kidney. I'm big enough to handle a bit of roughing. Plus, I saw where they were coming from. If it had been *my* team captain?" He snorts, as if that doesn't warrant explanation. Then he tips his head so he's looking right at me. Maybe right through me. "Let's be clear, Sera. At first, I *let* them have at it. They wanted someone to blame, and I looked like the right guy for the job. I figured it would blow over…"

He figured wrong. Nothing blows over in Marietta. Marietta has a million perks, but the high school scene features all the small-town drawbacks. My shoulders droop, arms gone heavy.

"Back then, the situation was fine," he says. "I was handling it. I had the metal shop, and yeah, maybe soccer was a bad idea, but I could still play football…until I couldn't."

"What do you mean you couldn't? I thought you were cleared."

"It doesn't matter. *No more sports.* That was what they decided—my parents and the coaches and the school board and probably some asshole PTA members. They loved that mighty *we*. *We* think it's best. *We* all want the same thing. *We* all know you don't mean to be a *danger*."

I don't know what to say. Nothing will help. Nothing will change what happened. I think of touching him, but he looks as if he might implode, so I stay still.

Lucas closes his eyes. "I never gave a shit what the rest of them thought, but when my parents decided I was a danger? Screw it, you know? If everyone's determined to be afraid of me anyway…"

"That's when you decided to fight back," I guess.

"Maybe. Or maybe I decided I believed them too."

It's not what I thought about him. It's worse because it makes me feel more. Pain spreads up from my middle, squeezing tight in my chest. I think that's my heart. But hearts lie.

I can't stand the idea of who I am right now, the girl with shaky knees and stars in her eyes. But when Lucas turns to walk away, I can't stand that either. I'm torn between impossibilities.

"That word on your arm isn't you," I say.

I don't even know if it's true, but it means something to him. He draws closer, and then his hands move to my hair, thumbs tracing the line of my jaw as he looks at me. "I'm going to get you out of here, Sera. And when we are home, I'm not going to sit by and shut up if you vanish again."

My knees turn to jelly. To liquid. To nothing at all. Any second, my legs will turn to dust, and I'll drop.

"I don't want to make promises out here. Let's just get through this," I say, but it comes out like a whimper.

His thumb drags down the column of my throat. "You don't have to promise me anything."

I kiss him this time, my good hand finding his, lacing our fingers together. Our palms connect, and Lucas tightens his hold around my waist, and everything just…disappears. No forest, no killer, no danger. It's magic. I don't care if it's a trick of the light; I am spellbound all the same.

CHAPTER 19

When we get back to camp, time crawls. Mr. Walker sleeps fitfully, and we stare at each other under filtered moonlight, waiting for the right time. It's colder tonight. I'm shivering, and sometimes, I can hear a faint tapping that's probably Emily's teeth chattering.

I scoot back and catch my left hand on my hip, hissing. It's a combination of scrapes and blisters from the sled handle, and it's turning into a real problem. I've had plenty of time to dwell on the pain and softly touch around the worst of the scrapes in the darkness. It's a little warm to the touch. Emily didn't say much when I asked earlier for her opinion, but I don't think it's good. Lucas ripped off one of his T-shirt sleeves for a bandage. It's better than nothing, I guess.

Jude discreetly dragged a six-pack of water away from the cooler when he headed off for another bathroom break. He's earning all the letters on his arm tonight. Between the water and telling Emily, I have no idea how he's pulling it off without getting caught. I never saw them speak, and Emily hasn't strayed from Mr. Walker's side, but she knows the plan. I can tell by her expression alone.

Mr. Walker starts to snore low, deep rumbles. Jude lifts his hands in question, but Emily raises one finger. We wait for *days*. Years. I count the snores because there's nothing else to do. I'm at eighty-three before Emily finally stands up.

It's time.

The four of us inch backward from the camp in slow motion. Jude's fashioned a pack out of an extra shirt I don't remember seeing, and he's got the water strapped to his chest like a baby in a sling. The food is gone, save the cracker set and yogurt we left behind.

Maybe twenty yards away, Lucas snaps a stick under his boot. We freeze, and the hair on the back of my neck rises. Did Mr. Walker hear us?

My ears ache, straining for noise. Crickets sing. There's a muffled hoot in the distance. Mr. Walker snores on.

We tiptoe slowly, inching from tree to tree, following the sound of each other's footsteps. North. God, I hope it's north anyway. I'm totally trusting Lucas and Jude on this one. They referred to the sun setting and a couple of other things, and it was all blah, blah, science, blah in my ears.

I scrape my arm across branches and trip over roots at first, but soon enough, I figure out a way to move that doesn't feel so dangerous. There isn't much light, but there's enough to see the tree trunks, columns of black interrupting the gray. I drag my good hand along the bark of each one to steady myself, keeping my steps light until I'm sure there's nothing to trip on.

Lucas holds the lead, but he moves faster than I'd like. I don't complain. I want out, and we can't get out if we tiptoe from one tree to the next. He doesn't slow until we've been walking for at least an hour. I think. Honestly, how would anyone know out here, but when we cluster up around his back, we're all breathing hard and smelling ripe.

"Are we lost?" Emily asks.

Lucas shakes his head. "No, I just thought…"

Jude snickers. "Please tell me you still remember where north is."

"Would you just shut the hell up?" Lucas is looking off ahead. He's very still. Focused. "I thought I heard something."

Heard what?

I look around, ears straining again. The darkness that had faded into the background suddenly rises up like a living thing. Ferns dance around my feet like giant spiders. Soot-black branches groan and creak overhead. Shadows reach for my arms, my face.

I'm going crazy, seeing things where there's nothing. But I don't hear what he's hearing.

"Let's just keep moving," Lucas says.

"We're still heading north, right?" I ask.

"We're doing good, Spielberg. How's the hand?"

"Fine." The lie goes bitter in my mouth. My hand is definitely not fine. It's seeping and throbbing in time with my pulse. I need real first aid.

Jude and Emily fall back a little, and Lucas nudges my shoulder. "Keep me company in the lead?" he asks.

I laugh. "I can try to—"

I'm cut off when he takes my good hand. The darkness recedes just a little, and the air tastes sweet and clean. Pine needles maybe?

189

"Do you think Mr. Walker woke up yet?" I ask.

Something clatters off to the west. Lucas stops, and my heart trips. There's cracking and rustling together. It's pretty far off, but I'm sure I heard it.

Jude almost stumbles into our back. "What the hell, Lu—"

Lucas stops him with a raised hand, then points in the direction of the noise. He touches his ear, and we all listen.

Silence.

Silence.

Crack. My next breath sticks in my throat. There's another noise I can't place after—a sound that goes low and then high. Almost like a bird or an animal.

Or a voice.

It comes again—a high-pitched grunt, like someone is struggling or in pain. Moving in from the west. Another vocalization, and this one's definitely human.

"No. No." Emily whimpers. I feel her fingers at my back, twisting in my shirt. I clutch Lucas's hand tighter while Jude swears over and over. We're all clustered so tight, we're breathing the same air, and we still aren't close enough.

"Let's move," Lucas whispers.

We're moving again, ever north, but fear makes us a stumbling mess. Lucas slams into a tree with a cry. A few feet after that, Jude goes down with a whump. We drag ourselves on. My foot hits a dip in the ground, and my ankle pops, but it's fine. I'm all right.

We are all grabby hands and harsh breathing now, desperate to escape the owner of that strange voice. We are so close that I don't know whose sounds are whose or what fingers are on me or which arms I'm grabbing. We're like one body, moving in an awful, terrified synchronicity up the tree-strewn mountain.

I bang my bad hand and jerk back with a hiss. My foot slips, and everyone scrambles, snagging my arm, even my hair, to keep me from falling.

Tears smear my vision. We're not going to make it. He's going to hear us.

Something calls in the distance. "Hello? *Hello?*"

It's a girl, a girl, so it can't be Mr. Walker. My insides unfurl.

Emily gasps. "Is that Madison?"

"I thought you said Madison was dead," Jude says.

"That's what we thought," I say. "There were flies everywhere, so we couldn't cross the—wait, how did she cross the river?"

"Hello? I need help!"

The thin, raw voice lays me open. It's definitely Madison.

"Help us! Please, please help!"

Adrenaline slams through my veins, throbbing in every joint. I force myself to answer. "We're coming!"

Jude snags my arm. In the watery snatch of moonlight filtering through the branches, his eyes gleam. "What if it isn't them? What if it's another trick?"

"*Please!*" Madison calls.

"Jude, it's *Madison!*" I shake him off at the sound that follows. I'm not close enough to be sure, but I think it's sobbing.

Lucas doesn't seem reluctant after that sound. We all jog down the west side of the hill we just climbed.

"Slow down," Lucas hisses.

"They need help! Listen to her!"

"You don't need a broken leg to go with that hand."

I stumble as if on cue, going down on my right knee in the center of a fern. I smell leaves and my own sweat when I look up.

"OK," I say, gulping in a breath that goes down like a pill that's too big. "Slower."

The clouds clear when we get closer. Or maybe I just shift into some sort of adrenaline-fueled super vision. I'm only sure of the fact that it's brighter. My feet are suddenly visible. Tree trunks aren't just muddy black lines on a charcoal canvas—they're trees.

And then I see Madison.

Long hair and a streaky shirt. She's sobbing. Holding out a stick like she might beat us to death if we get too close. The moment she recognizes us, she drops the stick and rushes Lucas. Her arms wrap around his middle, and he stands there, shoulders hunched and hands awkwardly patting her shoulders.

She pushes him away suddenly, her face and hair splotched with stains.

"Hurryhurryhurry." She says it all together, her raspy voice crawling up my spine like centipedes.

"Are you hurt?" Emily asks.

I try another angle. "Where's Hayley?"

Madison pushes clumps of hair back from her filthy face and starts to pace and mewl. "She's back—she's—hurry. Hurry."

Goose bumps prick up my arms in angry rows. She sounds

bad. Half-crazy. Lucas must hear it too because he frowns when she takes his arm in her filthy fingers.

I move closer, but my stupid hand whacks another tree, pain lancing into my shoulder socket. I bite back a howl, and Emily slows beside me, her face pale and round in the darkness.

"I think it's infected," she says.

"Yeah," I say because I already knew that. And there isn't one thing I can do about it until we get out of here, so I focus on our newest mess. Madison definitely fits the word.

Head to toe, she's streaked with dark stains I don't want to identify. Her knees droop, and her legs are pale and thin as sticks. I force myself to reach for her, and my hand shakes at even the barest pat at her sticky, slender arm.

"We're here now," I say. "Everything's all right."

"No," she says, licking cracked lips with a swollen tongue. Her eyes are like bruises. She's dehydrated. I reach for my water, but she can barely hold it. "Ms. Brighton—she's—Ms. Brighton is—"

"It's OK." I pat her again, try to ignore her tacky skin. "We know. We saw."

Emily pulls her away, and I can see the way Lucas's face relaxes. Jude still holds back, staying a few feet behind us with his arms tightly crossed over his middle.

"Madison?" It's Jude. His expression reminds me of Before Jude, the one with attached headphones and eyes that drifted over us like wallpaper. "How did you get across the river? Where is Hayley? Did you see Ms. Brighton?"

"There was a zip line." Madison clenches her fists with a sharp breath, and my stomach doubles up. "We followed the river for a while and found a zip line."

"Where is Hayley?" I ask because she's not here. I don't ask about Ms. Brighton. I already know too much.

Madison's eyes go huge and round.

"Where is she?" I ask again.

"It was an accident," Madison whispers. "Help me."

She says it again, and blood drains from my face until my cheeks ache and my lips go cold. Mr. Walker's words ring in my ears. Words about a dead girl and everyone getting it wrong. Is Hayley dead too? What do we have wrong this time?

"Hurry," Madison says, her voice scratching again like sandpaper. "Hurryhurryhurry."

CHAPTER 20

Emily and Jude take the lead following Madison, partly because my lungs are burning and partly because Lucas is holding my hand and keeping us back from the group.

I step over something. A root, a branch, some horrid nature thing. I hate trees now. The smell of them, the feel of them. I'm pretty sure as long as I live, I'll never voluntarily step foot in a forest again.

Emily falls with a cry, clutching her ankle. She's back up fast but obviously favoring her left foot. I knock into Lucas's side. He scrapes past a briar. No sleep makes you clumsy, I guess.

Lucas pulls me closer, "You all right? Your hand?"

"I'm fine," I say softly. "Better than Emily. A hell of a lot better than Ms. Brighton or even Mr. Walker."

He leans in, those rough fingers grazing the back of my arm, his hair brushing my neck briefly. "We could head north, Sera," he whispers. "Right now. Just you and me."

"What?" I catch myself and drop my voice, pulling even closer. Our gait is awkward like this, but I can't let them hear us. "We can't do that. We can't just leave them."

"We can." He looks around, shakes his hair out of his eyes. "I'm getting paranoid as shit around here. Especially with you at the center of all this."

"So?"

"So, I'm growing a chivalrous side or something," he says, stepping over a log. He helps me next, whispering, "I want you out of here, Sera."

"Because I'm too weak to take care of myself?"

He stops dead, his mouth so soft that I'm tempted to test it with my thumb. "No," he says. "Because you're the only one here who matters."

I hold my breath, and Lucas looks up at the sky like he's praying. Maybe he is. I can hear the click of a hard swallow. The hollow of his throat is right in front of me. *Right* in front of me.

I feel druggy and heavy, like I'm going to lean in. At the last second, I put up my hand, and it lands on his stomach, palm flat and fingers spread. I feel his heartbeat in my knees.

"Whatever this is, it's seriously messed-up timing," he says, sounding strained.

I jerk my hand back and press it to my own chest. My heart is thumping at a crazy rate. Too fast. "It's a chemical thing because of the danger. Jude says so."

He laughs. "What?" I don't know how to explain, but he steps back, and I feel cold. "Last chance. We split off now and run. Will you come?"

I wince. "I can't just leave them. Not Emily and Jude."

He grits his teeth, shakes his head once. He won't argue with that. Things are different now. "You'd better have Emily look at that hand."

Emily can't do anything for my hand, but it's a good enough way to end the conversation.

Dawn is just starting to smudge pale prints on the gray sky when we reach Hayley. She's by the river, propped up on what looks like a sleeping bag. That's what hits me first—

They have some of their stuff. They might have called for help.

"It happened yesterday," Madison says. She's sounding a lot less crazy now that we've given her some water. Or maybe it's because we're back with Hayley. "We followed the stream, and it started winding north. I remembered from the map that it followed the trail pretty closely."

"Did you try to call?" Lucas asks.

"No phones. We woke up with a lot of stuff missing, and Ms. Brighton…" She stops, looking stricken before she goes on. "We had to leave a lot behind when we woke up to all that blood. We tried to scream for you guys, but no one heard us."

"Because we were drugged," Lucas says. I can tell Madison wants to ask, but he waves. "We'll fill you in soon. Go back to how you got over here. What happened to her?"

She nods, and for a moment, that manic gleam flashes over her expression. "I figured there had to be another bridge. Something. A way. We found a zip line."

"A zip line?"

"It seemed like it would work. I got across OK. It was bumpy, and I lost our water, but I made it. But when Hayley went, it broke. She fell."

I tear my mind off the possibility of a phone and try to figure out what happened to Hayley. Emily's crouched over her now, and Jude's beside Emily, so I can't see much. When he finally steps to the side, I wish I hadn't tried so hard.

Hayley moans and turns her head on the wadded-up sweatshirt serving as a pillow. Her pale hair is soaked to the sides of her face, and the flesh under her eyes looks puffy and bruised.

My body goes cold when I see her injury. It's not good. Her left arm is strapped across her torso in a makeshift sling—a pretty good one from the look of it, but one glance tells me it won't help.

I don't think a registered nurse could help on this one. She needs a hospital. Probably surgery. Her hand is the color of a plum, and though the splint has her lower arm wrapped, I can see the misshapen lump in the center of her forearm. I can see the stain of blood too. Her bone has broken through the skin.

"It's a compound fracture," Madison says. "I tried to splint it to keep it steady. It broke when she fell."

Lucas startles. "Wait, how close is the river?"

"Not far. Maybe a twenty-minute walk. I wanted to go farther. I was hoping to hit that road on the map. I figured if the stream was heading north, we'd already cut out some of that distance."

I blink, surprised at how smart she suddenly sounds. That singsong lilt is gone from her voice, and shaken as she is, she sounds completely calm.

"We're trying to get to the road too," Lucas says. "Do you have a map?"

"No, but I don't think it should be much farther. I wanted to keep going, but Hayley had to stop."

"The sling looks great," Emily says, clearly reaching for something positive. "It's what I would have done too."

"Did you check for Ms. Brighton's phone?" I ask.

She shudders. "No. When we woke up that morning, ours were gone. And she was—we were too afraid to go near her tent. There was a trail of blood, and I saw the edge of something in the bushes. She wasn't moving. I know it sounds bad, but we just ran." Madison twists at the edges of her hair with filthy fingers. In the growing light, I can see the smudges and streaks all over her are blood. Hayley's blood, most likely.

"You actually saw her?" Jude asks.

"Barely. I could just see something..."

"Something that looked skinned, right?" Lucas asks.

I flinch. I didn't see *that* clearly, and now I'm grateful. My stomach rolls itself into a hard ball. He's been holding this in. All this time, he's had to live with that vision.

"I couldn't see much, but yes," Madison says.

"Me too," Lucas says. "Looked like her back."

"Where were you?" she asks, and for the first time since we got here, her voice wavers to that crackling edge that scared me before. "We screamed and screamed. We thought he killed you. We were sure he must have killed you just like her."

"We're OK. We were drugged. There's been weird stuff, but..." Jude trails off, gazing at Hayley. Because the four of us are alive. I've got an infected hand, and Emily is limping, but we're all basically intact. More than we can say for Hayley.

"We thought for sure he got you," Madison says, the words rippling across a sigh.

"Wait." I look up, my mind catching on that. "Wait. You keep saying *he*."

Lucas gets it at once, slipping up next to me with a steely expression. "Madison, do you know who killed Ms. Brighton?"

"Who?" She laughs then, and her serene expression splits like an overripe tomato. "Mr. Walker, who else?"

Something in me cracks. This shouldn't be a shock. It shouldn't be, but the world has turned to quicksand beneath my feet.

"You saw him?" Jude asks. "You *saw* Mr. Walker do this?"

"Mr. Walker is with us," Emily says, playing her hand closer to the vest. "He's very ill."

Madison's nostrils are flaring with every breath. She makes me think of frightened horses. "He's the only one who *could* have done it."

"Why?" Emily asks. She seems genuinely curious.

"Because he knows the land. Because he brought us out here. He left us on the other side of that river. He planned *all* of this."

Behind us, Hayley's soft groan rises in volume, turns to a scream that hooks through my middle. Madison's mouth forms a small O, but she doesn't move to help. Doesn't move at all.

Hayley's eyes pop open, and she scans our faces blearily, breathing hard, as if even moving her eyes hurts. It *looks* like it hurts. I feel a phantom ache just watching her.

"Thank God," she croaks. "Help me. Help me."

Emily eases forward with soft, hushing noises, but then

Hayley's eyes lock onto Madison behind her, and her face goes impossibly paler.

"No," she whispers, her eyes still on Madison. "No more! *Please*, noooo!"

She draws out the last word until it is a scream, a wail, a sound that goes on and on, turning me to ice and then to stone. I want to run or cover my ears. I want to bury myself down into the leaves and dirt and rot beneath my feet because anything is better than that sound.

Hayley struggles wildly, like she's going to try to get up. She passes out suddenly, her ragged breath the only thing left to puncture the quiet her scream left behind. I recoil, backing right into Lucas's chest. He wraps an arm around my middle, and I hold it there, pushing my fingers into his wrist until I know I'm leaving nail marks.

But my eyes never leave Madison. Hayley was terrified when she saw her. She was afraid of Madison.

CHAPTER 21

My vision has tunneled, narrowing to a thin point of focus somewhere across the stream. Night has given way to a pink-tinted morning. I can see a squirrel on the opposite bank. Smooth pebbles. Muddy water. Trees.

"Sera?"

Lucas. He's right behind me, squeezing my shoulder and pulling me away from that far-off place in my mind. I don't want to come back, but I do.

Their little makeshift camp is silent chaos. On the surface, we are soft words and polite conversation. Madison tells us that putting the sling on was very painful for Hayley, that she's in shock, associating Madison with that pain. We pretend all morning that we believe her, but I don't think we know what to believe.

The only thing I'm sure of is that we need to get out of these woods, and yesterday is not soon enough. We haven't figured out a strategy yet, and running isn't going to be a good enough plan. Hayley needs us, and Madison…I just don't know what to think about Madison.

My eyes drag to Emily and stick. She's still limping around—apparently, she twisted her ankle pretty good. Running, maybe even walking, is out for her.

Lucas offers me a water and leans in until his hair brushes my jaw. "I think we need to get the hell away from here."

I shiver and look to where Jude is pressed to a tree, eyes scanning the forest, his mouth a thin, hard line when he looks at Madison. I feel it too, but could she really be involved in this? It seems crazy. Until I remember the way Hayley looked at her.

"I think we should go," Lucas whispers, probably thinking I didn't hear him the first time.

"Jude and Emily," I breathe. Once, we were all one big school group. Now it is us and them, even though I know that's probably not fair.

Jude is not the problem. He's so ready to bolt, it's a wonder I can't see turbines spinning behind his brown eyes. We've got to do something about Emily though. I don't think either of the boys is strong enough to carry her for very long. And then there's Hayley. Pale and sick and in and out of consciousness. No way can we move her.

I look at Hayley now, and a lump grows in my throat. Emily and Madison are sitting near her, and I can tell Emily's scared to death. Her smile's stretched so tight that I'm sure it will snap.

Lucas pulls me to his chest again. I lean into him and listen as he picks at the bark on the maple behind us.

"Any ideas?" He says it so softly that I'm not sure I didn't imagine it, but he's looking down at me, eyes half-mast, though a muscle in his jaw is jumping. "What should we do?"

"I don't know how we could leave," I say.

"Shh," he says because I'm too loud. He glances over my

shoulder, where I'm guessing he can see Madison. He swallows hard and moves in until our foreheads kiss.

"Maybe you should get a room," Jude teases.

I lurch back, but Lucas's hand splays on my back, and he gives the barest shake of his head as he pulls us a couple steps away. We stop by an oak, and I let him curl me closer.

"He's trying to help us," he says softly. "So we can talk like this. Figure out a plan."

I close my eyes and feel the sting of my exhaustion. I'm almost swaying on my feet, but he's right. We have to do something. We all saw the way Hayley looked at Madison. We *heard* what she said.

What do I believe though? Madison's story is logical enough. It would have been excruciating, and Hayley's clearly in serious shock. But Hayley's expression? It looked bigger than reliving a traumatic moment. It looked like she was afraid for her life.

I dare a quick glance around Lucas's shoulder. Madison and Emily are both leaned over Hayley again, tending or whatever. But then Madison's eyes shoot up and fix on Lucas and me. The envy in her gaze is almost palpable. I turn away quickly, my cheeks hot.

"Do you think she's involved?" I whisper.

Lucas frowns, his thumb rubbing a slow circle on my spine. The touch turns my head even foggier. "She doesn't strike me as the type. My money's still on Mr. Walker. He likes you."

"He doesn't. Not like that," I whisper. "I know you think I'm not seeing it, but I'm telling you, I don't think it's there. There's *zero* motive. And the words? The dolls? That feels girly."

Lucas cocks his head and leans in again. "Sera, this is *Madison.*

She got excused from gym over a bad hangnail. Plus, if she's doing this, why would she be calling us in to help her?"

"No idea. But she's also the *only* one from *her* camp who's not dead or heading that way in a hurry. Maybe she called for us to bring us closer."

It isn't as hard to imagine as I'd like. Madison has a car. She could have gotten down here, set this all up beforehand. She's proven she's capable with first aid, that she's smarter than we thought. Plus, we found *her* granola bar wrappers around our camp. This whole nightmare isn't an exercise in brute force. It's just planning. Really careful planning.

"She could have done it," I breathe, and this time, I believe myself.

Lucas sighs. "OK. What motive?"

I'm pretty sure I already know. I look over my shoulder and catch Madison glancing our way. I lift my hands to Lucas's shoulders, and her mouth thins.

I drop my hands like he's on fire. "You. You're the motive."

"Then why am I *Dangerous*?"

"Because you could hurt her?"

He quirks a brow. "You're reaching. And why the hell would *you* be *Darling*?"

"Maybe in her eyes, I am a darling." I swallow hard enough to hear it. "*Your* darling. Does she know about us? About the party or last spring when I hung out in your shop?"

His expression clouds, and I can't hear his next breath. "She knows I'm out here for you. She tried to talk me into signing up with her, and I said no until…"

"Until you saw me on the list?"

It's his turn to swallow hard. His grip on my waist tightens. "OK. It's possible. Anything is possible. So I'll take her down. Right now."

I shake my head hard. Maybe too hard. The world spins, and this time, I grab Lucas's shoulders for real.

His eyes are wide with concern, but he says nothing.

"We're exhausted," I say. "We're stabbing in the dark, and we could be wrong. Plus, if it is her, she's almost definitely armed. It feels too risky."

"You're letting your tired talk," he says.

I scoff. "You've got bags under your eyes I could pack a lunch in."

He laughs. "I still think I can take a hundred-and-ten-pound girl."

"It feels like a bad idea. She could have a gun. She could have a *partner*." I dare a quick glance, but Madison's behind Emily, ducked low near Hayley. No way can we get to her without going through them. Could we call her out? Would she see it coming?

"Break it up already," Jude says. I didn't even hear him slip up, but he's suddenly right beside us. He drops his voice lower than a whisper. "Someone's paying awfully close attention to your sexual tension."

No way did Jude come over here just to pick at how close we're standing. He's got something on his mind. I watch his gaze move over Emily, his mouth going thin every time she limps. He's afraid for her. Afraid for all of us probably.

Jude isn't who I thought he was. Not that it would matter if he was. He's one of us now, which makes me wonder when we became an *us*.

Emily adjusts her spot beside Hayley. Madison is still crouched close, but I can see that Emily is moving awkwardly. Whatever's wrong with her ankle, it's bad.

"She won't be able to walk," I whisper. "And Hayley is wrecked."

"Plus, Mr. Walker could be following us," Lucas says with a sigh.

Jude nods, and something in his expression cracks when he looks back at Emily. I know that look. It's the way I look at Sophie when she's in the midst of a panic attack. Or the way Dad looks at me every day.

It's compassion. Worry. And it's so much bigger than the nine letters on his arm.

"I'm sorry for trying to define you." I say it because I'm not sorry for *whatever* now. I know what I did wrong.

Jude just raises his brows, his expression revealing nothing.

I scrape a nail across the *D* in *Darling*. "Whether I meant to or not, I *did* wonder about you. I made my guesses too, even though I didn't know you at all. I had no right. Your dating preferences have nothing to do with me. That's what I'm sorry for."

I force myself to meet Jude's eyes, and he watches me for what feels like forever. It isn't comfortable, but I don't look away. Looking away would cheapen everything I just said, and the words aren't worth much as they stand.

"Better," he says, and his sudden smile surprises me as much as his soft words. "I don't talk about it because I've seen the way people react to my dads."

"Is it hard?" This from Lucas. His soft sincerity surprises me.

"Not always. Lots of people want to be supportive, and most

people try. But there's always this moment when they hesitate. They're thinking about it, trying to sort it all out. Should Pop go in the dentist box or the gay father box?"

"More labels," I whisper.

He shrugs. "I was born into a stack of them. Cello prodigy. Person of color. Gay dads. I just want this part of me to be mine for now."

My chest blooms with warmth, and I try to bite back my smile. And fail spectacularly. "I think I get that."

"No, you don't," he says, but he smiles just enough that his words don't sting.

There's a rustling across camp, and I see Emily waving her hands gently, softly encouraging Madison to head out. My stomach flutters. Tightens.

"What's happening?" Lucas asks.

No one really answers. Madison checks Hayley one more time, pushes a hunk of her own sticky hair behind her shoulder, and stumbles into the trees. Her footsteps are loud at first but then softer and softer until they fade.

I lock on to Emily's gaze, and for one split second, I think this is it. We'll all run. We'll be out. Then Emily struggles to her feet, like she wants to approach. Her ankle buckles, and her face contorts. Jude swears, and we trip over each other trying to get to her.

I crouch down next to her, smelling sweat and blood and fecund things from the forest floor. Emily's letting out short puffs of air with a little whine at the end of each one.

"What can we do?" I ask.

"How long do we have?" Jude asks.

"She's using the bathroom," she says. "Stomach issues, but who knows."

"I'll carry you," Lucas says. "We'll run."

"No." Emily pushes his hands away hard and closes her fingers around my wrist. "You need to go. I can't leave Hayley."

"We can't leave *you*," I argue. "After the way Hayley acted, we can't let you stay here with Madison."

"She's right," Jude says. "Something's very wrong with that girl."

"Yeah, everything that's happened is wrong with her. She's crazy, but she's not behind this," Emily says. "I'd bet my life on that."

If we leave, I'm afraid that's exactly what she'll have to do.

"But everyone from her camp is dead or in very real trouble," I whisper softly. "And she has a *thing* for Lucas."

"If it *is* her, it's the two of you this is about," she says. She gestures at us. "More reason for you to go. Just send help fast."

"What if she hurts you?"

"If Madison is after someone, it's not me," Emily says, voice hard. "I *know* when someone's going to hurt me."

I study her red-rimmed eyes and stringy hair. I think about the old bruises I saw in the tent, the ones on her arms.

They were shaped like fingers, and I know why now. My throat feels thick. Emily catches me looking and clamps her hands over her biceps.

"Emily." I say it like a prayer.

"Please go," she says again. "I'm fine. Just hurry."

"They can go. I'm staying," Jude says.

"No," Emily says.

"Yes."

"You should be looking out for yourself," Emily tells him.

"Excuse me for evolving some empathy." Jude's words bite, but his look is gentle. "We can watch her better together. If she tries something, she'll have two of us to deal with."

Tears are glittering in Emily's eyes, and I can't do this. I can't leave them here. We are supposed to stay together. I wrap an arm around my aching middle, wincing against the throb in my hand. I try to speak, but Emily looks right over my head to Lucas.

"Get help," she tells him. "Be careful. Don't die getting out of here. Hayley looks stable, but she's going to need serious antibiotics. You two have to stay alive, or she won't."

My breath sticks halfway in. "Emily, I—"

Lucas curls his fingers around my arm. He should argue. Ask something. But he doesn't, and I knew he wouldn't because Lucas believes her. Us getting help is the best shot we have.

He takes my uninjured hand and eases us back toward the path. Thank God the trees are thinner here. There aren't leaves and sticks and things to pop under our every step. Before we're out of reach, I take a breath because I feel like I should say something important. Meaningful.

All we get is a long look at one another. Jude's hair is springing in a million directions, and Emily's got dark smudges beneath

211

both eyes. They look like the kind of people the world forgets, but they aren't forgettable to me.

Lucas pulls me slowly and carefully through the trees, and I let him. I know this is our best chance. But I can't help feeling like I'm betraying them.

CHAPTER 22

The light's gone golden, and there's an afternoon sleepiness to the air that makes my bones ache. I'm exhausted, we're low on water, and we're backtracking thanks to the steep slope of the mountain in front of us.

"I hate mountains," I say, panting.

"I hate backtracking."

I wrinkle my nose. "Are we near the speaker? The place we left Mr. Walker?"

He doesn't even slow down. "Yeah. We're basically heading back to where we were when Madison called us. I think it's easier to get north on the east side of the mountain. She and Hayley were sitting southwest of us. Pretty pathetic that we've probably all been in the same three or four square miles this whole time."

I look ahead at the narrow valley between the two mountains. It looks like the only way through—which scares me because it also looks like the perfect place for someone to be waiting for us. My arms prickle with goose bumps.

"Lucas, is there another way around? Could we go over?"

"We're about out of water and stupidly low on sleep. I want to avoid climbing unless we have no choice."

"But that feels like such an obvious place to go, like the mountains just naturally funnel you through that valley."

He nods. "Yeah, it does."

"Which means it's a pretty natural place for someone to be looking for us, right?"

"I just don't see a better option. Everything out here is a risk. If we go through that valley, we might run into our resident psycho. If we try to climb, we might collapse like Jude did when his dehydration set in. Thing is, either way could get us killed, and if we die, then everyone else dies, which is doubly shitty since they're all back there counting on us."

He's already thought all this through, and I didn't expect that. His concern alone stuns me to silence.

Lucas notices, wincing. "What?"

"You…you're worried about them."

His cheeks go pink, like I'd caught him with his hands in a cookie jar. "I'm just trying to think smart. If Mr. Walker catches up with them—"

"Why do you insist it's him? Madison's the only one with an actual motive. You saw the way she looked at you. Looked at *us*. Plus, none of this stuff requires a big person."

"Whoever did this killed Ms. Brighton."

"Ms. Brighton and Madison are about the same size," I argue. "With a weapon, it's definitely possible."

Lucas shrugs a shoulder, like he's not so sure. "OK, what about her finger? Do you think you could apply enough force to actually sever—"

"Let's just not," I say, the mental image making my stomach roll. "Look, I don't care what anybody says. Mr. Walker doesn't seem like a killer. I mean, not that Madison does, but…"

He lets out a low breath, and I feel like there's something he's not saying.

"Wait, are you defending her because of some sort of history between you two?"

He tilts his head right, then left, like he's sorting out his response. "She wanted to go there. Last year. Her brother and I got into it, and I think she took that as some sort of sign that I was interested. It was ridiculous, but she was…hard to shake off."

I arch a brow. "I'll bet. I knew she was hot for you, but is it like…obsession?"

"Nah. She's into *lots* of guys. She was probably trying to date me to get back at her brother for some stupid thing or just for drama's sake. Or, hell, maybe because she liked the idea of dating a big, bad criminal."

"You're not a criminal." He laughs, so I grab his shirt to make him stop. "Lucas, you're not a criminal. You're out here trying to be a hero, for God's sake."

"We can talk about heroics if I actually manage to get you out of here."

He looks up at the walls of the valley, which have grown steeper on either side of us. We're entering that narrow place that scared me. My insides shiver.

"I need to take a leak," he says. "I'll stay close."

"I've got to go too," I admit.

"I'll go with you first."

"Uh, yeah, no." I've lost almost everything that resembles dignity out here, but so help me God, I'm not going to have him stand three feet away while I pee. It's still daylight.

Lucas hesitates, so I throw up my arm to reveal the *Darling*. "Seems pretty unlikely that someone who goes to all this would finish me off on an unplanned pee break."

He smirks, but then he reaches down and hauls a long, dead branch off the ground. He turns it in his hand like he's testing the weight, then throws it javelin style into the ground. He braces one hand on the top and his boot on the center. Pushes hard.

It splinters, and he keeps pushing, twisting, until the bottom bit is broken off.

My stomach tenses as he holds up his handiwork, a pole, taller than him and jagged and sharp like a weapon. Because it *is* a weapon.

"What is that for?"

He offers it to me with a smirk. "Let's call it insurance."

He stomps off into the woods, and I head out the other direction, eyes searching the trees. A woodpecker's *tat-tat-tat-tat-tat-tat* echoes in the distance, and little pinpricks of sunlight are making their way through the canopy. It feels OK. Or as OK as it's going to feel out here. I prop the makeshift spear against a tree.

I've got my shorts around my knees when I hear the soft hiss of leaves rustling in the distance, opposite of where Lucas headed. A chill slides up my neck. There's something else too. Something that sounds like a child crying.

"Calm down," I tell myself. Because it's nothing. The wind. Some random squirrel doing a random squirrel thing.

And then I hear it again, and my heart turns to stone. It's not a squirrel or leaves or anything else. It's definitely someone crying.

I finish and yank up my shorts, heart thumping in my throat. I open my mouth to call for Lucas, but someone else beats me to the punch, a ragged voice that echoes strangely in the woods. It's too far away and too garbled to make out clearly through the sobs. I strain to catch the pieces, to tie the bits of sounds into words.

"—please come—Hannah!" it calls. It's not Mr. Walker. Madison maybe, but I don't think so. "Before he hurts—"

I'm already moving—moving around the tree I'd chosen, putting the thick trunk between me and whoever is out there. My hands are shaking, my heart pounding behind my temples. If I run, will I be fast enough? Will I get away?

More words filter through the wind. "Quickly, Hann—" More rustling.

Oh God, I have to run.

"—I'll help you!"

I push out from behind the trunk and dare one look back. It's nothing but trees, forest shadows, and distant birdsong. All is quiet. And then a black shadow peels off one of the tree trunks. I catch a glimpse of what could be an arm. It's reaching toward me.

I scream loud enough to split the sky in two.

CHAPTER 23

Lucas is already back in the valley when I burst out of the tree line. He's still buckling his jeans as he rushes for me, eyes searching for damage as he grabs my arms.

"Are you all right? Is Mr. Walker—"

"Not Mr. Walker. Someone's over there, crying." I can barely get the words out through my panting, so I point back to the direction where I'd heard it.

"Did you recognize the voice? Did you see him?"

"Not him." I gasp again. "A girl. Child maybe. They said they want to help. They said something about Hannah. Do you know a Hannah?"

Lucas shakes his head, his face blurring in front of me.

I rub my eyes. Maybe I'm seeing things. Maybe there was no shadow, no voice at all.

"I thought it was you," he says. "Before you screamed, I heard something. Not the words, but—"

We're cut off by another strangled cry. Closer now. I stumble back, and Lucas steps in front of me. Something shuffles in the distance. There's a soft thump. Three more thumps after that, and I flinch with every one. I search the trees—spot a shadow that turns me cold. Lucas points at it, but then it disappears. I hear footsteps retreating.

They're running away from us?

Lucas hesitates a second before heading after the footsteps.

"What are you doing?" I shriek.

"I'm checking it out."

"We should just go," I say, pulling his arm.

"Ms. Brighton's killer isn't crying in the woods over some girl named Hannah. Whoever that was, they might actually be trying to help. If they dropped something, I want to know what."

I can't argue with that, but I stay well behind him when we wander back up through the trees. Lucas shakes his head and moves forward, grabbing the broken stick I left against the tree.

"Maybe they just jumped or stomped hard," I say.

"I'm thinking definitely not."

Lucas crouches down, and I can see a stack of yellowed newspapers on the ground in front of him. They're all still creased, like they've been folded under someone's arm. Like someone just dropped them. My footprint is half-hidden in the soft, muddy earth beside them, so I know I didn't miss them. They weren't here before. The thumps I heard—that was these papers hitting the ground.

The papers were left here for us, just like the water and the dolls. And the first thing I see is an ornate number one in the upper corner, scripted like the letters on my arm.

My stomach rolls, and saliva pools in my mouth. Lucas adjusts his grip on the sharpened branch and holds a hand up, like he needs to stop me from speaking. As if I would speak. As if there are words for this. If I open my mouth, I will scream, and it will never end. So my lips stay closed, and my ribs ache with every heartbeat.

He sorts through the papers. One, two, three, four.

"There's something taped to them," Lucas says.

He scans the forest, looking wary, so I reach for a paper. It's a lock of straight black hair. I wince, thinking of the fresh cut I felt with my fingers. But this isn't my hair—it's Emily's.

I unfold the paper and find an article circled in black marker. The date is from eight years ago. A girl, Cora Timmons, from Marietta who'd committed suicide after years of drug abuse and mental health issues. There's no picture. Nothing scary. Just a few cold sentences reporting a tragedy with one line—*history of family issues*—underscored by that familiar ink.

My eyes fall to the hair again. So Emily's involved with Cora's death? Eight years ago? It's not possible. Wait, maybe she's supposed to be Cora.

Then who am I supposed to be?

"I think this is about Emily." I choke on her name. "It's about a woman with family and mental health issues. She committed suicide. I think it's supposed to be Emily."

"Like, what, a reincarnation or something?"

My exhale shudders out. "I don't know."

Lucas swears and grabs the next paper. It's his—I can tell by the short length of brown hair taped to the front. The next one up is a curly tendril that can't belong to anyone but Jude. And then there's mine. Tied with a tiny pink ribbon that makes my stomach twist like a pretzel.

I scan Jude's article, a short human interest piece about a man named Jeff Kohler, catching only that he surprised his wife with a secret dream vacation he'd saved for years to afford. Doesn't sound too sinister. And it's four years after Emily's article, so no connection there. I spot several words circled: *secret, hidden, undisclosed*. Really? Jude's marked *Deceptive* and linked with a thirtysomething guy over a surprise trip to Fiji?

Why would anyone want to hurt them for those things?

No one wants to hurt them. They want to hurt you.

I drop Jude's paper and focus on mine. It's got the same sinister number one written in the top-right corner. One day left, and our time is up.

And then what?

The headline for me is on the bottom half of the front page.

Local Girl Lost to Tragedy

The picture beside it swallows me like quicksand. From a distance, she could be me. Same shoulder-length hair and pointy chin. Same dark eyes and wide cheeks. She's not my doppelgänger, but it's close enough.

I shut my eyes, picturing the doll with my face and bloody hair. Hearing Mr. Walker tell us it was an accident. This girl who looked like me died out here.

Lucas swears and throws his paper on the ground. He storms a few paces away, but I don't ask. I can see the article from here. Brodie Jones. Star athlete with a history of trouble. Arrested for assault. It makes as much sense as the other two, I guess. Which means barely any sense at all.

My hands are shaking on my paper when Lucas joins me. There's nothing left to do but read it, so I do.

LOCAL GIRL LOST TO TRAGEDY

What started as an autumn hiking trip for four high school seniors ended with a family's worst nightmare when one of the teens, seventeen-year-old Hannah Grace Soral, died. Hannah's absence was reported by her three companions, and a search party located her partially consumed body late last night.

My intestines squirm like they've come alive. "Lucas, it's Hannah." I point at the name in the article, and he nods, looking grave.

Due to the condition of the remains, the circumstances surrounding Soral's death are uncertain. A spokesperson for the victim's family provided the following statement. "Our daughter didn't take risks. We believe something happened in those woods. Please help us find justice for Hannah." Despite the family's plea, authorities say there is no immediate indication of foul play. The official investigation remains—

The article continues on the next page, but I'm not sure I can go on. Lucas steps back, face pale.

"So is this some sort of re-creation of what happened to

Hannah?" Lucas asks. "The four of us are somehow living this over again? Is that the game we're playing?"

"Maybe."

"This is twisted."

Twisted but obvious. I know how this goes. Whatever script we're following out in these woods—this is *my* role. I play Hannah Grace Soral, and I'm supposed to die out here.

My vision goes smeary, and the words turn into squiggles that move and twist until I can't make out the letters. I blink hard and the words clear, but I still skim from one bit to the next. She died tomorrow, this girl who looks so much like me. Eighteen years ago, on tomorrow's date, she died out here.

Partially consumed. I flip the page open, pain buzzing through my bad hand, for the rest of the article, scan the paragraph for anything helpful. There isn't much. A few quotes from the community. Tragic loss. The principal's heartfelt condolences. And then a single name that stands out like a beacon. *Peter Walker,* a new, local teacher who grew up near the site of the incident.

"Hannah was a special girl," Walker said. "I hope her death serves as a warning. People die in those woods all the time."

The paper drops from my hands, rippling through the air like a falling bird. It lands in the dirt, and I leave it.

"What is it?" Lucas says, picking up the paper. He reads for a minute and then says, "Mr. Walker's in this article."

I nod, and he pulls in a long breath, tracing his finger under our teacher's name.

"He killed that girl, didn't he?" I ask, pacing three steps left and then back again. "He killed Hannah, and now he's coming after me."

Because I look like her. And I look like my mother. My face has brought me nothing but trouble.

I laugh. It dissolves into a shriek. And then a sob. I cover my mouth and shove it all back down.

Lucas drops the paper and wraps an arm around my back, his gaze flicking from tree to tree, shadow to shadow.

I grind my muddy boot into the newspaper. In the corner, the number one twists, and my eyes drag to the date on the paper. It's tomorrow. There's one more day left.

"Hannah died tomorrow," I say. "Tomorrow eighteen years ago."

Lucas's soft mouth goes impossibly hard. "Well, you're not Hannah."

CHAPTER 24

We make our way through the valley quickly, but there isn't a road on the other side. More mountains. More trees. Neither of us says a word as we weave our way through undergrowth that's denser with every step.

Shadows stretch longer as we walk. It's hard not to think about the figure I saw. Harder still to not imagine Mr. Walker in every rustle of leaves or snapping branch I hear. I'm jerking my head back and forth so much, I'm about to get whiplash.

"I don't think he'll come tonight," Lucas says. "I think it'll be tomorrow."

"Because that's the anniversary?"

"Makes sense, right?" he says. "None of this was spur of the moment. This all leads up to something, I think. And the article said she died tomorrow."

True. Doesn't mean he's not in the trees right now, waiting for midnight. Watching us walk. We crest over one mountain and collapse just past the top. It's grown dark, and the terrain is rough. The mountains are sharper here, rocky outcrops jutting up more often, the occasional drop-off reminding me of Ms. Brighton's ghosts.

Lucas offers me our remaining water. Thirsty as I am, I'm not sure I shouldn't use some of it on my hand. That situation is getting worse by the hour. It's throbbing up to my elbow now. The moon is high and bright, but I still can't see well enough to assess redness or swelling.

"Hand bothering you?"

"It needs to be dealt with."

"We're getting close," he says. "We're heading north again. I bet the road cuts right through one of those valleys up there. I've got a good feeling."

I don't feel good about anything. I'm convinced that even if we do manage to avoid Mr. Walker, we'll end up lost out here until my arm falls off and I die of gangrene.

"You don't believe me, do you?" he asks.

I smirk. "I wouldn't say I'm drowning in optimism."

"I could climb a tree when we get a little higher. I might be able to spot headlights."

"You're suggesting climbing a tree. *In the dark.* Do you want to end up like Hayley?"

"Good point." Lucas downs another few sips and stands up. "I don't like all the cliffs now that it's getting dark. We could fall if we're not careful."

It's a real risk. The drop-offs barely have rhyme or reason, cliffs that run along the ragged mountain ridges and fissures—those are even worse—that spring up without warning. Tree, tree, three-hundred-foot fall to our deaths.

Something snaps in the distance, and I flinch, scanning the darkness. Leaves rustle, and then I hear the scrabble of tiny claws on a trunk.

"Coon probably. Maybe a possum," Lucas says. "They come out at night."

I don't talk about who else could come out at night, but we're both thinking it.

Far in the distance, something calls in a rhythm. Once. Twice. Low and long in a way that makes me think human.

"Do you think...?" I ask him.

"An owl again? That one we heard made crazy noises."

When we hear it again, he doesn't look so sure. It's two-toned and too low to be a bird, and it's coming from the direction we came. Through the pass between the mountains, I think. I can't think of any animal that could make a noise like this. It sounds human.

It sounds like my name.

I stand up, knocking over my almost-empty water bottle.

Lucas saves it fast and rests a light hand on my leg. "Relax. Mr. Walker wouldn't go through all this stalking just to start screaming for us, right?"

I try to smile and ignore the cold sweat breaking under my arms as Lucas stretches and tightens the caps on the water. We're just moving when the noise comes again.

I clamp a hand over Lucas's arm because it *is* my name. Someone is calling my name.

"Do you hear that?"

He stops, and I can tell by his expression he did hear. I bite my lip and feel a mosquito puncture the back of my arm.

"Sera! Emily! Lucas! Jude!"

My blood frosts over in my veins. It's him—Mr. Walker.

CHAPTER 25

Lucas doesn't say a word—just grabs my good hand and starts marching. We're going faster than before, sloshing across ground that feels marshy. I smell old rain and rot, but it fades as we climb. Another mountain—we're heading up diagonally—and my legs are burning. Aching.

"Sera! Emily!"

I bite down a whimper and speed up. Mr. Walker's closer now. Below, I can hear the occasional thump of a footstep. God, can he hear us too? Lucas is silent as he climbs, but I'm panting too loud. My thighs shake with every step. I'm terrified I'll collapse and roll down this dark mountainside. And Mr. Walker will be waiting for me at the bottom with permanent markers and a knife.

I let go of Lucas's arm to grab at the trees, hauling myself up even though every muscle is shuddering. I have to get over this ridge because…because if I don't, I'm giving up. One step. Another. Another.

"Hey! Hello! If you can hear me, make some noise!"

Mr. Walker sounds a bit farther north of us now. He's continuing on the way we were going to go. But whatever, he's moving away, and thank God because I cannot take one more step. I cling to the tree, and the pain screams across my wound. I'm sucking air so hard, I can't tell Lucas to wait. He sees I've stopped. Maybe he can't go either.

Again, Mr. Walker calls our names, one after the next like he's doing a roll call. He sounds desperate.

Lucas moves closer and looks up the steep mountainside and then back at me. Is he thinking of carrying me? Please. He's sheet-white and soaked in sweat already.

Mr. Walker hollers again. "If you can hear me, stay where you are. I'm coming for you."

I shudder and watch Lucas's throat jump when he swallows. Funny he would use those words—*rescuer* words. Is he using them to lure us in? Lucas nods up at the mountain again, and I shake my head. My legs weigh two thousand pounds. Two *million* pounds. I am sinking into this forest floor, waiting for Mr. Walker to come for me.

"Sera, we have to keep going," Lucas says.

"He's going to get to the road first." The whisper comes out of me on the edge of a sob. "He'll cut us off. I can't keep going."

"Yes, you can," he says, and then his hands are on my face, and he's smiling at me like I'm chickening out on a ride at the fair. "It's a big road. We'll find another part of it. No option, right? The show must go on. Isn't that what you people say?"

My fumbling step forward is my answer. It's not easy going. We scrabble our way up, tree by tree, root by root. It's so slow that it's laughable, but the next time Mr. Walker calls, his voice is a distant echo to the north.

We reach a small clearing at the top, and Lucas waits, searching through the darkness for some indication that things are going right. I watch too, seeing nothing but a hazy white moon over-head and the veiled blinking of countless stars. The forest slopes down below us, and a cloud drifts away from the moon.

I see something. Something pale in the woods. I go very still, scanning the trees carefully. Nothing, nothing, and then I find it again. Pale and Twinkie-shaped and almost but not quite swal-lowed by the forest.

I clutch at Lucas's shirt and point down the slope. He follows my line of vision, and I can see the moment he spots it. His wide shoulders tense, and a low breath comes out of him.

"What do you think that is?" I ask.

"I don't think. I *know*." His smile gleams a little bit wicked in the moonlight. "That's a camper trailer."

It has a broken window, cinder block steps, and a ripped *God Bless America* flag, and it is the most gorgeous thing in the world. Or it is until I see the half-tarp-covered four-wheeler parked beside it. Lucas tells me at least ten times to slow down, heading down that mountainside, but I don't care. I run.

My feet thud to a sudden stop twenty feet or so from the front of the camper. It's a once-silver cigar with rust and trash around the base and a few thornbushes draped over the front door. I don't think anyone's been home in a while.

My smile falters, but I force it to stay put. It doesn't matter. We don't need a person really. We just need to get that four-wheeler running so we can get the hell out of here.

I pull in a deep breath and move from the front of the camper to the four-wheeler. Lucas is already pulling the tarp loose, checking over the engine.

"Do you think it's usable?" I ask.

"Battery would be my first worry." He starts rummaging around the pile of wood and scraps around the quad. "No keys either."

"Can you hotwire it?"

"You mean from my stint in *Grand Theft Auto: The Reality Show*?" He smirks up at me, holding something long and metal. "A few fights does not make me a car thief."

"I'm sorry." I bite my lip and look back at the camper. "Do you think they'd just leave it if it's running? Is that…convenient?"

Lucas shrugs, leaning in. "I don't know. I've got an uncle who lives about seventy miles from here. He leaves a dirt bike at his hunting shack sometimes."

"Doesn't he worry about someone stealing it?"

"He always says anyone who could find it would be riding something better. This thing is a rusted piece of junk, so I'm betting the same logic applies."

He taps the heavy metal file he's holding to something inside the engine area. There's a crack and a sudden spark, flaring white and brilliant and brief in the darkness.

"Battery's good," he says, dropping the file. "We should check inside for keys."

Looking at the camper sends spiderweb chills up my back. I don't know if I want to go inside. "I still think it's weird it's out here."

"Well, they didn't leave the keys, and I'll bet the camper is locked tight."

My eyes drag back to the broken-down trailer, sticking on those long, draping branches, each one covered in thorns. I square my shoulders. Thorns are not going to stand in the way of me getting out of here.

Lucas heads for the steps, swearing before he even reaches for the first sticker branch.

I catch up and pluck at the shirt between his shoulder blades. "Let's be smart here. We'll use the file and sticks to push some of this crap away."

He turns back, chuckling. "See? I knew that bossy side was still in there."

"No sense in making an easy job hard."

It's not an easy job. By the time we uncover the door, we're both covered in bleeding scratches, my bad hand is burning like I've doused it in gasoline and lit it on fire, and I've got thorns in my hair.

Lucas rattles the shiny padlock on the front door with a sad laugh. And then his shoulders sag, and he drops his forehead softly to the door. Something in me aches at that gesture. It's the first time he's looked weak.

It's the first time I've wondered if he was going to cry.

I reach for him, fingertips grazing his sweat-damp shirt. It feels like slow motion when he turns, tears glittering in his eyes even as he forces that cocky grin back into place.

"Yeah, I'm real dangerous. I can't even get into this rickety-ass trailer."

I rest my palm against his chest until he takes a breath that shakes as badly as my fingers. I press harder, hoping to steady him. He leans back into the trailer like I pushed him, watching me with heavily lidded eyes.

"You could have left us two days ago," I say, only just realizing it. On his own, he would have made it. Lucas is built for this sort of adventure. He's made to survive.

He snorts. "Sure, I could have just—"

"Yes, you could have. You could have walked north on that first day like you wanted to. Like we *all* probably should have. You could have left us, left me. And you didn't."

His heart thumps at my fingers like a bass line, and I step in close.

"But you're still out here," he says. "We're all still out here, so what does it matter?"

I feel everything I felt on the back deck and more, but I don't hate it right now. This feeling I mocked and ran from and despised is the thing that's keeping me going.

"It matters," I say, and I kiss him softly, stretching up so high on my toes that the arches of my feet ache. I taste the salt on his lips and maybe a little dirt, but then his hand is so soft on my neck that everything goes feather-light at the edges. The darkness and fear melt away. Even my stupid hand dulls to a throb.

Lucas pulls back. I can feel his eyes on me, but his expression is hidden by the camper's shadow. He brushes a thumb over my lips and then takes me back down the concrete block stairs that wobble under every step.

"Stay down here for a minute."

I'm opening my mouth to ask when he launches back up the stairs, grabbing the file off the ground. He wedges it in the seam beside the door. After grunting and shifting, he slips it farther into the frame and pushes against the end for leverage. Metal and wood creak. I hold my breath—the file slips with a pop.

Lucas cries out, yanking his hand back and shaking it. Blood is dripping from his middle finger.

"Lucas—"

He waves me off, and then he's pushing until he's groaning and the door is groaning and I'm biting my lip. A snap rocks through the air, and something clatters on the concrete steps.

The file. Half of it. It broke off in the door.

Lucas explodes, fists and feet and words flying at the door like bullets. I step farther back as he rages, kicking one of the concrete blocks in the steps three feet away as he brutalizes the door. I don't even think he notices it's gone. He's too busy cursing a blue streak and rocking the camper on its deflated wheels.

My heart climbs into my mouth, trapped there by my gritted teeth. I have to do something. Stop him before Mr. Walker hears and comes back. We're in a valley, but it could echo, couldn't it?

"Lucas," I say.

He doesn't stop, shoving and punching at the door like it's all he sees. The frame splinters a little, but he's still slamming over and over, muttering to himself.

"Outofhere. Outofhere. I'mgettingheroutofhere!"

"Lucas!"

He doesn't stop, throwing his shoulder, his whole body, against the door. Once, it rocks. Twice, something snaps underneath the trailer. A third time, and the door gives with a symphony of snaps and rips.

Then there is quiet. The door dangles off one half-busted hinge. Lucas lands on his side, shoulders and head inside the darkness of the camper.

CHAPTER 26

I make my way up the stairs on Play-Doh legs, crouching at his side and helping him sit up inside the busted door frame.

He looks up at me, cuts on his face and a dazed look in his eyes. "Shit, I actually got in."

"You did," I say, brushing his hair back from his forehead. "You really did."

It's so dark inside that the trailer is mostly things I feel and smell. A sticky floor under our boots and sleeping benches I bump into with every step. It smells like spilled beer and cigarettes, but it does not smell like blood or death or trees. And I am grateful.

There's a plastic-wrapped carton of bottles on the counter, mostly empty. I find a couple of bottles of Gatorade in the back and crack one open. I offer the first to Lucas before opening my own. For a while, we stand there in the dark and quiet, staring at the door he destroyed while we drink our fill.

Lucas finds a flashlight strapped by a window, and the sudden brightness is disarming, illuminating duct-tape-repaired cushions and cracks on the tiny metal table hinged to the wall. Someone moves across from me, and I flinch. Nope, not a person. A mirror.

I stare, Lucas's left shoulder shielding the worst of my stained clothes. My view of my face is clear as day though, and it's the face of a stranger. My dark eyes are sunken, my hair clumped around my neck in dull hanks. I have a scrape under one eye I don't remember getting and sweat and dirt ground into my forehead and chin. I sure don't look like my mother now.

Do I still look like Hannah?

Lucas isn't much better. He's like an extra from a zombie movie, his features beyond hollow and patches of stubble showing through on his chin. He's rooting around in cabinets, hunched over because he's too tall to stand up in here. He takes up every inch of available space, like a cartoon character in a too-small bed.

"Let me see that hand," he says, reaching for me. I can see a red metal box in his other hand. First aid kit.

I turn over my hand and let out a low breath. It isn't pretty. Like the worst case of road rash I've ever seen. It's puffy and pink, and I see places where it's weeping yellow pus.

Lucas opens a bottle of peroxide and looks at me. I can tell his jaw is tight, but he just tells me to grit my teeth and hold on to the table. Nothing has ever hurt like the peroxide he pours over my hand. It hits my tender flesh like lava, flashfire painful and leaving a loud throb in its place.

"Breathe, Sera," he says.

I do, and I cry a little too but try to hide it because Lucas knows me as the girl with her crap together. I had clipboards, flouncy dresses, and a *plan*. Even when our rotating *Les Misérables* set broke mid-show last year, I held my shit together and got us all to curtain call.

Now I cry over every damn thing and swoon when Lucas glances at me sideways, and I'm going with my gut so much, I should hate myself. I really should.

I feel cool pressure and look up to see him pressing a white gauze pad over the palm of my hand. He frowns at it.

"I squirted a bunch of antibiotic ointment on it. It's not perfect."

"It's better than nothing."

"It's not good enough." He rummages in the kit again, finding a ratty-looking ACE bandage, and starting at the webbing between my thumb and forefinger, he wraps my entire hand and wrist. "It'll keep it padded and clean. Cleaner anyway."

I pick at the table. Stare at my lap. Think about the last time I cut my hand. It wasn't as bad, of course—just a paper cut—but it was in that tender webbing between my thumb and index finger, and God, it hurt for a week.

I got it on the one and only thing my mother has sent me since she left. I'd ripped open the envelope so fast, desperate for some sort of explanation. A letter. Maybe a late birthday card. Or at least a check.

It was a holiday card, one of those preprinted photo things you can order from the drugstore. This one featured Mom and Charlie by a palm tree strewn with Christmas lights. On the back, she wrote four words—*Always thinking of you*—and a little ink heart.

I look up at the mirror, and now I can see her. Just a spark in my eyes, but it hurts. What did I expect though? There aren't enough scrapes and bruises in the world to take her out. She's in the marrow of my bones. Some part of that person who believes a greeting card somehow makes up for four years of not *being* there—it's inside me.

"Are you OK?" Lucas asks.

I stand up abruptly. "Sorry, got distracted. We should find a key for the quad, right?" Then I turn to the four doorless cabinets and hinged counter over the cooler. I guess it's supposed to be the kitchen, pathetic as it is. There's a camping set and something made of grass and sticks that's too shadowy to investigate in the corner of the counter. It's probably a nest.

"There's got to be one somewhere," I say.

"Got it." I hear him stand up, feel him move behind me, all strength and heat and absolute patience. Lucas is always patient. Always waiting.

He reaches past me, hand grazing my hip. My whole body goes tight, heat surging behind my rib cage. Something jingles, and then I see the keys in his hands.

"How did you see that?" I ask, looking behind me. There's a small hook screwed into the edge of the counter I'm leaning on. They must have been hanging there.

"Lucky spot," he says.

"Thank God! So, we're going north?" I turn for the door, eyes on my feet as I try to edge past him in the narrow space.

He steps in front of me, a simple move that stops me in my tracks.

"We can't leave until dawn."

"Are you kidding? Mr. Walker could be out there right now!"

"You know what's definitely out there? Cliffs. A shit-ton of them." He shakes his head. "Dawn is four hours away, tops. Mr. Walker was headed north, so he's probably to the road already, unless by some miracle the Cherokee ghosts led his ass off a cliff."

I bite my lip. "I'm afraid to wait."

"Me too," he admits. "But I'm more afraid to go when we can't see. We'll keep watch. We'll hear him coming long before he gets here, if it comes to that."

"And then what? What if he does come?"

"Then we fire up the quad and take our chances with driving off a cliff," he says. "We have to be smart, Sera. Driving in the dark around cliffs is how people die."

"It feels crazy to just sit here."

He nods, and I can tell he's still watching me. I try not to fidget, but it's hard.

"Sera, what were you thinking back there? When you were sitting at the table, you were a million miles away."

I stop, arms crossed around my middle and hair covering my face. I can see his shirt move as he breathes. In and out. In and out. I feel like a diva with a broken voice. This isn't me marching across a stage, laying out battle plans and leading the charge. I have no control here.

"This is almost over," he says, misreading my fear. "Dawn will come. Mr. Walker will look for us at the road, not here. We're going home."

"I know." And that's part of why I'm terrified.

He steps close enough to thumb the edges of my dirty hair. He traces the scrape under my eye, a touch that leaves a trail of liquid fire in its wake. His fingers graze the place in my neck where my pulse races.

"Long way from that night on your friend's back porch, huh?" His voice is rough.

"Yeah." The word comes out too breathy. I try to force a laugh, pushing lightness into the heavy air. "I really was so screwed up after that. I'm sorry."

"Don't be. Let's just call *this* the beginning if you want."

I do. Even though it terrifies me, I want it more than I've ever wanted anything.

He leans in slow, thumb stroking my chin down to the hollow of my throat. When we kiss, there isn't darkness or panic to muddy the reality of what I'm doing, the contact I'm craving with him.

Every look he gives me makes me want another. Every brush of his hand spins my world into more pieces.

We scoot back on the narrow floor, shoulder to shoulder and backs against the filthy cabinets. I feel the sigh he lets out, close my eyes at the tickle of his hair against my temple.

"It's almost over," he says again.

"Yes."

With Lucas beside me, I can almost believe it will be different this time. That I'll be brave enough to be with him and good enough to not turn out like her. That I'll find some sort of balance in the middle.

But will I? Out here, it's another world. It's easy when it's life and death and he's laying everything on the line to keep me alive. But at home with my life and my friends and my father? I don't know.

Maybe I can find a way to be with Lucas without feeding the part of me that is like my mother. Or maybe that part will grow like a cancer, quietly snagging bits and pieces of my organs, taking me over cell by cell until there's nothing good left.

CHAPTER 27

A bacon cheeseburger," he says.

"Bleh. Too much meat for me." I wrinkle my nose, checking the window again, willing the sky to grow lighter. It doesn't. We're leaned against opposite sides of the camper now, his back to the bench seats, mine to the camper wall. My calves are on his lap, feet dangling off his knees. His legs are everywhere. He's a praying mantis in a matchbox.

"So, what do you want?" he asks, drumming his fingers on my shin. "Food-wise."

"Tabbouleh." I close my eyes at the idea. "*Tons* of it."

"What the hell is that?"

"It's a salad with parsley and mint and lemon—"

"This is your comfort food?" he asks. "It sounds like the contents of a tea bag."

"It's not a tea bag. It's healthy and fresh and way better than the crap granola bars and—" I clutch my growling stomach. "We have to talk about something else. This is torture."

Something cracks outside. My shoulders jerk back, hit the side of the camper.

Lucas is already up, staring out the broken window, his neck tendons roped tight.

"Raccoon," he says. "It's almost time. The stars are fading, so dawn's close. The second we can see, we're out of here."

He's right. This will be over. *And then what?*

I watch him through my lashes, trying to sort out what will happen back in the real world. In Marietta. Will I…date him? Is that where this is going?

"You're thinking about what comes next, aren't you?"

I tip my head, trying to decide how to answer. "I think I know. But I'm…I might spook. It could be messy dating me."

"Who said I wanted to date you?" he asks, but he's grinning, and then I'm grinning too.

Lucas kisses me, quick and hard on the mouth. "I don't need all the answers. We can feel our way one day at a time."

My laugh feels good. "Of course you'd say that. So are we getting out of here or what? By the time you get it started, it will be light enough."

He should get a patent for that grin. "Hell yes. Let's do this."

Going back outside is scarier when I stand up. Dread settles heavy in my chest. Lucas joins me, still half hunched over in this too-small space. Outside, the air is cool and damp, and my stomach sinks at the first smell of leaves. I'm checking every tree, every shadow—waiting for something to jump.

Lucas is watching too, but he's moving toward the quad with steady strides. He's done hiding, jangling the keys in a way that pricks my hope to attention.

He slides behind the handlebars and tries the key. Once, and the grinding sets my teeth on edge. Again, and it's trying to turn over, but no go. Lucas hops off and messes with wires. A hawk cries out as it soars overhead, and I think I'm going to come apart. This really has to work. I can't handle a universe where this doesn't go right.

He's crouching now, adjusting this, muttering about that. Then he's back in the seat, and the engine is grinding with a little *phutphutphut* before it goes dead again. Lucas isn't stressed, but I'm so tense, I'm probably going to snap a shoulder blade in two. He blows on something on the side of the engine, knocks something else, and heads back to the key again.

I hold my breath. It has to work. It has to—

The motor starts, and I nearly collapse with relief.

Lucas's smile is as wide as I've ever seen it. The engine is an almost deafening roar, and when he revs it, I laugh, my spirit lifting like birthday balloons. A hawk takes flight from a nearby maple, and my laughter catches in the back of my throat, sticking on sudden fear.

We aren't alone out here. And that engine was probably heard for miles.

"We should go," I say.

Lucas climbs off, grinning, then his eyes catch on my hand, and he frowns. I check the bandage, which is red in a few places. I'm bleeding through.

"I should probably see someone about that." I laugh, but Lucas's expression is grim.

"Yeah. Sooner the better." He nods at the trailer. "I'm going to grab the first aid kit just in case."

He dashes inside before I can argue. I can hear his heavy feet thunk-groaning on the sloping floor. My insides tighten, praying for it to hold. All around me, the leaves twitch and flutter. Birds flit at the very edge of my vision, leaving me jumpy.

"Lucas, I really want to go."

He reappears in the doorway, grin in place. "Keep your pants on. Mr. Walker isn't going to catch us on this thing."

I try to smile, but I'm shaking too hard. It slides right off my lips. "Let's just get moving."

He chuckles on his first step out of the camper, and I see it before it even happens. The stair wobbles, and then his left foot searches for the next step, but a huge chunk is gone. Missing from where he kicked the cinder block out yesterday. I can't even scream before it's happening. He's falling.

His balance pitches, and the first aid kit flies. Bandages flutter like moths as Lucas hurtles down. His fingers flail for the door frame, but he misses. The impact is awful, shoulder first into the dirt and limbs falling every which way.

Everything is screaming. Me and Lucas and the engine of the quad, still idling, ready to carry us to safety. I crouch beside Lucas, afraid to look or touch anything. He rolls over, face twisted in agony. When he tries to sit up, he's gone ash-gray. Something's really wrong. I look for a head wound first. No. It's his shoulder. It's crooked or his arm is too low or—

Oh no.

His eyes are screwed shut, and he's pulling his arm across his middle like that will fix this, but it won't. I've never seen a dislocated shoulder, but I'm pretty sure that's what this is. And it's way beyond fixing with the yellowed bandages and boxes of rolled gauze in our first aid kit.

CHAPTER 28

Lucas," I say, feeling close to tears.

His eyes pop open, searching the sky and finally landing on my face. "My shoulder."

"I know."

He groans, then lets out something that's supposed to be a laugh, I think. "Escape a killer, get taken down by a stair."

Technically, it was the absence of a stair, but it's not important. I touch his stomach, afraid to get anywhere near his misshapen shoulder. "What do I do? What do we—"

He grits his teeth and braces his good arm on the ground, and I can tell he's going to try to stand up. "We get the hell out of here."

"You can't drive like this," I say.

He laughs, not looking like he's inclined to disagree.

My face goes cold, lips numb as I stare at the rumbling four-wheeler. "I have no idea how to drive that, Lucas."

"You can do anything, Sera," he says, and he believes it, so I have to believe it too. "I'll tell you how."

My hands shake as I help him onto the seat. My whole body is rattling when I settle in front of him. I will do this. We don't have any options left, so I follow his instructions and put it in gear.

We keep it in lower gears because there isn't a trail. There's barely enough space between the trees to weave in and out. At first, it was awful—I was bad with the clutch and worse with the brakes, and Lucas gritted through cries that made me flinch.

I learned fast. Maybe I'm not doing it like a pro, and maybe I'm going slow, but we are crossing through the forest fast enough to let the wind hit my face. We climb straight up when it gets steep. I tried to take it at a diagonal, and Lucas hollered about that right away. Too much danger of rolling. Instead, we have to stand up and kind of lean forward. It was uncomfortable for me, so I can't even imagine what it was like for him.

At the top of one crest, I catch my first glimpse of the road, a winding gray snake with a yellow stripe, cutting its way through the green mountains. My heart bubbles up. It's really happening. Help is one mountain away. We just have to get there.

The forest isn't making it easy on us. The backside of the mountain is treacherous, stone ledges rising up so sharply, it's hard to find a path down from the rim of the peak. In other spots, the mountain drops off a cliff and into nothing.

I turn left around a line of rocks that jut up like a hobbled fence. We're completely turned around—this is not getting us closer to the road. I tighten my grip and try to ignore the stabbing bolts of pain shooting from my hand to my armpit. I also ignore the tightening in my chest because I know panic won't help. There has to be a way through. I just need to find it.

Clouds are gathering, thick and gray in the sky overhead.

It brings me right back to our early days here, when we were annoyed by a storm. Back then, rain was the low point.

My eyes scan the horizon in hopes of a break in the rocks—a place where I can shift us north so we're back on track. I catch another glimpse of the road, and my heart clenches.

"Damn these rocks," I mutter.

Lucas doesn't respond. He's tense and sweating behind me, and his good arm has gone damp around my middle. My whole body aches, imagining what he's going through back there. There can't be words for pain like that.

I ease the throttle as we finally start down the opposite side. The terrain turns even worse. A sharp, rocky outcropping flanks the west side, and the trees are thicker here. We're forced to curve to the southeast, and my stomach is dropping into my feet. If Mr. Walker followed the valleys, he might have walked through here. If he kept moving at night, he might be ahead of us. Waiting for us.

But we are faster, and I'm not above running him over if it means saving our lives.

The quad crawls over dead leaves, and I keep our speed slow, picking the smoothest path I can as I search the sharp slope on the left. There's got to be a way through this. A gap in the rocks or—

"Sera!"

Lucas's grip releases my waist, his fingers jabbing in front of me to tug the left handlebar. The quad hurls left, and my body slings against it. Something sprays underneath the tire, and I yelp, spotting the drop-off just inches from the right side of the quad.

Oh my God, we almost went over. The earth drops into nothing *right there.*

I pull the brakes when we're a few more feet away, my stomach heaving into my mouth as my eyes drag to that narrow gorge we almost slipped into. I can't see the bottom. I could have killed us. We could have died, and we are *so* close to living.

Guilt smothers me. "I'm sorry," I say, inching us forward at a crawl, my voice choked with terror. "I'm so sorry."

Lucas presses the crown of his head to the back of my neck. He's breathing hard and ragged. "'S OK."

My throat goes fist-tight, and distant thunder rumbles. It's absolutely *not* OK. I shake my head and continue, much slower now. I start edging to the left, farther from the ridge, where it's safer.

I sigh at the piles of sharp, moss-strewn rocks. "We've got to get back north," I say as if he needs the reminder. As if we aren't both perfectly aware we've been funneled into a channel, a one-way road heading the absolute wrong direction.

I grit my teeth and release the throttle even further. It's easier to hear Lucas now, to feel the sticks snap and pop under the tires and his answering groans. I can't see the road, but I imagine it up there, a gray line of salvation tucked behind a forest that is eating me alive.

There's a craggy overhang on my right and what looks like a footpath. Is that the trail? Too small, but it could be something. I spot an orange-red box next to the overhang and muddy boot tracks.

I hit the brakes gently. There's an opening, but I don't think the quad will fit through. Those are definitely boot tracks too. Lots of them.

"Do you see that?" I ask, nodding at the red stuff. "Is that a first aid kit?"

Lucas shudders behind me, his pain spelled out in a strangled groan.

I switch the quad out of gear and try to get a closer look at the plastic box. It's closed with white latches. When my eyes adjust, I see there are letters on the side. I can only read part of them.

F L A R

Flare. That's a flare gun.

CHAPTER 29

Hope uncurls, warming my throat and cheeks. My heartbeat quickens as I stop us just past the box and cut the engine. There's a red rain slicker and a thermos next to it. Everything looks clean. Recent. None of this has been here long. Someone might be close.

The stuff is all situated against a ledge, and I can see that the ledge disappears downward behind another craggy formation. It's a hallway of stone, one that curves down and to the left.

We might already be rescued.

I turn off the quad and consider the box with the flare gun. Should I shoot one off, or would that just bring Mr. Walker back? I mean, he doesn't know we have it, right?

"What's wrong?" Lucas's speech has gone muddy. Slurred.

"That box is a flare gun. And I think whoever owns that stuff is down there." I jut my chin toward the corridor between the two rocks. "Maybe it's another hiking group."

His only answer is a series of sharp breaths.

I turn in my seat to look at him and gasp. "Lucas!"

I clutch the front of his shirt even as he sags sideways. He looks beyond awful. His shirt is soaked, hair dripping on his forehead. He also weighs more than this quad, and I'm sure we're both going to go sideways off the seat. At the last second, he jams his good hand onto the back tire and grunts.

"I'm fine," he says, righting himself on the seat.

"Like hell you're fine! Why didn't you stop me?" I ask, voice cracking.

He smirks, that devil-may-care spark reduced to a bare flicker in his hooded eyes. "Only way out is through, right?"

He tries a smile, but I can tell it's beyond painful, and there's nothing I can do. He's too big, too heavy. I have nothing to secure his arm with, and frankly, I wouldn't know how even if I did. If someone else were here…

My eyes stray to the slicker, and hope burns, ember-bright, in my center. "Lucas, I want you to sit tight. I'm going to check to see if someone's down there. Or if there's a good place to shoot one of these flares."

The wind picks up, carrying the smell of rain on its back.

He shakes his head once. "No. North."

"You'll fall off, and you know it." I move an arm around his waist, my words floating along the tears in my voice. "You said I was in charge, so I say we're stopping."

"I said you were bossy," he says. "That's different."

I help him off the quad, and he slings a long arm over my shoulders. I take a breath that's heavy with sweat and pain and bite my lip when we awkwardly work him off the seat. His hand shakes against my side, so I try to be steady. I have to fix this. He's out here for *me*—to protect me. I'm at the center of *all* of this, and I have to get us out of here.

"Dammit," he mutters as we ease his back against a tree.

"Is it bad? Was the quad better?"

"Not that." He looks up, and whatever's swimming in his eyes tears me apart. "I'm sorry. We didn't need this."

"Shut up," I whisper, wishing instantly I'd picked better words. Nicer words. "Just…just don't say that. We're getting out of here."

I touch his forehead, my palm kissing his sweaty brow. I clench my teeth and straighten my spine. "Stay put. I'm going to get help."

I ease toward the stack of flares and the slicker, but Lucas lifts his hand, his eyes clearing.

"Don't just…don't charge down there," he says.

It's not Mr. Walker. I know what he's worried about, but the bright-red slicker and emergency flares don't exactly scream *clandestine murderer*. Still, he's right. We've been fooled before. I need to be careful.

I tilt my head, looking through the tracks. Some of them are too smeared to make out, just a bit of heel or toe. I finally find a full print a few feet from the quad. I settle my own boot next to it and smile.

The print is smaller than mine would be. Not a guy. Definitely not Mr. Walker, whose boots were almost as big as Lucas's.

"It's not Mr. Walker down there, Lucas. The prints are too small. I checked."

He seems mollified, but I still unlatch the flare box and take the gun out. It is very orange and very basic. I load a cartridge in and smile up at Lucas. "See? Now I'm armed to blind and burn. Extra careful."

"Extra careful," he repeats.

"Hey, maybe these belong to a pair of picnicking paramedics." I grin. "They could be down there right now, wondering who will eat their extra bacon cheeseburgers."

He almost laughs. "Let's hope those burgers are slathered in morphine. The expired ibuprofen from the first aid kit is not cutting it."

I smile as I ease my way farther along the stone wall, my good hand gripping the flare gun. Rocks slither down in a series of natural steps curving into darkness. I go slowly to let my eyes adjust as I move through the tight crevice. I don't know what's on the other side. It could be a cliff. Or a cavern.

Or something worse.

I lick my lips but stay quiet. Careful. That was my promise. I'm not going to stumble off a cliff because I'm rushing. The stones are smooth and slicked with mud under my feet. Even in the darkness, I can see the smear of footprints here and there along the edges. One person couldn't have made all these passing through. Not unless they've been in and out of here a dozen times.

As I curve around farther, light leaks into the narrow channel, and some crazy part of me thinks I smell food. Burgers, just like Lucas wants. I move just a little faster, my feet a quiet scrape against the stones. I can see the opening. My heart falls because what's out there is not what I want. It is not a way out. It's practically a cave. And there's no one here to help.

I step into the light and stumble forward, my vision blurring, eyes blinking like crazy. I'm in a clearing, a roofless stone alcove, with shadowy crevices and overhangs and what once might have been a cool place to see before it was littered with all this trash from campers long gone.

We're still alone. The thought snatches the air out of my lungs with hot fingers. The floor tilts…or no—no, that's me. I'm just dizzy. I stumble to a wall and lean my shoulder against it. Blink until my vision clears at the edges.

OK. OK, so we're alone. I'll figure out a way to get Lucas back on the quad. We'll shoot flares and keep driving. Someone will be looking for us, so we just keep moving and—

Something familiar catches my eye. My gaze trails over the trash strewn in the shadows of the cavern, and I find it again. A backpack with a familiar white granola wrapper.

That's from one of Madison's granola bars. Is that Madison's backpack?

I shuffle away from the wall, assessing the litter along the walls. There are piles of twigs and twine in various sizes. A stack of ratty sleeping bags in the shadows. Black and gray bits of plastic. A striped backpack strap.

My heart hurls sideways like a skipping rock. That's my backpack strap. The sticks that made the dolls. I find more things. A crushed box of yogurts. The cap of a black marker that makes my fingers scratch at the letters on my arm.

It's like bracing myself for a fall one second too late. I can't save myself now. I've walked into my killer's lair.

CHAPTER 30

I turn for the exit slowly. I think my heart is thundering in my ears, but it's not. That's *real* thunder, a low ripple that picks at my edges. I clench my fists to hold myself together. He's not here. I found his hidey hole, his little backstage setup area, but Mr. Walker isn't inside. He's out looking for me.

Time to go.

I blink back furious tears and start toward the stairs. My feet stutter-stop after two steps. The small, boxy GPS device is sitting on the back wall, strapped in its bright holster with *Walker* printed neatly down the side in familiar permanent ink. My vision narrows until it is all I see.

He used this to keep help from coming. This is how he lied to our parents, to my father, clicking a few buttons and letting them sleep at night, believing we are OK.

We are not OK. And now I am going to tell them.

My heart grows strangely steady as I cross the cavern floor. I tuck the flare gun under my arm and reach for the GPS. He taught us how to call for emergencies. His one mistake, it seems. When my fingers graze the canvas holder, they are buzzing with anticipation. It's easy to activate the emergency call. As easy as putting in my locker combination.

I check it again because I'm not sure I did it right, but the message is there.

Confirmed.

Help is coming. It feels like the tide rolling away. I step back on wooden limbs and look up the channel that will lead me back out to Lucas.

Something moves out of the corner of my eye. It's just the sleeping bag.

No.

It's something *inside* the sleeping bag. And it's moving.

I can't muster a scream, so I scramble for the tunnel as the mound shifts and twists in the shadows. Gun. I have a gun. Flare gun or not, it's something. I raise my weapon and face the sleeping bag, trying to back my way up and out.

The bag bends. Folds. Someone is in there, trying to sit up. An awful gurgling cough comes from inside all that fabric. Then a bloody face emerges in the light.

Mr. Walker. My finger is on the trigger when he slumps sideways, shaking violently. I lower the gun an inch because Emily was right. He is sick. It wasn't an act. Not before and not now. Something is very wrong with him.

He opens his mouth and closes it. I can almost see his lips forming around my name, and it makes me want to burn the *Darling* off my arm, but I don't need to. I put in the distress call, so help *will* come now. They will find us and rescue us.

Mr. Walker lets out a breath that gurgles, and I really look at him. At the blood on his shirt. The blood around his mouth, like he's been coughing it up. Spitting it out.

I think we're already rescued. I didn't rescue myself. Lucas didn't do it either. We aren't the heroes. Whatever is killing Mr. Walker, that fever burning him from the inside out? That's the hero.

I force my shoulders down as his eyes find mine. I want him to look at me. I want him to face what he's done and to know I'm not afraid anymore. He won't get up and relive his little eighteen-year-old murder scene. He might not ever get up again.

My stomach knots as I look at him because he still doesn't watch me like I'm a *Darling*. Or like I'm something he wants to destroy. It doesn't matter. Getting out of here matters. I force myself forward, and Mr. Walker startles, another wet cough rattling in his throat as he tries to talk to me.

He works one arm out of the bag, and I can see a paper folded in his hand. I can't read it from here, but I can see there's a girl's picture. Is that Hannah? From her funeral maybe?

Yeah, it's her picture, her face under Mr. Walker's smeared crimson fingerprints. He squirms, one arm still pinned in the sleeping bag. He's a bloody, hacking worm, and looking at him clenches my stomach. And it makes me angry.

I lift the flare gun and take a step toward him. Because I want him to know I'm not the girl he thinks I am. For one sliver of a second, I think I might pull the trigger.

But I am not that girl either.

I lower the weapon, and he tries to say something. His breath is a sticky rattle, telling me he doesn't have long. Finally, he shapes the words, pushes them out of his mouth with a croak of voice.

"Run, Sera."

Anger flares through me at the words. Screw him. I will not run from him. Not one more minute. I'll walk away when I'm good and ready because it's crystal clear he's not hurting *anyone* anymore.

He nudges the paper with his chin, but it goes nowhere, just flutters to his lap, her face bending over one of his thighs. He makes a noise that I think is supposed to be a laugh and a sob all mixed together. It is a monstrosity of both. Bile blooms at the back of my throat.

"I thought it was you," he says. "I thought you were down here, hiding. I thought—"

I look down at the girl who isn't me. The memorial card from her funeral, I guess. Her face is framed in appropriately somber ivy, her smile frozen beneath the bloody stamp of Mr. Walker's fingerprints.

Hannah Grace Soral. Beloved daughter and stepsister.

Stepsister. His stepsister? Is that what he thinks? Is that why he looked out for me? Fed me? Called me *Darling*?

"I am not Hannah!" The words fire out of me without warning. "I am Sera Khoury."

I don't know if it's rage or exhaustion or some need to hold on to the truth of my identity, but I see it now. I understand. I am not this girl, and I am not my mother. I'm just Sera, a theater director and a mediocre student and a girl who's going to survive this hell.

"I'm not your sister." I feel better for saying it—lighter maybe because I know it's over. I will not end here, a bloody heap in this forest like him.

Mr. Walker moves his head so slowly, chin back and forth. He's shaking his head, but I look away. I've seen enough I don't want to see.

It's time to go back to Lucas.

"Run!" Mr. Walker cries out. "Before she comes—" A cough. Some awful, stomach-curdling noise in his throat that swallows up half of his next words. I catch all the sticky bits that come between his hacks. "—pushed me down—zipped me in—can't move my legs—it's the *anniversary*, Sera—she thinks you're Hannah—she thinks Lucas—"

He cuts off with another soul-shattering hack and something about a deer, I think, but after that, he doesn't speak again. I've already heard enough. I move closer, look at the spattered paper on his stomach.

She. He said she. Oh God. Was it really Madison? Did we leave her with Jude and Emily? Panic tingles through my limbs.

"Run, Sera!" he says again, dissolving into a fit of coughing that spatters the paper and the bags with more blood.

"Who did this?" My voice is nearly as shattered as his. "Who killed Ms. Brighton?"

He's coughing too much to speak, to even breathe well, but he jabs his hands at the paper again and again. Flipping it over at last. The words on the back are hard to read, smeared brown-red and turning my stomach to a bag of worms.

He gives a groan, and I flinch away, but he's not reaching for me. He's holding it out, letting me see. I scan the rest of it, focus on the line he's jabbing.

When I read it, the world tilts under my feet. My eyes lock with Mr. Walker's. He doesn't have to tell me again to run.

CHAPTER 31

I slip, bashing my elbow, smacking my knees into a jagged rock. *Up! Get up!*

I'm on my feet. Climbing. My knees are weak, my muscles like Silly Putty. Like my old dollies that wouldn't sit up or stay standing. I should not stumble like this. I *cannot* fall. I *can't.*

I judge wrong in the dark of the crevice, and my foot slips. I reach to catch myself and drop the flare gun. It clatters and bangs all the way down the tunnel, landing somewhere at the bottom. I leave it.

There's no time. I move forward again, bracing myself on the walls on either side, though pain slices through my bad palm and up my arm. I bite back my cry. *Keep going. Just go.*

I move up, one rock, then another, then the ground goes level, and I am out. Birdsong descends with a soft occasional patter from high above. I tear out from the gap between the stone outcrops, the not-a-bridge, the not-a-canyon, the not-a-path. Out of the cave where a man is dying and the truth took my legs out from underneath me.

A fat raindrop slaps into my forehead. Another on my arm. They feel like tears and burn like shame. How did we get it so wrong?

No. Don't think about that now. Find Lucas. Make sure he's OK.

My heart is pounding double time as I search. Trees, trees, the quad. *Lucas.*

He's dozing where I left him, sweat-damp hair over his eyes and those soft lips parted in sleep.

My heart swells, and there is no time for me to think—not of the things I want or the fact that I can't understand why I spent sixty-two days avoiding this face or all the kisses we shared in the last two days. But I think of all those things as I cross to him now.

I could have lost him. God, I could have *lost* him before I know what it means to have him in my life.

You could still lose him if you don't move.

My feet lurch forward, and a sob rips through me that startles him awake. He is OK. He's alive. Still with me.

Concern creases his features in an instant, his eyes straying from my tears to my elbow to the warm trickle I feel leaking down my knee.

"What happened?" he asks.

"We have—" I'm beyond breathless. Forcing words out in chunks while I scan the trees for danger. "Go. Have to go." Another shaky breath, my good hand tugging at his shirt. "Mr. Walker."

His eyes go wide. "Mr. Walker's here?"

"Yes." I touch his arm, tears dripping off my chin. I'm crying? When did that happen? It doesn't matter. I can't talk. Can't think, so I'll explain while we go. I pull him again. Trucks weigh less than Lucas. Mountains maybe. "It's not him. Help's coming, but—"

But we need to go. We need to go before we are found.

Thankfully, Lucas doesn't require much explaining. He scoots around, grabbing the trunk of the tree. He groans, and I push him up like a piece of furniture, using shoulders and knees and urging him off the ground.

He bumps his bad shoulder and lets out a cry that cleaves my insides in two. Lucas slumps against the tree, and I stroke his back, still watching. I want to apologize, want to tell him what I know, but I am choked on terror and tears, and we just need to go. If we're on the quad, we are fast. We can run.

I pull him off the tree, and he swallows down most of the next groan, eyes drifting as he forces himself through one step and then another. He stops all of a sudden, pale face going paler, until he's sheet white.

"Do you have the keys?" he asks.

"What keys?" I follow his gaze to the quad, and there are no keys in the ignition. Did I pocket them? God, how could I not know this? How could I flake out about this?

I pat my pockets, front and back, and swear, digging in each one to be sure, but I don't have the keys. I don't remember taking them out of the quad. I search the ground and look around. Nothing.

"Oh my God, Lucas. I left them in the quad. They should be there."

"It's OK," he says. "Just breathe."

Oh, I'm breathing all right. I'm gulping air so fast and hard that my cheeks feel fuzzy and my vision is graying at the edges. I reach for a tree and slow down.

I just need to think. The keys have to be here. I just need to open my eyes and look. I take a slow breath, and something shuffles ahead of me in the trees.

Wait.

My eyes pop open, and Lucas shifts behind me. He's *behind* me.

"I saw something up there," I whisper.

Lucas goes stone-still, and we both search the trees beyond the quad. The rain is falling harder now, heavy drops plopping into my hair, onto my shoulders. Another shuffle, and my eyes catch on a shadow.

There's a flicker of movement behind the quad. The jangling sound of keys that sends my heart into freefall.

My face goes cold as the shadow emerges, stretching into an arm. A hand. My throat cinches shut as fingers wrap around the trunk of a baby maple. I catch a glimpse of purple nails and one charred, bloody stump.

A stump where Ms. Brighton's finger should be.

CHAPTER 32

It's her," I say, still breathless. Panting out every word. "Ms. Brighton is Hannah's stepsister. She did this to us."

Ms. Brighton's mud-dyed shirt is stained with things I can't look at. Her smile twists, and my head swims. Spins.

"Do you see how the forest brings the rain again?" she asks. "It was my sacrifices. I pledged my devotion, and look what the forest gave me."

It's a little kid voice, shrill with delight. Like the one I heard in the valley. God, it's really her. Even after reading Ms. Brighton's name on Hannah's memorial card, I couldn't quite swallow this. Now I have no choice, and the truth is going down like fishhooks.

"Your finger," I say. "That's a sacrifice?"

She inclines her head. "And the deer."

"You're alive," Lucas says, a bit of wonder in his face.

I bump my back into him to hold him away from her because he doesn't know. He hasn't put all the pieces together yet, but I have. Lucas and Madison didn't see Ms. Brighton's body, and neither did we. She killed a deer and skinned it. That's what we saw.

Lucas moves, and I snag his arm to hold him back. She is *not* here to save us.

"I can't believe you're alive," he says again, obviously confused. He's probably in shock.

"I'm *full* of lives," she says. "We are all full of lives. Do you feel yours now? The past stays with us, even when we wish it would go."

She scowls and is transformed. Her quirky crystal earrings dangle like broken teeth. The streaks on her hand-dyed shirt look more like blood than earth, and that mouth that once smiled so easily now gapes like a maw.

"What the hell are you talking about?" Lucas asks. He shifts on his feet, tries to move past me.

I pull at the back of his shirt. "Lucas, don't."

Ms. Brighton laughs. I can see black grime caked under her nails and marker stains on her fingers. The rain is sending filth running down her arms and legs in murky rivulets.

"Let him come, Hannah. Let the forest find its justice."

"I'm not Hannah."

"But you were last time. You were Hannah, and he was Brodie. I've waited for the forest to show me who defiled you all those years ago. And it did, *darling*. It did."

Darling. The word sends snakes slithering in my chest. She lifts a hand, and I spot a flash of metal in her fingers. A knife. Old-looking, with an antler handle. That's what she used to cut her own finger off.

I take a step back, and Lucas comes with me, stumbling.

"What is this?" he asks. "Who cut off her finger?"

I can practically feel him trying to wrap his brain around what's unfolding in front of us.

"She cut it off herself," I say, swiping rain out of my face. "She did this, Lucas. All of it, for some twisted version of justice for Hannah. She thinks we're the reincarnation of those four kids. That's what the papers were about. I'm Hannah and you're Brodie."

Ms. Brighton is moving around the quad. "I don't *think* it. Look at yourself, Sera. Look how you love to direct the tragedies, the plays where someone dies at the end. Look how you know to avoid men. You know who you really are."

"Holy shit, she's crazy," Lucas says.

I don't respond because I'm trying to find a way out. The path that leads down to Mr. Walker is beside me, but that's a dead end. She's by the quad, trapping us from the direction we came. The only way out is to go on ahead, to just run up the cliff side and hope to God we find a way around the mountain and to the road.

"I'll rush her," Lucas says.

"You're barely standing! We have to go up the cliff side."

"We don't know if we can get through up there," he says, but he's already moving because it's the only way. The only chance unless we want to run headfirst into Ms. Brighton or climb down into the alcove with Mr. Walker.

Ms. Brighton is getting closer and picking up speed. There's a stone ledge to our right and a sharp incline to the left, covered in brambles and briars. We're still in that damn channel we were trapped in on the quad. And we've got to break out because she's gaining.

I cry out for help, though there's no one to hear us but

Mr. Walker. Mr. Walker, who was innocent all this time and who might have to hear us die when he gave everything he had trying to save us.

Lucas kicks a fallen log into her path, but she's going to catch up. She's already closing the distance. Twenty feet. Fifteen feet.

"Help!" I scream. Like there's someone to help.

Something pop-hisses, and the gray sky tinges red. I gulp a breath and look over to track the spark of light in the sky. Ms. Brighton stops. It's coming from down in the alcove—Mr. Walker fired the flare gun.

Mr. Walker.

In my mind, I hear him tell me to run. *Run, Sera.*

I do, one hand against the stone and every breath burning hotter. My feet shift for purchase. The incline isn't as harsh now on the left, but the undergrowth is blanket-thick, spun of thorns. Impossible choices everywhere.

I have to find a way through because this stone will lead to a cliff, and if we can't find a hole, a thin spot—no. No, we *have* to find it. We will.

My legs wobble, and Lucas groans. I glance over my shoulder, hoping Ms. Brighton took the bait with Mr. Walker's flare. No dice. It stalled her, but not for long. She's heading our way, and she'll gain on us. Lucas just isn't moving fast enough.

"Wait!" I say, lifting a hand. There's no way to outrun her and nothing within reach that looks like a weapon. There has to be something I can use, but all I can think of is Hannah. How do I use *that*?

"I don't understand," I cry, trying to play the part she chose for me. "I could die again! Do you want me to die *again*?"

"You're already dead, Hannah! You were brought back to this place, and I promise you this time, it will be right. Your soul can finally be with the spirits of your people."

My chest squeezes. Oh God. That stuff about the Cherokee spirits—those weren't ghost stories to her. She twisted bits and pieces into her own warped version of reality. She was warning us. There's no logic I can appeal to here.

But I can still play my role. And I can change my lines.

"I could live again in this body," I say, laying it on thick. If being Hannah gives me power, I'll take it. "We could be sisters again."

She makes a wounded noise. Shakes her head. "You belong to the forest, darling," she says. She's crying now, and I recognize those sobs. I heard them in the forest before we got the newspapers. She was trying to get me away from Lucas. "These trees revealed your killer. He will be punished. You will be delivered."

He'll be punished? She's going to kill Lucas. The certainty of it rocks me.

Ms. Brighton stalks forward with that knife, and I feel like there should be thunder, but there isn't. No wind. No lightning. Just the steady patter of early autumn rain and her eyes, wide and pale and brimming with conviction.

We're moving again, but Lucas is going slowly, groaning with every step. We hit a clump of trees, branches shaking more water onto our heads as we squeeze past. There is no break in the thorns on the other side. We are still pinned between underbrush and the mountainside. And the woman who will kill us both.

My throat tightens and my chest throbs. We're in serious trouble. The cliff is closer now, and Ms. Brighton is almost in striking distance. We have to go faster.

Lucas trips, goes down on one knee with a grunt. Ms. Brighton takes her chance, lunging through a sheet of hard rain. He kicks out, screaming in pain, but his foot connects with something. Her knee? Her stomach? I don't know, but she slams into the ground back first, feet rolling up. I see her filthy hiking boots in the air, and I'm pulling Lucas to his feet. It's so hard. *So* hard.

"It's OK, Hannah," she says, hearing my cry. "It's almost over, and you'll be free."

"I am free! Lucas didn't hurt me!"

She lunges again, and I kick this time, catching her injured hand. She yowls, and the knife skitters. We have to move. *Move!*

We run. Lucas is too slow, but we try. We pull-scramble-rush along the rain-soaked stone, looking for a way out. A way through. Please, please, let there be a way because I know we are close to the edge of this mountain, and it might as well be the edge of the world.

"Hannah." Ms. Brighton's close again. I hear the drag of her blade against the face of the mountain. "Your spirit will be free like your ancestors when I end this. Let him go."

"You've got to run," Lucas tells me. He sounds like he's in agony. He *is* in agony.

It's not even worth a response, so I dig my fingers into his good shoulder and steer him on. My feet slip sideways, and I look down in horror. The rain is turning the soil to wet clay. It's slipping under my soles worse here, sending every step in the wrong direction.

"Sera?"

Lucas's voice sends chills through my spine. I look up, and dread turns my limbs to ice. End of the road. Fifteen feet ahead, the stone drops off, and the trees thin. There is gray sky and the promise of a fall we will not walk away from. We take our chances climbing down a cliff in the rain, or we face the tangle of thorns, hoping to get to the forest on the other side. Or Ms. Brighton.

Ms. Brighton slips too, crying out. She's already too close again. We have to choose.

The thorns it is. I reach ruthlessly, pushing some of the briar away. Thorns puncture my good palm like needles, and when I tug it loose, three more limbs snake over my back, tangling in my shirt, my hair. I rip myself free with a cry.

Ms. Brighton goes down, but she'll get back up. She'll be here in seconds.

"We're trapped," Lucas says.

"I know."

We inch back closer to the cliff. I eye the cliff, the thorns, and then the woman with the braids who wants to end a boy who never hurt me. Ms. Brighton barrels toward us, and I pick up the heavy stick Lucas is kicking my way.

Ms. Brighton raises the knife, and I brace myself. This is how it ends.

"I'll make this right, Hannah," she says to me.

She lunges but not at me. It's at Lucas. I slam the stick at her arm. She dodges until it is only a graze. The momentum spins me around and sends her staggering back. But she'll come again.

Lucas tries to strike, but he topples sideways. He's going to fall, and she's going to kill him. And then I see a plan so bad it is almost no plan. It is the *only* thing.

Ms. Brighton moves in, and Lucas kicks again, groaning, because it must hurt. Everything must be hurting him now. His balance is off, and he sways heavily to the left. Toward the thorns.

"I'm so sorry," I whisper. And then I shove him with everything I've got.

It doesn't take as much force as it should. He crashes into the thorns, and I choke on my sob. Lucas the tall. Lucas the mighty. But the bigger you are, the harder you fall, and Lucas goes down like a small building, crashing through the thorns with a symphony of screams that cuts my soul to pieces.

CHAPTER 33

No," Ms. Brighton says, the word choked and almost lost on Lucas's groans. She says it again, louder, because my bet paid off. It worked. He's buried in those thorns. It's like the worst cocoon and the best.

Because she can't get to him without me getting to her.

Lucas is on the ground, groaning. Everything but his feet is tangled in thorns. My stomach rolls at his pained cries. I did that. But he's still alive, and she can't get to him in there.

Ms. Brighton snags one of his boots, and I shove her with everything I've got. "Leave him alone!" She recoils, and I kick at his boots, tears streaming. "Pull your feet in! Pull them in!" I yell at Lucas.

Ms. Brighton turns on me. Chills steamroll my insides. It's my turn now.

"I waited for the one who led you away, darling," she says, knife raised, her eyes darting so that I'm not sure what she's aiming for—me or Lucas? "You will be safe from him now."

She lunges for the thorns, stabs at his leg. I don't know who screams louder, me or him.

I plow into her with everything I've got. She flies backward, and I go down hard on my knees. The rain is sending rivers of mud down the ground beneath me. Ms. Brighton struggles to her feet, but her knife has spun backward. Closer to the cliff.

Ms. Brighton rushes for it. "Let go of your desire for this boy! He is what ruined you!"

My desire for this boy?

Oh God. She thinks he's guilty because I kissed him? My *desire* did this. I followed my heart, and it might kill him.

No. *Ms. Brighton* might kill him.

She has the knife. She's on the edge of the cliff and rising like the sea.

I run at her like a crazy person. If I keep her away from Lucas, there is a chance. Someone might come. With the flares and the emergency call, someone *will* come.

Ms. Brighton tries to push past me, but I snag a fistful of her hair and haul her back. We both stumble. I slam into the side wall, and she scrabbles backward. Closer to the cliff.

Everything is slick. I slide down onto one hip, but she skitters back, trying to hold her footing, searching for something to grab. She's dangerously close to the edge.

Please. *Please.*

For one second, one breathless instant, I think she'll go over. Then her good hand catches a tree. Her eyes meet mine, and I can already see the smile spreading on her lips. She's found an opening in the thorns.

I scramble up, elbows and butt and feet, and nothing works right. I am cold and wet and shaking so badly. She's four feet away from him. Lifting the knife—

"Help me!" I cry to her, stretching out my hand. Pleading with my eyes. This plan is as crazy as my last, just a random impulse to keep her away. To keep Lucas safe.

I make sure she can see me because my face is my only weapon—the face that reminds her of her long-dead sister and me of my absent mother. Right now, I hope I look like them both. I plead with my eyes and soften my mouth and hope.

She turns to me, so I twist onto my side, clutching a hip that doesn't hurt at all. "I can't get up. My leg. It won't move."

"Hannah?" Her voice warbles, part cold and part madness.

"Sera!" Lucas twists, and I can hear the thornbushes crack. "Run!"

I'm not going to run. Not this time.

She takes a step toward me, and I swing my foot around fast, swiping her legs. I fling myself to a crouch. She goes down hard, but she scrambles right back up. She's not quite to her feet when I launch myself into her.

If I can trap Lucas in the thorns, I can trap her too.

Ms. Brighton dodges the worst of my blow. She spins to avoid the briars, and Lucas is shouting again as I lurch to my feet. This time, when she lifts her knife, she's not aiming for Lucas. She's coming for me. Lucas is shouting, but it's his words from earlier that float through my overloaded mind.

Some hits go bad.

Yeah, they do. Ms. Brighton stabs, and I duck, feeling the flash of sharp metal nick my ear before I lower my head and plow into her stomach. We both slam into the ground, and half her body is sprawled over mine.

I struggle underneath her, squirm and wrestle to get away from her heavy body. I manage to push my head and arms free, and the rain feels warm on my arms.

And then I see the crimson line rushing over my wrist. It isn't rain. It's blood.

I writhe like a fish on the bank of a creek, flopping and gasping until I kick myself free of Ms. Brighton's body. I don't know where she got me. There's no pain. I can't see the knife. I search my arms, my face—find nothing.

Heart still pounding insanely, my hands go still on my back, and my gaze turns to Ms. Brighton. My body is still ready for a fight, but it's over.

Ms. Brighton is curling in on herself, twitching quietly on the ground. It's her blood. I can see the handle of her knife from where she landed all wrong. Where her plan fell to pieces.

There is one instant where her face clears, where the insanity recedes and I see my teacher, with her recycling campaigns and indie music and her terrible ghost stories. And then it's gone. And so is she.

CHAPTER 34

My insides churn as I stare at her body. The forest is the same. Leaves shiver, dirt settles, and the world keeps turning.

I close my eyes and feel my heart slow even as my stomach rolls. A mourning dove coos softly. Sadly. Rain drips. My hand burns. Nothing is different, and nothing is the same either.

Lucas.

My heart thumps a funny beat as I turn to the thorns where I left him. Where I pushed him. I crawl because I cannot walk. And then I peel back the slender, cruel branches one by one, calling his name. I can barely see him, and every thread I untangle sends four more lashing at me.

"Lucas? Lucas, say something!"

He suddenly moans, rustles like he's going to try to escape.

"Be careful," I say, every word a croak. "I can't get you out. We need tools. Help should be coming. There were flares, and I sent a distress call on the GPS." I stop myself, thinking of Mr. Walker and knowing there is no way to help him. No way I could make it back down there, even if I wanted to. "Someone will come soon."

"Where is she? Where's Ms. Brighton?"

"Gone." The word takes all my air and a piece of my soul.

He rustles again, cries out, and my breath hitches. "Where are you, Sera?"

"I'm here," I say.

"Where are you?" he asks again, sounding a little frantic. He's hurt so badly. And part of that is my fault, isn't it? If I hadn't attached myself to him out here, Ms. Brighton would not have—

No. I shove that thought away hard. All the broken bits of things Ms. Brighton believed—that's what brought her here. She lost someone, but she never let go. It was holding on too tight that drove her to this. Hell, holding on too tight drives a lot of us to the worst places, doesn't it?

"Sera?" Lucas calls again, sounding on the verge of tears.

"I'm here," I say again, stronger now. I worm my hand in to the thornbushes, stretching out on the ground so I can reach better. Thorns prick my palm, cut my wrist, then my elbow. It doesn't matter.

I find his fingers. He curls them around mine, and I rest my face on the soft, wet earth and hold on tight.

The rain fades to a mist and then to nothing at all. Finally, the *whomp, whomp, whomp* of helicopter blades tells me it's over. I walk Lucas through everything I see, only releasing him when I see the ropes drop down from the helicopter. Our heroes have come to save us.

Funny how it doesn't feel much like salvation at all.

Still, when I hear the steady hum of voices shouting, I am grateful we aren't alone. Grateful, too, that there will be someone else to climb down that hole to check on Mr. Walker. To find him bloody and used up and hopefully, *hopefully*, still alive.

"We're here!" I cry out. "Over here!"

"That's them?" Lucas asks, and I can tell he's only half-conscious. He's slurring his words, but it could be worse. My gaze drags to Ms. Brighton's body. It could be much worse.

"Yes," I say finally. "Yes, that's them. It's over."

He laughs inside that tomb of thorns, and I startle at the sound.

"See? Told you you'd rescue us," he says.

It starts as a laugh but ends with tears. I am still crying when the rescuers find us. They wrap me in a gray blanket and untangle Lucas with pliers and gloved hands and soft voices. They keep us apart, and I let them because the rest can wait.

There is a woman with me though. She has dark skin and close-cropped hair. Her hands brush over me, warm and dry and so beautifully clean that it's hard not to press them to my nose and breathe deep.

She tells me the park rangers found the rest of us shortly after, and they're getting the help they need. They've been looking for us all day because our parents worried after the rain and when the signal check-in didn't follow the right path. I nod along, only hearing half of what she says.

Things happen, and I let them. I'm lost in a blur of dark pants and simple questions and warm blankets and trees moving overhead as they take me through the forest. Then, quite suddenly, a patch of gray sky grows between the trees. The branches crisscrossing over my head are gone, and there are misty clouds marching in my vision. I blink, and there are still more clouds, and after that, the phantom strobe of red emergency lights that grows stronger with every heartbeat. I take a breath that tastes like rain and diesel fuel.

Like a road.

I open my eyes wide as someone clicks down the wheels on the stretcher. When did they put me on this thing? Where is Lucas? I want to ask, but they roll me swiftly across the two-lane road, and the words get lost in the noise.

So many noises. Voices, engines, and the groan of doors opening. It's been a thousand years since I've heard these sounds. I want to cry and laugh at the same time, but I only manage to lift my head, searching for Lucas, wondering if he hears them too.

The doors on his ambulance are closed. The taillights move down the ribbon of black, and I hold my breath until they dip below the next hill and out of sight.

CHAPTER 35

It's all very anticlimactic at the fire station. Hayley was airlifted all the way to Columbus for emergency surgery, and Madison and Lucas were transported to our hospital back in Marietta. Jude, Emily, and I were lucky enough to score the fire station evaluation and treatment center while we wait for more ambulances to arrive. Madison was moved to mine. Apparently, emergency vehicles aren't falling from the sky here in the middle of godforsaken nowhere.

They're making calls, they've assured us. Two ambulances within reasonable distance, nine parents on the way to various meeting points. The three of us are all stable, so who will go first when the cavalry arrives? It feels like a real-world math problem, and I can't help but wonder what Mr. Walker would think.

Mr. Walker wouldn't think anything. Not anymore.

My grip tightens on my musty fold-out cot. The rest of the room smells like stale coffee and sweat—a mix of odors that zaps my appetite. But I sip at my plastic cup of Gatorade and keep my head ducked so I won't be tempted to ask questions. The last time I asked a question, I found out Mr. Walker didn't make it. They carried me out on a stretcher. They carried him out in a bag.

My gut clenches, and I look right, where the same woman who helped me turns Emily's wrist over when she checks her pulse. Her gaze trails over the word on her wrist—police officers took dozens of pictures of us already—but stops on the finger-length bruises that are fading to gray-green on her upper arms.

When she releases Emily's hand, her eyes stay warm, but her smile is tight. "Your vitals look very strong," she says to Emily. "Now you hold tight. I'll be back soon."

Emily nods, two spots of pink high on her cheeks. As soon as the woman is away, Emily utters a word that makes my head snap in her direction. I can't believe it came out of her mouth, but it did. My eyes drift to her bruises, and by the burn in her stare, I know she catches me.

I look to the other side, where I hope Jude will say something. He's the one who's talked to her most since we've gotten here. Whatever happened with all of us bonded the two of them. But Jude's got a man in a flannel shirt asking him to follow a flashlight with his eyes. So I guess I have to say something.

"I'm so sorry," I say softly. It's the first thing I've said in a long while, and it feels wrong. Maybe I should keep pretending I don't see the bruises.

Or maybe I should stop pretending we haven't seen the ugliest things imaginable in the last three days. I want her to know I can handle whatever is behind those bruises.

I try to pore through my brain for her family situation. It's a small school. I should know her. I should know *more*. My mind finds an image. A tiny woman—much older—behind the wheel of a large SUV. A thin man with big hands and a hard face. He has Emily's eyes.

Her father? Did her father do this to her?

I force a smile for Emily. It won't pass any tests, so I let it fade. "So, who's coming to take you home?"

"My dad."

"Oh." I can't pick the right expression fast enough, so my face falls. Emily's eyes narrow, and my chest goes tight with panic. "I'm sorry. I didn't mean to pry."

"You're wrong," she says. "You're wrong about him."

"I…" My gaze drifts to the bruises. Her father's the one I pegged as dangerous. I think of the word on Lucas's arm, and my breath catches. Things aren't always what they seem.

"Your grandmother," I say.

It's a guess, but she stiffens as soon as my words are out, her face going tight and her hands balled at her sides. I can't imagine it—that tiny, stern woman. It's hard to believe she'd be capable of leaving bruises like that.

"But you thought it was him," Emily cries, tears brightening her yes. "Just like *everybody* else."

Is that why she doesn't tell? Because she wants to protect her dad from the accusation?

I get the motivation. Isn't that why I ran away from Lucas all those months ago? I thought if I could be reliable enough, *different* enough, from my lovesick mother, maybe I could protect my father too.

But the truth about Lucas and me *will* come out now. There

will be interviews. Discussions. I will have to tell the police that Ms. Brighton came after Lucas and me because she thought we were together.

No. Because we *were* together and still *are* together, and all those things I told my dad he'd never have to worry about with me? Yeah, it's going to be different.

"You were wrong about Madison too," Jude says, jerking my attention back. He's at her side now, his arm stretched to accommodate the tube leading to a bag of fluids. "The next time Hayley woke up, she was crying for Madison. Emily's got good instincts. She was right."

"Yeah, you do," I tell her. I want to tell her I hope her instincts will prompt her to talk to someone, but I don't. I want to tell her I'll be there, but I still don't know how it's all going to work when we get back home.

Will it ever be the four of us again? Will we even talk? I have a sudden raw aching to stay here with these people who are anything but strangers, but the nurse is back, and that means one of us will go.

The door at the end of the room opens, and two men in blue paramedic shirts enter. A radio on one man's hip chirps, and I think of the speaker in the woods and bark stinging my hands, and all these memories are a hive of hornets, buzzing and buzzing with no meaning for me at all.

"It's OK," Jude says.

His words snag my attention like a hook. I turn my head just a little, just enough to see Jude's hand rest on Emily's shoulder. She's trembling. His eyes meet mine, and there's zero mistake he knows I've heard or that his next words are for me.

"Things are different now," he says. He never breaks my gaze, but when he nods, I nod back. This isn't normal friendship. It's stickier and darker, but I don't think I'll wash my hands of it either. It's harder to wash away things once they're buried this deep.

"Looks like you're up, Sera," the woman says.

I whirl to the paramedics, an argument sputtering on my lips as they mention my elevated temperature and the infection in my hand. They will take me to Marietta too. My dad will meet me there.

Dad.

I can barely hold back tears at the idea. Paramedics help me onto the stretcher and chatter about how long it will take and what their names are... I don't listen to any of it. I smell the sharp tang of trees and close my eyes tight against an onslaught of memories I'd rather forget.

CHAPTER 36

It seems like sleep will never come, but it does, and it sticks hard. I doze the entire way home to Marietta, waking when the ambulance doors fling open and drifting off again when I see bright-white rectangles—ceiling lights, I guess—whipping by above me.

I sleep until my dad is there with quiet words and gentle hands, until the cops come with their questions, until Sophie and Liv leave flowers and ask my dad if I'm all right, until I've heard all the updates about Lucas being fine and Hayley making it and, of course, that Mr. Walker didn't. I already knew, but it's still a sucker punch when they say it again.

I don't tell my dad how much I saw Mr. Walker endure or that I was the last person who heard him speak. It will come out, but I'm not sure he can handle that now, so I close my eyes like all the news exhausts me. It's not a lie.

The next time I wake, the room is dim, and there are two people sitting in the chairs across from me. Neither is my dad. One of them has a plastic tub, and there's a faint smell of cologne in the air.

"Jude?"

My voice scratches, and my vision stretches everything like I'm underwater. I blink until it clears, and then their faces sharpen. An ache swells in my chest, and I don't know what that means. I barely recognize them, clean like this. I guess I'm clean too now.

I was in the shower so long, Dad knocked on the door to check on me. After I was out and dressed, he helped me comb my hair. He's never done that before, not even when I was little. But he did today, and I let him. I stared at my freshly scrubbed, still-scratched face in the mirror while he brushed my shoulder-length hair into a gleaming ribbon of black.

He told me I was beautiful.

He did not tell me I look like my mother.

"How are you feeling?" Jude asks.

"Cleaner."

Jude smiles. He's back in his element, in an outfit that's crisp and clean and probably worth more than my bedroom furniture. Aside from dark circles under his eyes, he looks good. Emily looks good too, though there are still scratches on her left cheek.

There are three of us, but there should be four. Six if you count Madison and Hayley, but I don't, even if I know that's not fair. I can't feel their absence, but I can feel the space Lucas would fill. The emptiness of having him down the hall.

"Hey," Emily says, shifting the basket on her lap.

I scooch up in the bed, reaching for my plastic mug of water. What time is it? My eyes find the digital clock above the TV. Three thirty in the morning.

I sip some water because my throat's parched. It's lukewarm through the plastic straw, so I must have slept awhile. I spot a note on my end table. Dad. Home for a nap because the nurses begged him. I begged too. He looked so tired. Still, he insisted on waiting until I fell asleep, and the note promises he'll be back before I wake up.

"What are you doing here?" I ask the others. "I didn't know they released you."

"We weren't admitted," Emily says.

"I was deemed healthy, but they wanted to keep her longer," Jude says, eyes narrowed just the tiniest amount.

"I'm fine," Emily says, but the circles under her eyes tell me otherwise. "Just couldn't sleep much."

Her grandmother made her leave the hospital? Makes me wonder how on earth she's here at zero-dark-thirty in the morning.

"She's a deep sleeper," Emily says, reading my mind. "I snuck out."

"So you're here to visit?" I don't sound convinced.

Jude swallows hard. "Not exactly. We thought we should take them off together."

I'm not sure what he means, but then Emily tucks her hair behind her ear, and I see the *Damaged* on her arm. My eyes flick down to the *Darling* on mine. It didn't come off in the shower. I think I'd take a wire brush to my skin to see it gone, so I nod.

Her plastic basket includes bottles and cleaning supplies. One that looks like nail polish remover and another I think is bleach.

I frown, worry pricking at the back of my neck. "Is that safe to mix?"

"We're not mixing them," Jude says. "We looked up recipes. We're going to try a few. Can you walk?"

I'm sure I can, and I know why they're asking. Because Lucas is here too, so there's one more of us to collect. I haven't seen him since that moment in the forest, and every time I've wondered why, I've pushed the question back, locked it in a box at the far corner of my mind.

I already know the answer. I'm afraid of what I'll see.

I went sixty-two days without looking at him after the first time we kissed, but that was then. And now is very different. When I see him, I'll have to face what happened in the woods. Mr. Walker. Ms. Brighton. The thorns. He is wound into every memory of that terror, especially the awful end. Seeing him might be like reliving a nightmare.

"Come on," Emily says. "I'll walk with you."

"I don't…" I don't know how to finish, so I shrug lamely and look at the floor. There's a black scuff on the pale linoleum, like the letters on our arms. I think too many things in that second, flashes that jar me like punches. Bottled water on my parched tongue. Black flies buzzing in a cloud. Mr. Walker's bloody fingers. Ms. Brighton falling onto her knife. How can anything good come of what happened out there?

The door to my hospital room snicks open. We tense with one collective breath, and then someone shuffles into the shadows. His height betrays him before he says a single word.

"Sera?"

My whole body goes warm as he crosses the room to my bed. If he's surprised to see Jude and Emily, he doesn't show it. No one speaks or explains. Lucas just looks at the box on Emily's lap and helps me out of bed.

He laces his fingers with mine, and we sneak our way to an on-floor waiting area because we all know staying in my room is an invitation to get caught. It's tomb-quiet at night and dark in the hallways, so it's easy to go unnoticed.

No one says much when Jude unfolds the instructions and Emily starts pulling out stacks of cotton pads and swiping us down, one by one. The nail polish remover takes off about half the ink. The alcohol is pretty useless.

"Hell," Lucas says, wrinkling his nose at the fumes. "Are we trying to get high or clean here?"

Emily just purses her lips and directs us all to the sink. We rinse off, and then she's back at it with detergent and bleach, warning us not to mix the bleach with anything else. She sets in on Jude with a toothbrush, and he doesn't look thrilled with her enthusiastic scrubbing.

"A little harder and they'll think my very white dads are bio-logical," he teases, and Emily just laughs and eases her touch.

"You want to go first?" I ask Lucas.

He looks at me like we're still on Sophie's back deck. Like we're still by the stream with his hands in my hair and my eyes spilling out secrets he's dying to hear.

"Hey," he says, eyes cashmere-gray and voice softer than that. His arm is in a sling, and he's scraped and raw in too many places to count. He's beautiful.

I smile. "Hey."

He turns up his good wrist, and I scoop a little bit of the detergent mix onto his arm, see the scratches on his hand and his wrist, the bandage around his ankle where Ms. Brighton stabbed him inside the thorns. We're both in hospital gowns, and we must have had the same nurse because we've both got an extra gown on as a robe, keeping our butts from waving in the breeze.

I graze his arm when I turn with the powdered bleach and detergent mix, and my eyes tear up. I could blame it on the bleach, but I won't.

Lucas hisses when a little gets in his cut, and I flinch. "I'm sorry. Sorry."

"It's OK." Then I'm tearing up, and his hand is on my arm, my face. "Hey. I'm all right. What you did—"

"*Hurt* you." The words come out with tears.

"*Saved* me," he corrects softly.

His face is the worst. There's a puncture in his left brow, a row of scratches down his jaw and neck. I pull him to the sink and rinse quickly because I can't put him through more pain.

The *D* and the *OUS* are still easy to read, but the rest is gone— just a smear of gray, spelling something that isn't him.

"What's with the words?" Jude asks after he rinses. "Was it a random part of her crazy?"

"Not random," I say. "The girl who died out there before was Ms. Brighton's stepsister. Her name was Hannah. She looked like me."

I close my eyes and see the brightness of Hannah's smile, frozen on the blood-stained memorial program. When I open them, they are waiting. "I guess it was an accident, but Ms. Brighton couldn't accept that. She needed someone to blame, so she investigated the kids who were with Hannah. She stalked them really."

"So we're supposed to be the reincarnation of those kids?" Jude asks.

I sigh. "I guess so."

"You don't look like a Hannah," Emily muses.

I lift my chin. "No, I look like a Sera."

"I still don't get the words," Lucas says.

"We're never going to know for sure," Jude says. "That woman was a full-fledged lunatic."

"I think she was sad. She was looking for motive," I say. "Some reason or trait that might make one of you guilty. She wanted words to explain, words that would give her someone to blame."

"Labels," Emily says.

"Tidy little boxes to tuck us into," Jude says.

"You and your damn boxes." Lucas's words hold no bite. The boys exchange a look that isn't the same as before. We're still us. At least, some part of us anyway.

"She was wrong." I have to say it because I need to make sure they hear it. "She didn't know you at all. She didn't know any of us."

There's nothing left to say, so we curl onto the stiff waiting room couches and flip through the news. They've got everything mixed-up already.

"Two points for every time they call me Judah," Jude says.

Lucas chuckles. "Five for every time they mention my violent past."

"At least they don't have our faces on the screen," Emily says, but they flash Hannah's face up, and we all take a breath.

I catalogue her features one by one. They do not add up to me.

In the end, we change the channel to old cartoons. Emily finds a bag of microwave popcorn, and Jude treats us all to soda. Lucas is leaned against my chest—we propped him up with every pillow we found in the closet—and his legs are everywhere, but his free arm is resting on my leg, his fingers pressed to my bare knee where my hospital gown has ridden up.

Jude is telling Emily to listen to the orchestra rise behind the action scene. I hear the soft rumble of her reply, feel Lucas's deep breath against me. I catch a glimpse of my reflection in the mirror beside the window. The world rights itself, all the tilted things leveling. Here—far from the trees and the terror and the blood—there are no ghosts waiting in my reflection. Not my mother or Hannah. The only one looking back is me.

ACKNOWLEDGMENTS

Probably the greatest blessing of being a writer is all the amazing people I meet along the way. I find myself encouraged, inspired, and kept on track in so many different ways by just as many people.

As always, my thanks to God for blessing me with joy throughout every step of *One Was Lost*. This book was a breath of fresh air, scares and all, and I am so grateful to have written it.

Thanks to Cori Deyoe with Three Seas Literary, who helped me tremendously in shining my initial draft and who is wonderful, wise, and kind in countless ways. Words can't express!

Thanks to my unbeatable team at Sourcebooks Fire: Todd, Amelia, Stephanie, Elizabeth, Stephanie, and my super sparkly unicorn, Alex. A special thanks to Annette for getting me to the finish line with some seriously brilliant insight! And most of all, thank you, Aubrey. Your vision for this book made it a joy to revise, and your wisdom made it the project I'm proudest of to date. Thank you so much!

To my critique partner and dear friend, Romily Bernard, who sees all the ugly parts I hide from everyone else and still picks up the phone when I call. Thank you doesn't cut it, but still…

A special thanks goes to Dr. Mark Gittins (Boots!) for the

injury advice, to Justin Hall (thank you!) for the help with all the quad stuff, to Liz and Susan and Margs for theater advice, and to my cousin, Angela, for talking me through a scary choice, and to Leigh Anne for constant cheer.

I'm blessed with friendships with so many talented writers who make my life brighter. To Julia Devillers, Margaret Peterson Haddix, Erin McCahan, Lisa Klein, Jody Casella, Edith Patou, Kristen Orlando, Pintip Dunn, Meg Kassel, Stephanie Winklehake, Sheri Adkins, Robin Gianna, and others I'm missing. Thanks for pushing me on and making me laugh.

There are several librarians, readers, bloggers, and teachers who have championed me in my writing journey. Amanda, Donna, Erin, Teddi, Sara, Stephanie, Cath, Pam V., and many more. Thank you with all my heart! You mean the world to me!

And, of course, my biggest thanks are always saved for my wonderful husband and our three beautiful children. They are my light in every dark place. All of this, every word, is only possible because of the four of you. I love you.

ABOUT THE AUTHOR

A lifelong Ohioan, Natalie D. Richards spent many years applying her writing skills to stunningly boring business documents. Fortunately, she realized she's much better at making things up and has been writing for teens ever since. A champion of aspiring authors, Richards is a frequent speaker at schools, libraries, and writing groups. She lives in Ohio with a Yeti and a Wookie (her dogs) and her wonderful husband and children. *One Was Lost* is her fourth novel.